CW00552557

"This is a fascinating acco
workers in Singapore who
Revealing as it does the po
workers, the novel demonstrates the humanity and resilience
of a community that had fallen out of history. This painstaking
and beautifully illustrated translation brings this story to a wider
audience offering not just a story but an ethnographic account of
a particular chapter in the story of colonial exploitation."

Professor Bill Ashcroft
Emeritus Professor, University of New South Wales

"Kamaladevi Aravindan's *Sembawang* is a compelling tale that
evokes Singapore at a time of rapid change, told through the
eyes of Tamil and Malayalee migrant workers whose lives were
bound up with the Sembawang naval base. With its strong
female characters and its keen ear for language, *Sembawang* does
a brilliant job of bringing to life the cadences of everyday life
and speech in this polyglot society. It also dramatises the sense
of loss that can accompany rapid economic development. We
are fortunate to have this lively and sensitive translation by the
author's daughter, Anitha Devi Pillai."

Professor Sunil Amrith
Professor of History, Yale University
Recipient of MacArthur Fellowship 2017

"Kamaladevi Aravindan's *Sembawang*, translated from
the original in Tamil to English by Anitha Devi Pillai,
is an enthralling novel set in a village on the 13th mile
of the northern borderlands of Singapore in the 1960s.
Finely poised between fiction and history, it delves
into the interconnected world of the descendants of

indentured and *kangani* servitude from southern India. What emerges is a powerful exposé of the severe, capricious and unrelenting journey of Tamil and Malayalee women — a hitherto obscure fragment in the story of Singapore's pioneer generation."

Associate Professor Rajesh Rai

Head of South Asian Studies, National University of Singapore

Leading authority on the history of Indians in Singapore

"*Sembawang* has all the lived-in qualities of an immersive historical novel. Evocative period details backed by solid research, a complex web of characters you want — no, demand — to follow through their ups and downs, and a narrative that holds you spellbound. Thanks to this great translation by her daughter, Anitha Devi Pillai, Kamaladevi Aravindan's novel is finally available for an English-reading public."

Felix Cheong

Young Artist Award recipient 2000

"Kamaladevi's fascinating narrative, set mainly in the 1960s and 1970s in Singapore, is dominated by forceful women originally from Kerala and Tamil Nadu who fearlessly shaped their own destinies. Translated skilfully and with infinite tenderness by her daughter, it captures not only the vicissitudes of a vast canvas of characters but also the varied cultural and linguistic features that determine their regional identities."

Gita Krishnankutty

Translator

"This fast-paced, hyper-informed, eclectic and highly readable saga from 'below' makes a doubly valuable contribution to Singapore writing: a rich, deep and wide bricolage slice of local historical literature, *Sembawang* also affectionately captures forever a rich and genuine portrait of a long lost, never again so intense migrant microculture at a key moment in Singapore's history. Its empowering gynocentric lens on an often shockingly violent, patriarchy dominated milieu of ordinary people at 13th Mile fifty years ago illuminatingly resonates with many of our present-day Singaporean issues and challenges. Anitha Devi Pillai's meticulous research for and curation of this transcreation of her mother's novel adds a further enriching layer to this fascinating text."

Dr Angus Whitehead
National Institute of Education, NTU
Editor of *Singapore Literature and Culture* (2017)

"*Sembawang* is essential reading for any Singaporean. The author's deft portrayal of the Tamil and Malayalee communities in the area from pre-independence days, is rendered through a vast array of women characters and their experiences. No single voice dominates, and mundane joys and sufferings bring home the message that the largest historical events are secondary to lived realities. This is a novel that sings."

Ann Ang
Author of *Bang My Car* (2012)

"A vast, richly detailed epic set in the Tamil community in Singapore. Evocative, poignant, and shot through with colour, drama, and light, *Sembawang* is guaranteed to transport you to a magical world."

David Davidar
Author of *The House of Blue Mangoes*

SEMBAWANG

A NOVEL

Kamaladevi Aravindan

Translated by Anitha Devi Pillai

Marshall Cavendish
Editions

Published by Marshall Cavendish Editions
An imprint of Marshall Cavendish International

A member of the
Times Publishing Group

Other Marshall Cavendish Offices:
Marshall Cavendish Corporation, 800 Westchester Ave, Suite N-641, Rye Brook,
NY 10573, USA • Marshall Cavendish International (Thailand) Co Ltd, 253 Asoke,
16th Floor, Sukhumvit 21 Road, Klongtoey Nua, Wattana, Bangkok 10110, Thailand •
Marshall Cavendish (Malaysia) Sdn Bhd, Times Subang, Lot 46, Subang Hi-Tech
Industrial Park, Batu Tiga, 40000 Shah Alam, Selangor Darul Ehsan, Malaysia

Marshall Cavendish is a registered trademark of Times Publishing Limited

National Library Board, Singapore Cataloguing in Publication Data

Name(s): Kamalātēvi Aravintan. | Pillai, Anitha Devi, translator.
Title: Sembawang : a novel / Kamaladevi Aravindan ; translated by Anitha
    Devi Pillai.
Description: Singapore : Marshall Cavendish Editions, [2020]
Identifier(s): OCN 1164595378 | ISBN 978-981-48-9328-2 (paperback)
Subject(s): LCSH: Sembawang (Singapore)--Fiction. | Families--Fiction.
Classification: DDC 894.8113--dc23

Printed in Singapore

Cover photographs by Binod Therat

For Theijes Therrat Menon
You are my greatest strength
and weakness

AUTHOR'S NOTE

THIS NOVEL AND the characters are a work of fiction and a product of the author's imagination. Any resemblance to actual persons, living or dead, is purely coincidental.

The story begins in Sembawang, Singapore, in the 1960s and spans the next fifty years. Several key historical moments and events are referred to in the narrative. It was written based on interviews with residents who had lived in the area, in order to reflect elements of the way of life during that era.

Photographs of people and places are included in this book for the same purpose, as a reflection of what life was like at that time. All photographs of people featured here do not relate to any of the characters or events in the novel.

The details of the actual historical events are described in the Historical Notes & References section.

MAP OF SEMBAWANG

12TH MILE

HOT SPRINGS

JALAN ULU SEMBAWANG

LORONG MAHA

CHONG PANG VILLAGE

CHYE KA VILLAGE

13TH MILE

METHODIST TAMIL SCHOOL

KEDONGDONG RD

J. SEMBAWANG KECHIL

SEMBAWANG ROAD

TO OLD NEE SOON VILLAGE

SEMBAWANG 1960s
ILLUSTRATED BY SHALYN AND FAIROZ

MELODY ZACCHEUS (*The Straits Times*, 22 June 2015) reports that before the 1970s, milestones were used to mark and identify places in Singapore, for instance in the case of Sembawang, 13th miles, 14th miles and 15th miles, as

shown in the map. These markers were found 1.6km apart from one another and the starting point — or point zero — was the General Post Office, where Fullerton Hotel is located today.

SETHULAKSHMI AND PAARUKUTTY HOUSEHOLDS

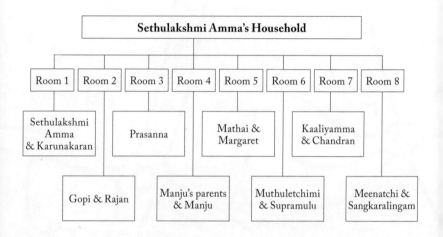

Sethulakshmi Amma's Household

Room 1	Room 2	Room 3	Room 4	Room 5	Room 6	Room 7	Room 8
Sethulakshmi Amma & Karunakaran		Prasanna		Mathai & Margaret		Kaaliyamma & Chandran	
	Gopi & Rajan		Manju's parents & Manju		Muthuletchimi & Supramulu		Meenatchi & Sangkaralingam

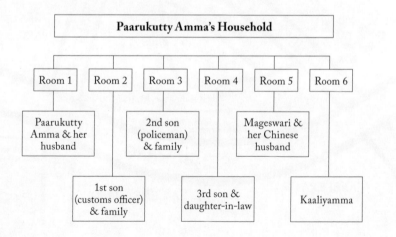

Paarukutty Amma's Household

Room 1	Room 2	Room 3	Room 4	Room 5	Room 6
Paarukutty Amma & her husband		2nd son (policeman) & family		Mageswari & her Chinese husband	
	1st son (customs officer) & family		3rd son & daughter-in-law		Kaaliyamma

CAST OF CHARACTERS

In order of appearance by chapter:

Kaaliyamma / Kaali	main character
Munusamy	Kaaliyamma's first husband
Krani Appadurai	Kaaliyamma's immediate supervisor at Anjarai Kattai
Raasu / Raasu Boy	Kaaliyamma and Munusamy's son
Chandran	Kaaliyamma's second husband and Perumaayi's cousin
Perumaayi	Chandran's cousin; Kaaliyamma's colleague
Mandor Maarimuthu	one of the mandors in Anjarai Kattai
Anjalai	Chandran's mother
Sethulakshmi Amma	houseowner of the first house Kaaliyamma stayed in in Sembawang
Karunakaran	Sethulakshmi Amma's husband
Muthuletchimi / Muthu	Supramulu's wife and Kaaliyamma's friend, a Telugu tenant in Sethulakshmi Amma's house
Manju's mother	A Malayalee tenant in Sethulakshmi Amma's house

Mathai	A Malayalee tenant in Sethulakshmi Amma's house
Manju's father	A Malayalee tenant in Sethulakshmi Amma's house
Margaret	Mathai's wife
Chinnadurai, Murugan and Vellaya	Three friends who lived in Sembawang
Machappu	Vellaya's father
Sinnasee's wife	Machappu's second wife
Chinnasamy	Vellaya's grandfather
Ramasamy	Vellaya's uncle and boss
Sangkaralingam	A tenant in Sethulakshmi Amma's house
Meenatchi	Sangkaralingam's wife
Maasilamani	Sangkaralingam's friend
Rangan	Maasilamani's friend
Shanthi	*Thevaram* and *Thiruvasagam* teacher who later married Maasilamani
Prasanna	Sethulakshmi Amma's daughter
Mallika	Vellaya's girlfriend
Mohan	a teacher and owner of the house in which Mallika and her mother stayed in
Sembakam	Mallika's mother
Appunni	Sethulakshmi Amma's neighbour

Supramulu	Muthuletchimi's husband
Koshy	Margaret's father
Abdul Kader	also called Kader Bhai, Mathai's boss
Mayilvasagam	moneylender in Sembawang
Meena Amma	yogurt lady in Sembawang
Dr Raamasamy	Tamil patriot doctor in Ramu's Clinic, Sembawang
Akhilandam	a lady betrothed to Chinnadurai
Chinthamani	resident of the kampong who owns a chicken farm
Kuttan Pillai	a high-ranking officer / *Krani* at the Naval Base
Omana	Kuttan Pillai's wife
Chinnasami	vegetable store owner and Kaaliyamma's boss
Kochappu Maama	Prasanna's second uncle
Kamatchi Paati	Margaret's neighbour
Prema Akka	Kaaliyamma's friend
Paarukutty Amma	houseowner of the second house Kaaliyamma stayed in in Sembawang
Mageswari	Paarukutty Amma's tenant
Jameela Akka	Kaaliyamma's friend

Manohari	Paarukutty Amma's neighbour
Sasidharan	Prasanna's husband
Chithamparam / Chithamparam *Ayya* / Clerk Thambi	An educated man in Sembawang
Vaani	The daughter of Chithamparam's first houseowners in Sembawang
Chua	Chithamparam's colleague
Unnithan *Ayya*	A successful mill owner in Sembawang
Rajan	Sethulakshmi's second son
Mottai / Raani	Chinnathaayi's daughter
Anjalai	Buttermilk seller
Usman	Houseowner of the room Vellaya rented and Mumtaj's first husband
Mumtaj	Usman's second wife and Dawood Maraikkayar's daughter
Dawood Maraikkayar	Butcher shop owner and Mumtaj's father
Seeni Chettiar	Moneylender
Gopi	Sethulakshmi Amma's eldest son
Meena	Chithamparam's wife
Siam Thaatha / Sangayya	Meena's grandfather; one of the workers who escaped from the Siam Railway
Mala	Sangayya's wife
Rajathi	Sangayya and Mala's daughter
Ramasamy	Rajathi's husband

Sarojini	One of the nurses appointed to Maternal and Child Health Clinic in the later years
Chinna Akka	Mumtaj's childhood friend
Moosa *Ayya*	Frequent customer at Vellaya's butcher shop
Elizi	Mumtaj's maid
Gilbert	Vellaya's Chinese friend and an ex-convict
Mei Ling	Raasu's wife
Thakkan	Munusamy's childhood friend

Minor characters have been excluded from this list.

GLOSSARY

* Terms of address
** Tamil, Malayalam and Malay words used by Indians in Malaya

Term	Meaning
ada * / *aye*	Tamil equivalent of hey
Akka *	Tamil word to address older sister; also used as a term of respect for an older woman
achhu murukku	Flower-shaped South Indian fried snack; in Tamil, *murukku* means twist and *achhu* means mould
aluru **	Tamil word for drain
Ambaal	Goddess Ambal or Mariamman is generally known as a Hindu Tamil Goddess; she is worshipped by Hindus in different forms
Amma / *Yemma* *	expressions to address mother in Tamil; also used as a term of respect for an older woman or well-respected woman in the community
ang pow	a gift of money packed into a red packet (or 'ang pow' as it is known in some Chinese dialects) and given during auspicious occasions such as Chinese New Year and weddings
Anna / *Annachi* *	Tamil word to address older brother; also used as a term of respect for an older man
Appa / *Yeppa* / *Yeppoi* *	expressions to address father in Tamil
archanai	Tamil word for special worship and prayers done by Hindu temple priests in which the name, birth star and family lineage of a devotee are recited to invoke individual guidance and blessings
arinju	Malayalam phrase that means 'have known'
arishtam	popular medicinal herb containing alcohol, that is used for Ayurvedic treatment
aviyal	traditional Kerala dish that is a thick mixture of vegetables in a coconut curry base, and is part of Onam and marriage feasts

*Ayya**	Tamil word to address any older male relative or acquaintance
baju kurung	type of traditional dress worn by Malay female descendants that is a kind of frock coat, whose sleeve length is to the wrist and skirt is of ankle length; in Malay, *baju* is shirt and *kurung* means confine or imprison
Bhai *	Hindi word for older brother
bhajan	Sanskrit word for a devotional song
chakkara	type of traditional gold necklace
chapatti	type of griddle-baked unleavened bread
char siew	Chinese word for barbecued marinated pork
Chechi *	Malayalam word to address older sister; also used as a term of respect for an older woman
chendol	traditional dessert drink found in Malaysia and Singapore which is laden with tiny bits of green pandan-flavoured jelly, coconut milk, red beans, *gula melaka* (palm sugar) and crushed ice
Chetta *	Malayalam word to address older brother; also used as a term of respect for an older man
*Chinna Durai**	small boss or a junior officer
'chopped' **	local English term for getting the passport stamped
chutney	a sweet or savoury but usually spicy sauce, made of fruits or vegetables with vinegar, spices and sugar, originating from the Indian subcontinent
dalcha	Hyderabadi Indian curry made from split chickpeas and tamarind
Deepavali	Hindu festival in October/November that is a celebration of light and of hopes for the following year
*dei**	said in anger or affection to address a man/boy or amongst male friends

dosa (sometimes spelt locally as *thosai*)	South Indian thin pancake made from rice flour and fermented pulses, cooked on a flat griddle that is a popular breakfast item among South Indians
drumsticks	fruit of the moringa tree
Ganesha	Hindu God of wisdom, success and good fortune and remover of obstacles
goreng pisang	Malay word for deep fried bananas
hurry-burry	an Indian English word to refer to doing things in a hurry; derived from a Tamil phrase *arakka parakka*
ice kachang	Malaysian/Singaporean dessert made of shaved ice, red beans, jelly and sweet syrup; in Malay, it means 'iced beans'
idli	South Indian steamed cake of rice that is a popular breakfast item among South Indians
injipuli (also known as *puli inji*)	a dark-brown sweet-sour and spicy curry originating from Kerala and is served as part of a *sadhya* or banquet
*jaga***	term used in Malaysia and Singapore to refer to a guard
jemput-jemput	Malay name for a popular tea-time snack in Singapore/Malaysia made of banana, flour and sugar
kaara kuzhampu	Tamil phrase that means spicy curry
kaasu-maala	traditional long necklace with a whole lot of gold coins assembled together; *kaasu* in Malayalam and Tamil means coin and *maala* denotes necklace
kaavadi	Tamil word for the heavy, decorative structure carried on one shoulder by a Hindu devotee during the Thaipusam festival in worship of the Lord Murugan
kaili	Malayalam word for lungi worn casually at home or at work and can be of any colour, unlike a dhoti

Kakka *	Malayalam word to address an older Indian Muslim man; it means brother
kampong **	Malay word for village
kangani	Tamil word for an overseer of labour in Sri Lanka, India and Malaysia
kanthaka-bhoomi	Tamil word for land (*bhoomi*) rich with sulphur
karimani maala	a gold chain with dozens of small black beads
karuvadu	Tamil word for dried fish
kasha kasha	poppy seeds, used in small amounts for cooking
kati **	old unit of measurement of weight
Kavuni rice	black glutinous rice popular in Chettiar and Burmese cuisine
keema	minced meat; the traditional Indian dish made from this minced meat, peas or potatoes and spices is also referred to as keema
kesari	South Indian dessert that has a rich orange golden colour
ketti urundai	Tamil word for a traditional Indian delicacy that is hard in texture and requires some effort to eat it
kithakaadu	Tamil word for rubber estate
kittangi	Tamil word for warehouse but in the Singapore/Malaysia context, refers to a warehouse containing a Chettiar's office, which was situated on the ground floor of a shophouse
Kochu / Kutti Keralam	Malayalam word which means 'Small Keralam'
krani *	supervisor
kueh	Malay word for a bite-sized cake/snack or dessert of Malay, Chinese or Indian origin
kumkum	red turmeric powder used, ceremonially and cosmetically, by Hindu women to make a small distinctive mark on the forehead

kusini **	Tamil and Malayalam word for kitchen, believed to be derived from Portuguese/French
kuzhalappams	a tube-shaped rice flour cannoli that is prepared with rice flour along with onion, garlic, sesame seeds and cumin; a popular dish amongst Malayalee Christians in Trissur, Kerala
kway teow goreng	dish of stir-fried flat or wide rice noodles
laddu	Indian dessert made out of flour, ghee, sugar, chopped nuts and dried raisins
laksa	Malaysian dish consisting of rice noodles, seafood, tofu puffs and bean sprouts served in thick broth of coconut or tamarind
lallang	a plant that is commonly known as cogongrass; it is highly invasive and treated as weeds
Lord Krishna	Hindu God who is worshipped as the supreme god or as the eighth incarnation of Vishnu, the Preserver
Lord Murugan	Hindu God of war
Lord Yama	Hindu God of death
maadi-veedu	Tamil word used to describe terrace houses with two or more storeys
*ma**	Tamil term to affectionately address a younger female
Maama *	Tamil term to address mother's brother or an older man who is not necessarily related
Maami *	Tamil term to address mother's brother's wife or one's mother-in-law
maapu	Malayalam word used to ask for forgiveness
*machan**	Tamil term to address one's brother-in-law; informally used to address a friend or buddy
mandor *	foreman or overseer of a plantation
'marketing'	a local term used in Malaysia and Singapore in the early years to refer to buying groceries and meat from a wet market
masala	a mixture of ground spices used in Indian cooking

mee goreng	Malay term for a dish of fried egg noodles
murukku	Indian snack made from semi-solid dough, which consists primarily of rice or dal flour, formed into a twisty shape and then deep fried
Muniswarar	a Hindu deity whose name translates to saint (*muni*) and Lord Shiva (Ishwarar); he is worshipped as a family deity amongst many sub-communities
Navarathri	nine-night celebration dedicated to Durga, the Hindu mother goddess
neli ring	South Indian traditional gold ring that looks curved and may have gemstones
nendra pazham	lengthiest and biggest of all banana varieties available in Kerala which tastes different at every stage of development so is used to make a variety of food items
*nerai***	Tamil word referring to a plot of land
Onam	annual harvest festival celebrated in August/September in Kerala.
Onasadhya (or *onasadya*)	a traditional vegetarian 26-course meal served on Onam day for lunch
oodukali	Tamil curse word which refers to a woman who has run away from her marriage
*paapa**	Tamil word that means baby or child and is used to address a child or someone younger
*Paati**	Tamil term for grandmother
pallu	loose end of a sari that is generally draped over the shoulder
pappadam	thin crispy Indian flatbread, prepared using lentil flour, that is usually eaten with rice and curries
parang	Malay word for machete
paranju	Malayalam phrase that means 'have told'
pasar	Malay word for market

pasar malam	Malay word for a night market with temporary stores
pathiyam (*pathiya samayal* in Tamil)	Ayurvedic diet
payasam / pradhaman	*Payasams* and *pradhaman* are different types of milk-based desserts
peratu **	Tamil word for roll-call
periya durai *	big boss or senior officer
poda	Tamil phrase for 'get lost man/boy'
Pongal	a four-day-long harvest festival — celebrated by Tamils as a thanksgiving ceremony for the year's harvest — that falls in the month of Thai (i.e., the January–February season) when crops like rice, sugar cane, turmeric, etc. are harvested; Tamil term '*pongal*' means 'to boil'
Pongala	a ritual in which women prepare sweet payasam and offer it to the Goddess during the Attukal Pongala festival held at the Attukal Bhagavathi Temple in Thiruvananthapuram, Kerala; the word means 'boil over' in Malayalam
pooja	Tamil and Sanskrit word for worship
prasadam	Tamil word for food that is offered to a Hindu god
prata	South Indian flatbread made by frying stretched dough flavoured with ghee
pulisseri	yogurt-based curry that is flavoured with ground coconut and a few spices
puttu	breakfast dish originating from Kerala, made using steamed cylinders of ground rice layered with coconut
rasam	South Indian spicy soup-like dish that is tangy in flavour
Saar *	Sir

sambal	Malay word for a hot sauce or paste made from a mixture of a various chilli peppers, shrimp paste, fish, garlic, ginger and shallots
sambar	South Indian lentil-based vegetable curry cooked in tamarind broth
samsu (also known as *samshu*)	alcoholic drink of the Chinese, made of fermented rice and also known as rice wine
sarong kebaya	traditional Indonesian/Peranakan/Malay dress, consisting of a traditional blouse (kebaya) made of sheer material and worn with a batik or sarong
seekumaram	Tamil word for an old rubber tree with very little sap
seluar **	Malay word for trousers as well as pants reaching just below the knees
string hoppers	a rice noodle dish, made of rice flour that is steamed; also known as *nool puttu* in Tamil, it is popular in Kerala, Tamil Nadu and Sri Lanka
sundal	Tamil word for traditional Tamil Nadu dish consisting of chickpeas that is prepared as a food offering for religious worship
sundari	Malayalam and Tamil word to describe a beautiful woman
Thaatha *	Tamil word to address grandfather
thaayi *	Tamil term of affection to address a younger lady/mother
Thaipusam	important festival observed by Hindus during the Tamil month of Thai (January–February), which is dedicated to Lord Murugan
Thambi *	Tamil term to address younger brother
tharavad	Malayalam word for ancestral home
Thevaram	collection of ancient Tamil hymns of the foremost of the Shaivite Nayanmars (Appar, Sambandar and Sundarar), sung in temples as part of worship, which have a profound influence on the growth of Karnatic music

Thiruvasagam	collection of ancient Tamil hymns by the 9th century Shaivite poet Manikkavasagar
*thongal***	Tamil word for corner
Thoondamani vilakku	Tamil word referring to a type of decorated hanging brass lamp; vilakku means lamp
thoran	dry coconut-based vegetable dish in Kerala which is a common menu item for a feast
*towkay**	Chinese word for businessman; also means sir or master; it was also used to refer to anyone who owned a shop or ran any sort of business
*udang***	Malay word for prawn
ull paavadai	Tamil and Malayalam word to refer to an underskirt worn by Indian women beneath their saris
Vaappa *	Malayalam word for father used by Malayalee Muslims
vadai	Tamil word for a South Indian savoury snack made from soaked or fermented pulses moulded into balls or a doughnut shape and deep fried
vanakkam	Tamil greeting that is said with both palms together
*vangsa kadai***	Tamil word for provision shop
vatti kadai	Tamil word for a moneylender's shop
velai	Tamil word for work
velikaadu velai	Tamil word for cleaning weeds from a rubber estate/plantation
vibhuti	Sanskrit word for scared ash used in Hindu rituals
*yellai**	Tamil word to hail someone
yu char kueh	deep-fried dough fritter, a Chinese breakfast food; also known as *youtiao* or Chinese cruller

PROLOGUE

"We want Indians as indentured labourers. We don't want free men in Malaya," called out a Sir Thomas Hyslop. This quote would become synonymous with how many South Indians arrived in Malaya as coolies — lowly paid indentured labour.

The period of 1844 to 1941 was known to be a period of rampant poverty in South India. Coolies arrived in Malaya from Tamil Nadu (Thiruchirapalli, Madurai, Ramanathapuram, Salem, Thanjavur, Chengalpattu, North Arcot — 'a former district in Madras State' — and from Tirunelveli districts). Malayalee coolies came from the Malabar kingdom, and Telugu coolies from Visakhapatnam, East and West Godavari, Kondoor and Nellore in Andhra.

Many did not know then that their lives and their descendants' fates would change forever. Ship owners hired *kanganis* who would visit villages with tales of how they could make their fortunes in Malaya. For each adult coolie that they managed to recruit, the *kanganis* received ten rupees. There were female *kanganis* who tricked women who had a quarrel with their husbands or parents into leaving their homes for the shores of Malaya. These *kanganis* made seven rupees for the pretty ones. Boys were reportedly kidnapped from villages. The *kanganis* received less for boys who were not in great demand but much higher rates for young good-looking women. For these boys, they were given five or six rupees. The ship only left for the Straits ports when it was full to its brim with people. Some brought with them their meagre possessions in a bag, leaving everything that was familiar to them. They were packed like sardines in these ships and arrived to find themselves working for the rest of their lives, clearing the forests and building roads for a paltry salary. They came to be known as coolies.

The *kanganis* were known to have enticed the workers with the promise that their lives would be far better in Malaya — a land where they would receive sky-high salaries that were equivalent to gold. The truth was far from it. It was only when these coolies arrived in Malaya that they realised that the promised wages were an illusion. Some say that the way the coolies were brought into the Malayan jungles and treated bore many resemblances to the way African slaves were treated at the hands of the 'Europeans'. It was a time when all Caucasians were called Europeans in Malaya. No one really bothered to find out if one was British or an Irishman.

The coolies were subjected to long working hours and harsh conditions in Malaya. Many succumbed to hunger, cholera, typhoid and dysentery; others to poisonous snake bites and passed away. Those who survived did not fare much better as they did not have nutritious food and died a slow painful death. Up to ten men and women were housed in the same room. There are tales of women resisting this arrangement in the beginning. Over time they got accustomed to not even having any privacy or a place to call their own. Many women were raped. Others sought refuge in marriages to much older men as a means to escape the prying eyes of the men in the rooms they lived in. That didn't always save them from the lecherous *kanganis*. In time, their dreams of returning to India and building their own home were forgotten.

Many of the descendants of these coolies worked in rubber estates, tapping rubber, cleaning weeds from the estate which they referred to as *velikaadu velai*. The lucky ones worked as storemen in the rubber estates. If, at all, any of them were paid, it was a meagre sum. It was often a hand-to-mouth existence. Life was hard in the estates. The coolies were lorded over by the estate managers, whom the coolies had christened *Periya Durai* or 'Big Boss' for the main *krani*-in-charge. The second in-charge was called *Chinna Durai* ('Small Boss'). The others were called Store *Krani*, *Velikaadu Krani* and *Kithakaadu Krani* depending on the specific jobs that they did. The dresser, who was really an assistant to the doctor, was called 'Doctor' by all.

The estate workers lived in a row of tiny houses. In the evenings, the men queued up outside the toddy shops for their daily fill. While the *kranis* and the workers both loved a glass of toddy in the evening, the *kranis* felt that it was beneath them to queue with the workers for their drink. So, they had their workers, who were only happy to oblige their bosses, buy their toddy for them. The worker tasked with the job of buying the toddy enjoyed a slightly elevated position to his peers.

The British primarily hired educated Sri Lankan Tamils and Malayalees from Kerala as *kranis* as they were educated and fluent in English. These *kranis* lived in better homes which the coolies called bungalows. The truth was far from it, of course. These only looked like bungalows in the eyes of the coolies in comparison to their own humble dwellings. The womenfolk who worked in the estates also doubled as servants in the homes of the *kranis* in the early evenings. The work in the estate would begin before dawn and end early which left them with time to spare before dark; that is if they were not all spent by the demands of their day job. The women welcomed the additional income. More income meant more food on the table. Sometimes, if the wives of the *kranis* were in a good mood or during festive occasions, they would 'gift' their old and worn-out clothes to their servants.

There was very little to do in the estates and the workers found respite at toddy shops, occasional movie screenings and with one another. Once in every two to three months, Tamil movies would be screened on the outskirts of the rubber estate in an open space. No one really knew if anyone paid attention to the obligatory advertisement that came on before the movie started. The popular comedy stars of yesteryears, Nagesh and Manorama, would often appear with a message on family planning. That was the cue for the movie to start.

This is the story of a sixth-generation descendant of two coolies from Tamil Nadu who had lived their whole lives in these estates, fighting off mosquito bites and working themselves to the bone. This is the story of a woman named Kaaliyamma — Kaali.

"THE MOVIE VAN is here! The movie van is here!"

The air was filled with the voices of squealing young children and teenagers. The boys ran after the van which drove through the narrow lanes of their estates. The huge speakers announced the arrival of the movie for the night.

Kaaliyamma was irritated. She had walked home with a heavy heart after a long day of work. *Krani* Appadurai had yelled at her for a slight oversight at work. She knew that she should not worry herself unnecessarily about being scolded by the *krani*. After all, she was just a rubber tapper.

To add fuel to the fire burning in her heart, she spotted her son running after the movie van, with one hand holding onto his loose *seluar*. He must have just returned from school. His homework lay untouched at home. She knew that her son would only return home after watching the movie in the open space under the night dew. He could not have eaten anything yet. Kaali knew the routine. On the days when the movie van came into the estate, her son would disappear for a few hours. She would have to go in search of him and cajole him to return home to have his dinner. Even when she was successful in getting him to return, all he would do was to gobble down a few mouthfuls of rice and dash off into the field.

Today, it didn't look like she would have any luck in dragging him back for dinner. Kaali sighed and went in search of her little boy in the open space where the movie was being shown, with his dinner in hand. A family planning advertisement was running. She sat down to feed him.

When she returned, Munusamy too walked into their home. As usual, the man was reeking of toddy. Like his son, he too hurriedly ate his dinner and promptly fell asleep. It is only now that Kaali could do the odd jobs around the home. She set out to wash the dirty dishes in the pail of water outside her home. She noticed that the edge of her earthen pot was chipped. *Goodness, now this too?* She refilled the pail with a generous amount of water and picked up the dirty clothes that they had worn that day — her *kaili* and blouse, Munusamy's *seluar* and shirt, and Raasu's clothes. She hit them against the washboard, willing the dirt out of them. She then soaked the clothes once again in the pail of water, pulled them up and twisted them tightly to get rid of the water from the clothes. She flicked off the water from the wet clothes gingerly before draping them across the metal strings strung across her metal laundry poles. A searing sharp pain on her back made her pause. Someone had thrown a stone at her.

"Won't you leave me alone today either?"

Her angry outburst was laced with a tinge of shyness. Calming her racing heart, she continued to drape the wet clothes. Another stone fell on her back. She refused to turn around. The whole estate was at the open space watching the movie. There was not a soul in sight on the street. The night was lit by the light bulb in her *kusini* and the sky. Chandran emerged stealthily from the shadows of the estate, dressed in a short-sleeved T-shirt and a half-pant *seluar*. She continued to ignore him.

The next moment it happened.

Her false anger melted away. Half an hour later, they both slowly emerged from the back of the chicken coop. She flicked the dirt off her *kaili*.

"Kaali, won't you think about what I have told you?" pleaded Chandran softly. She was irritated.

"Give me two days. I will tell you later. Now, go!" She sent him away. Chandran did not want to leave. As Chandran moved away, half-heartedly, Kaali stood rooted to the ground. *What am I going to do when I go into the house anyway?*

As she had predicted, Munusamy was sprawled on the bed, fast asleep in a drunken stupor. The mere sight of him angered her. *Now he would only wake up when it was time for the peratu* (roll call) *tomorrow morning, that too rather sleepily. What does he need a wife for, anyway?*

Raasu was born after a rare late-night romp. That too happened once in a blue moon. Munusamy would feel amorous only when he was drunk. It was a routine. He would jump on her, rip her apart and let her go once he was done.

Then, he would wake up at dawn, in time for the *peratu* just as she was about to leave the home. Munusamy would run into the forest to take care of his morning business, pour a few buckets of water over his head in a jiffy, in an attempt to wash himself. Next, he would drink the coffee that Kaali made for him in the morning, take a bite of the Singapore bread, put on his *seluar* and shirt, and rush out of the door before Kaali for his *peratu*.

She would be right on his heels to report to her job. As soon as the *Poonai Kannu Krani* (Cat-eyed *Krani*) told her which *nerai*, or section, she was assigned to that day, she would pick up her pails and the long wooden pole that she would use to balance the pails on after collecting the latex, and head off to board the lorry. The lorry took them to the respective sections. There, she would collect latex in the plates from the night before. She would then slice a groove into the bark of the tree with a hooked knife, taking care to ensure that it was a quarter inch, and peel back the bark diagonally. Once work started, she generally never had a moment to stand or sit. One time, she did not even notice that a snake had crawled over her rubber-stained slippers. Thankfully, it was not a poisonous snake.

About twelve o'clock or whenever she got hungry, she would stop and have the meal that she had packed in the morning — fried rice and black coffee. If Perumaayi was close by in the next *nerai*, which was often the case, she would chat with her for a short while. It was during one of these lunch breaks that she met Perumaayi's cousin, Chandran.

"My cousin is here for one week from Singapore," introduced Perumaayi. But Chandran, who was initially just there for a one-week holiday, showed no sign of leaving even after a month. It wasn't clear if Kaali was the reason that he stayed. On her part, Kaali did not find him particularly interesting nor attractive when she saw him for the first time.

There was nothing unusual about that day. She was at work at the rubber estate, cutting the rubber trees, cleaning the latex plates, pouring the latex into the pail over her shoulder and hurriedly moving from one tree to another when she screamed, "Ayo!" and fell to the ground. Hearing her scream, Perumaayi and Chandran, who were in the next *nerai*, came running to her. As soon as Perumaayi saw her, she knew that Kaali needed immediate medical attention.

"Thambi, carry her, carry her! We need to take her to the doctor."

Chandran didn't hesitate for a moment. Carrying her down the muddy path, he managed to stop a Chinese man's van. The driver was returning to the estate after dropping off his children at the English-medium school in town. Perumaayi put both Kaali and Chandran on the van and told Chandran to take Kaali to the doctor. Perumaayi then ran all the way back to tell the mandor the news. Fortunately, it turned out to be a scorpion bite, and not a snake bite as was initially feared. Dresser Varghese gave her medication and a jab before sending her away.

That was how it all started.

Kaali's gratitude knew no boundaries. She acted like a woman who was rescued from being shot at the enemy lines. She treated Chandran like the God who had rescued her from death. She described the incident to everyone in the estate, making Chandran's act sound larger than life. She boasted of Perumaayi's and Chandran's quick thinking. Munusamy too treated Chandran with a lot of respect after that incident. He invited Chandran home whenever he saw him for a cup of coffee. Chandran and Kaali barely spoke to each other in front of Munusamy except for a brief cursory greeting. Sometimes, when Raasu Boy was naughty, Munusamy admonished him with the threat, "I will tell the Singapore Maama that you're being naughty." Chandran was rather pleased to hear Munusamy's words. It was clear how important he was to Kaali's family.

The sky was still dark that day when Kaali got off from the lorry in front of the eighth *nerai*. She set out to work and must have completed about ten trees when somebody hugged her from behind in a tight embrace. She froze for a moment. She couldn't turn around. His huge fingers roamed her body freely. He grabbed her tighter as she wriggled, making it impossible

for her to turn around. When she couldn't contain herself
anymore, she screamed, "Chee! Leave me alone!" She pushed
him away using all her strength, trying to catch her breath. The
next moment, in a flash of lightning, he pushed towards her
again and buried his face at the nape of her neck. He moved his
lips down her body slowly. By now, it was clear that he did not
need to hurry. Everything that happened afterwards, happened
according to his wishes. Soon, he started visiting Kaali once the
neighbours had retired for the night.

Chandran filled a huge gap in Kaali's life. In fact, he
made her life more bearable. Suddenly, she was able to escape
from everything that was wrong with her life — the lack of
affection from Munusamy, the machine-like work that she
did at the rubber estate, the scolding that she endured from
the mandors and the *kranis* who looked at her as though
she was a worm. It was a novel experience for her and she
was overwhelmed by his amorous love. She was also secretly
pleased that a 'modern man' from Singapore, who was unlike
the men in her estate, had chosen her out of all the women
in Anjarai Kattai.

*Would he not have met several women in Singapore… and yet…
and yet he likes me, doesn't he? All I have done from birth is to live in
this estate. I have not seen anything other than this estate. At most, I
must have gone to town to buy new clothes on rare occasions. Doesn't
my life deserve to be brightened up? My husband has never even
taken me to watch a movie. Oh well, he does not even go to watch the
movies shown at the estate himself. All he does after work is to head
to the toddy shop. What else does he know?*

One day at the dawn of a new day, Kaali packed up her
belongings and her life in Anjarai Kattai to elope with
Chandran to Singapore. The place they arrived at was 13th

Mile Sembawang or Sembawang Kechil. The first sight that greeted her in the new land was a row of kampong houses.

Out of the blue, Raasu Boy was told that his father, Munusamy, had come to pick him up from school that day. Wondering if something had happened to his mother, Raasu came out to meet his father.

WHEN RAASU BOY saw his father standing at the school gate, he leapt into his arms screaming, "*Yeppo!*" For some reason, that day Munusamy did not draw his son close to him as he usually did. Raasu Boy was puzzled. This father held his hand but did not say a word all the way home. As they walked past the *Kakka* Shop, he looked at his father and said, "*Yeppa*, colour sweet" pointing to the coloured candy in the store. The next minute, he felt a searing pain across his cheek.

As soon as they got home, Raasu Boy ran into the home. "Amma, Appa hit me!" He sniffed a little and then started crying. His father slapped him again. Raasu Boy could not bear it anymore and started crying loudly. A neighbour was sitting in the corner of his home crying.

"Your mum is not here, my dear Raasu. How could your mum do this?" she said.

"Where is Amma, Paati? Where is Amma?" yelled out Raasu Boy, kicking his leg in the air as he fell to the ground crying. That was it. As though he had been waiting for that moment, Munusamy started berating her.

"How could she run away without even a thought about this boy?"

Munusamy found himself weeping along with his son.

He could not believe what had just happened. He would never have believed anyone if they had told him that his wife — the quiet one — would do this.

When he got up that morning to go to the *peratu*, there was no one around. *Maybe she had left early.* He walked into the *kusini* and found his usual black coffee and fried rice waiting for him. He gulped down the black coffee and fried rice that Kaali had made for him that morning and walked out of the house. That is when he saw her rubber-stained slippers lying outside the front door. *"Aye,* Kaali!" he yelled into the pitch-black forest. There was no reply. The pail, the sickle and the sack she took to work lay in a corner outside the home next to the slippers.

Munusamy was irritated. *Where was she? She clearly had not gone to work. She was not home either. Oh, maybe she had gone into the woods to relieve herself.* Raasu Boy was curled up and fast asleep in bed. It was time for school. *Why isn't she getting the boy ready for school? Where on earth is she?* But Kaali was nowhere to be found even at 10 a.m. This was highly unusual. The estate was coming alive. It was then that Lorry Driver Ahamad came by to tell him that he had seen Kaali walking down the path with a man at dawn. News started to trickle into the estate. Mookan's wife too had seen her. She told him how she had had a bad case of diarrhoea that morning and had rushed into the estate woods twice to relieve herself. That was when she had seen Kaali in a green sari walking away from Anjarai Kattai.

Other folks in the estate who had sighted Kaali at dawn came by to report what they had seen to Munusamy. When Munusamy learnt that Chandran and his clothes too were missing from his home, he was heartbroken. Kaali had also taken her two-pound gold necklace. The estate-folk gathered around his house.

"Kaali ran away with that boy from Singapore, that Chandran," they whispered.

It was the topic of the day. The women at the rubber plantation could not refrain themselves from talking about Kaali and Chandran. For once, they ignored the mandors who were on duty. The conversation continued throughout the day. Even as they returned home in the lorries, they continued to discuss the scandal. One could not blame them. Hardly anything ever happened at Anjarai Kattai.

The incident left Mandor Maarimuthu bristling with rage and disappointment. *Bloody fool! I was after her for such a long time and she ignored me. She even pretended to be virtuous! In the end, she became the talk of the town.* Mandor Maarimuthu had a hard time believing Kaali had eloped. *How could she?*

Perumaayi too was in a state of shock. "Of all the people, why did he have to run away with her? I didn't see it coming. I thought she was a good person. How could that filthy woman do this to my cousin?" Unable to contain her anger at Kaali's betrayal, she spewed vulgarities about Kaali to whoever was close by.

In Singapore, with some difficulty, Kaali and Chandran were able to get a room for rent in Sethulakshmi Amma's house in Sembawang Kechil. There were six other tenants in the other rooms. Once they moved into the house, Kaali was finally able to sleep in peace. Both her heart and body were weary from the week's happenings. They had gone to Chandran's home in Naval Base Quarters when they had first arrived a week ago. Chandran's mother, Anjalai, did not allow them to enter the flat initially. Anjalai wasn't pleased with her son arriving at her doorstep with a strange woman. She was far less pleased when her son announced, "From now on, she is my wife." Anjalai barricaded herself for several hours in the *kusini* in protest. Then all hell broke loose when Perumaayi's husband, Pichaimuthu, returned to Singapore that evening.

"How could you do this? Do you look down on us, the estate people?" he said as he grabbed Chandran's collar and shook him violently.

Hearing that Kaali had left behind a husband and a child, Anjalai bellowed out revolting vulgarities at the top of her voice. There was no stopping her. The neighbours' ears must have melted with the filth that came out of their flat that night. In Anjalai's eyes, a married woman had seduced her innocent unmarried son. Anjalai lunged towards Kaali, in an attempt to yank her long hair and beat her senseless. The neighbours managed to stop her in time. But they could not stop her from continuing to yell out unpalatable words at Kaali. Chandran and Kaali left the flat briskly after that and sought refuge at the entrance of the Holy Tree Sri Balasubramaniar Temple.

Hearing their plight, Chandran's friend, Ponnusamy, came to their rescue. He told Chandran that there was a vacant room at his older sister's neighbour's home. He accompanied them to Sethulakshmi Amma's house to vouch for Chandran as well. Sethulakshmi Amma had not heard about what had happened in the Naval Base Quarters yet. Unfortunately, she didn't like Kaali.

"Why has she tied her sari like this? She doesn't even speak well. There are so many people in this house and yet, she is locked up in the room all the time. Doesn't that woman have any shame?"

But that was not Kaali's fault really. Chandran wanted her all the time. Whenever Kaali walked into their room to pass him something, he would pull her onto the bed and pin her down. He wanted her to feed him. He wanted her to sit close to him. Even though Sethulakshmi Amma did not come into her room, Kaali was worried about what the women in the house thought about her. She was embarrassed to face the other woman when she stepped out of the room. Understandably so, because almost on cue, the moment she walked out of the room, Sethulakshmi Amma would start questioning her. That day was no different. As soon as she stepped out, she was met by a disgusted Sethulakshmi Amma who asked, "Haven't you gone to wash your clothes yet?"

Kaali had indeed forgotten the dirty laundry that needed to be washed. She needed to go to the main pipe to do so. One had to walk four houses away to what the residents called the main pipe to wash their clothes. Kaali was frequently late and that meant that by the time she got to the main pipe, there would be a lot of women there already. Like the women around her, she too would hurriedly wash her clothes. It's not that there wasn't any running water in the home. There was. But Sethulakshmi Amma did not want her tenants to run up the utilities bill.

Chandran's devotion to her did not cloud her longing for Raasu Boy in her mind. But Chandran had told her rather firmly that she should not talk about any of her family members or her past in their home.

"You're not going to work at all! How long can we keep borrowing money to feed ourselves?" asked Kaali on the third day after moving into Sethulakshmi Amma's house. Her question irritated him.

"I know that! I know what to do! If I know how to bring you along with me, I know how to look after you too!"

Most of the tenants in that house were Malayalees from Kerala. There were only two other Tamil-speaking tenants —

Muthuletchimi and her husband. What surprised her more was that in Sembawang, everywhere she turned, she ran into Malayalees.

"Didn't you know that this place is called *Kochu Keralam* or *Kutti Keralam?* This is where a lot of Malayalees live in Singapore. Most of them work at the Naval Base. Even the Tamils in Sembawang speak Malayalam, don't you know?" said Muthuletchimi. Muthuletchimi was her window to understanding Sembawang. Kaali was baffled by the news. She really did not like Malayalees.

In the estate where she came from, the *kranis* were either Sri Lankans or Malayalees and all of them looked down on the estate workers. They screamed at the workers if there was an additional cut on the rubber trees or the plates used to collect the latex were not cleaned properly. This was despite them working as quickly as they could to collect as much latex as possible for the day. The punishment for any mistakes that they did would be to work on old trees which had little sap. The womenfolk called it *seekumaram* or 'sick tree'. Their stomachs would burn in agony as they bent over repeatedly to cut the row of old trees which had very little sap and hard barks. They had to strain with all their might to coax the trees into giving latex. The strain made their eyes feel like they were bleeding.

In retaliation, the workers gave the *kranis* hilarious nicknames: *Kungkumutti Krani, Lol Lol Krani, Mandai Moonji Krani. Kungkumutti Krani* looked like a huge barrel with his massive tummy. *Lol Lol Krani* barked like a dog and was named 'lol lol' to mimic the bark of a dog. *Mandai Moonji Krani* or 'head-faced *Krani*' would constantly scold them by asking, "Is there anything in your head?"

Having grown up in these circumstances, Kaali found herself in a quandary — she had run away from these men only to be placed in an environment where everywhere she turned, she heard Malayalam being spoken and Malayalee voices. All day long, she heard Malayalam words that sounded like "*paranju... arinju*". It was sheer torture to hear or be surrounded by the Malayalees.

But there was no way out of the situation. Chandran was already having difficulties paying the ten-dollar rent for this room. He spent his day asking for a loan to help to pay the rent. She really had no room to complain. Plus the Malayalee female tenants in the house and next door treated her with love and care. Their affection soothed her heart somewhat.

After one week, Kaali started going to the pasar on her own. On the first two days, she had gone with some of the fellow female tenants in the house. Then she started going alone. She did not understand what the fuss was. *Was going to the market and buying fish a job?* Having cut three hundred to four hundred trees a day, collected their rubber from those trees and carried that in pails balanced on a wooden pole to the collection centre, she didn't think 'marketing' for the household was a chore at all. For 20 cents, she would buy sardines and for another 20 cents, she could buy green leafy vegetables. She would spend 10 cents on a nice big potato. That would be sufficient for two meals for both Chandran and her, with plenty of leftovers.

After one month of begging *Kunjampoo Krani* for a job, Chandran managed to get a small job at the Naval Base. Friday was payday at the Naval Base. The weekly payment made things easy for her. Slowly, she started buying pots and pans, and other things for the *kusini*.

Her fellow tenant friend, Muthuletchimi, warned her about Sethulakshmi Amma, the houseowner. Sethulakshmi Amma did not like her tenants to stand in front of her house to brush their teeth. Nor were they allowed to leave the water running at any time; failing which, she would complain that the electricity and water bill had gone up and charge them more money. Kaali was careful to abide by all the rules. She did not want to cause any trouble.

There were eight tenants in the house. Sethulakshmi Amma, the houseowner, and her husband, Karunakaran, as well as their three children had two rooms at the back of the house. Karunakaran was really dark and was twenty years older than Sethulakshmi Amma. He never raised his voice at his wife nor reacted to her constant questions.

Sethulakshmi was from a small village in Kerala. She had been brought over to Singapore by a relative and married off to a much older Karunakaran. Her resentment towards her husband had not receded over the years and could be seen in the way she spoke to him. Ironically, she used the same tone when she spoke to the tenants as well. Not even God was spared from her sharp tongue that day.

"The gas stove in the *kusini* is stinking! Which idiot put the dirty underwear in front of the house to dry? Which one of you idiots doesn't know that you shouldn't display your bra and underwear in front of the house for the world to see?" These sharp needle-like comments on the tenants would only be met with pin-drop silence in a house full of tenants and family.

The house next to Sethulakshmi's was filled with tenants who were bachelors as well as those who had left their wives in Kerala. All of them worked at the Naval Base but, for some reason, were not eligible for housing quarters at the base. The houses were built really close to one another. The room across from Chandran and Kaali's housed four men. One of the men would constantly stand by his window that overlooked her room and, when no one was looking, would wink at Kaali. Kaali was embarrassed. But whom could she complain to?

One day, as she was returning from the market and walking by Jalan Kadai, she saw the man from the house next door walking towards her. There was no place for her to run away to hide. When he got close to her, he asked her in Tamil, "Have you eaten?" in his heavy Malayalam accent. She giggled. *Goodness, is this what I was worried about?*

"*Aye, aye,* why are you not talking and walking away?"

When she finally asked Muthuletchimi about their neighbour, she was surprised to hear that Muthuletchimi actually liked the man.

"He is a gentle soul. He left his family in Kerala. Whenever he sees us, he sees us as a family member. He is really warm. Don't misunderstand him."

For the life of her, Kaali could not fathom why a family member would wink at her with a funny expression.

A few days later, the whole town was in a festive mood. Muthuletchimi explained that the Malayalees were getting ready to celebrate Onam. Kaali was roped in to help the women cut unripe bananas into very thin slices and fry these pieces into crisp chips. These banana chips were filled in biscuit tins. There were several other sweetmeats like *murukku, achhu murukku* and *kuzhalappams* that were made in several batches. The festive air and preparations around Kaali and Muthu occupied them for days. On the eve of Onam, her houseowner taught her to prepare a ginger dish, *injipuli*, and mango pickles.

On Onam day, the Malayalees in Sembawang wore new clothes or *Onakodi* as they called it. The women's attire reflected their husbands' status or rather what they could afford. The boys' attire puzzled Kaali. They were dressed in white shirts and blue pants or rather in what looked like new school uniforms. The girls wore silk skirts and blouses.

The smell of the multi-course strictly vegetarian *Onasadya* was intoxicating and engulfed the air around the village. There were vegetable curries made of yogurt and coconut. Even the men pitched in to fry several dozen pappadams. Once the men and children were served, Sethulakshmi Amma, Kaali and Muthu finally sat down to have their meal. Kaali had never eaten such a wide variety of vegetable dishes in a single meal. The vegetarian meal on a banana leaf actually tasted pretty good. The *injipuli* was out of the world. But Kaali didn't particularly like the cabbage *thoran* nor the long beans *thoran*. The only curry she recognised was sambar — the lentil and vegetable curry. She loved the traditional Malayalee dessert, *pradhaman*. Once they had eaten, Kaali and Muthu set out to clean all the utensils.

Since all meals at home on Onam day would be vegetarian, the men headed off to the shops to have their fill of laksa and *mee goreng* in the evenings, as they were craving for some meat dishes. Some couples headed to the Sultan Theatre to watch the newly released Malayalam movies. That was Kaali's introduction to the Malayalee Onam festival.

The next morning Kaali watched the children head off to school in their new uniforms. Muthu explained that most families with five or six children would purchase uniforms for their children on festive occasions as these doubled up as new clothes.

Three days after Onam, Kaali had just finished her household chores when Manju's mother in the third room asked if she could accompany her on an errand. She did not ask where they were going. Kaali carried Manju in her arms as they walked for a bit, past Sembawang Kechil, until they reached Ulu Sembawang. Manju's mum joined a queue and told Kaali that was Sembawang Hot Springs and that if one were to drink the water in the hot spring or bathe children in that water, the aches and pains in the body would be removed. Based on the long queue that was gathered there that day, it was clear that this was a widespread belief. But it was an orderly queue. Soon, it was their turn. Manju's mother took the child from Kaali's hands and placed Manju near the hot spring well. She poured the water all over the child and even made Manju take a few gulps of the water. Manju was an obliging child and she was a delight to watch. Following Manju's mother's actions, Kaali too put her hand out to scoop up some water and drank it. The hot spring water tasted slightly different but that was it. There was nothing else unusual about it.

When Chandran heard that she had visited the hot springs, his first question was, "Did you watch the men having a bath in their tiny underwear?"

She had. But it didn't strike her as something unusual. She had grown up seeing men in the estate taking their bath in a loin cloth and nothing else. Grown men in their underwear did not faze her.

"I don't like it, Kaali. Don't go to the hot springs without me in the future."

He was rather quiet for the rest of the day. But his words had warmed the cockles of her heart, thinking how much Chandran must love her to be jealous of the mere thought of her gaze falling on another man's body.

DAWN WAS JUST breaking when Kaali heard a commotion outside her room. She tried to jump out of bed but Chandran tightened his grip around her waist. It sounded like someone was being beaten up. She managed to break free from Chandran's tight embrace. When she opened the door of her room, she saw all the other tenants standing outside the *kusini*.

"Leave her alone, leave her!" The houseowner, Karunakaran, was yelling at Mathai.

"I should just kill her for what she did!" retorted Mathai. He continued to kick his wife who was curled up on the floor. Manju's father and a few others managed to pull Mathai away from his wife. Later in the day, once the children had left for school and the men for work, Muthuletchimi told Kaali what had happened.

As she walked to the pasar that morning, Kaali's thoughts drifted to Margaret. She felt sorry for Margaret. Margaret had just received a letter from Kerala informing her that her mother was not well. Without telling Mathai, Margaret had promptly taken the money that her husband had given her for 'marketing' purposes as well as their savings and given them to their neighbour, Devagi Chechi, to send to her mother in Kerala. When word of what she had done reached Mathai's ears, he beat up his wife who was six months pregnant.

Margaret was curled up on the floor sobbing her eyes out when Kaali entered her room with a plate of rice, dal and two pieces of dried fried fish (*karuvadu*). Kaali helped Margaret off the floor.

"Don't cry, Margaret. Come, have something to eat."

Margaret managed to swallow one or two mouthfuls of the food. Tears continued to stream down Margaret's cheeks. The two women became fast friends after that. Whenever Margaret made Kaali's favourite Kerala fish curry with grated coconut, she would make extra for Kaali. Margaret tried teaching Kaali how to make the curry, but Kaali could just never get the taste right or cook it the way Margaret did.

One Saturday evening, Chandran took Kaali to the pasar malam, the night market, that was set up between the shops in Sembawang and the market. Kaali had never been to a pasar malam before. Once in a blue moon, Munusamy had taken her to town to the shops, but he would be the one to choose the clothes for her and her son. He never once asked her if she liked what he bought for her. Kaali only received new clothes on Pongal and Deepavali.

During one of those trips with Munusamy and her son, she saw people drinking *chendol* in tall glasses. It was a green drink and had ice floating at the top of the glass. Drooling at the sight of the drink, she asked Munusamy, "Can you buy me and Raasu Boy a glass of that?" Munusamy's grim expression had left her silent.

Here at the pasar malam, there were so many shops. Her eyes lit up at the sight of it. It had everything. "Is this a pasar malam? My goodness. Look at the number of things there are." Kaali's eyes grew wide. And she could not stop staring at the sights around her.

Chandran bought two huge glasses of sour plum juice for the both of them. Because her bras were torn, she went to the shop selling feminine products and bought herself two bras and two pieces of cotton underwear. Chandran seemed to hesitate for a second before paying for the items. Kaali's eyes then fell on a hair clip that was similar to the one worn by Muthuletchimi. Kaali had never worn a hair clip in her life. She bought herself one that night at the pasar malam.

"Do you want anything else?" asked Chandran. She was too blind to notice that his voice sounded lifeless.

"It's okay. We can buy more things next Friday when you get your salary," said Kaali feeling rather very self-righteous about her self-discipline. *What else would I want out of life?* That night she melted into Chandran's arms and forgot herself.

Chinnadurai was feeling frustrated. He had completed his primary school education at Methodist Tamil Primary School and his secondary education at Umar Pulavar Tamil School. But to date, he had not found himself a job. Like his father, Ezhumalai, he washed the *aluru* (drain) by the blocks too and in the evenings, he took on odd jobs in the homes of some of the British officers who lived in Sembawang. He was embarrassed to tell anyone what he did for a living. He was hoping to land a job as a Tamil teacher and relentlessly searched day and night for such a job. The truth was that he had failed his English Language paper and to make matters worse, scored zero for his Mathematics paper. His former Tamil teacher, Mr Joseph, had even mocked his desire to become a Tamil teacher. With his grades, it did indeed seem like it was an impossible dream.

"Why do you want to work as a teacher? Just go work with your father cleaning the *aluru*. At least, then you can decrease the burden on your father."

Unable to take his parents' constant nagging about his future, Chinnadurai enrolled himself in night school. It was here that he met Murugan and Vellaya. Both of them had stopped their education at the primary level and neither had any ambition to study further like he did.

In fact, Murugan's family had lost all hope in him. Like Chinnadurai, he too had completed his primary education at Methodist Tamil Primary School. At ten, his teacher, Mr Chellam, had caught him red-handed stealing something. At fifteen, he started smoking. He was also in love with a married woman who lived in the next block of flats, to whom he had one day penned a love letter. The woman's husband confronted him rather angrily. Hearing the news, his mother beat him up with a broom. It was his older sister who enrolled him in the night class to keep him occupied.

Vellaya, however, had no parents to worry about. His mother had died at childbirth because of incessant bleeding within a half hour of giving birth to him. Vellaya's father, Machappu, had an affair with Sinnasee's wife. How long could they keep their affair a secret? Unable to bear living alone for a long time and tired of hiding their relationship, he eloped with Sinnasee's wife. A few months later, Vellaya's grandfather, Chinnasamy, heard that the couple were seen working as sweepers in the Kolam Ayer area. Chinnasamy did not pay much heed to the news. He knew he could raise Vellaya on his own. Not wanting to give up when he realised Vellaya was not good in his studies, he enrolled Vellaya in night classes. Vellaya didn't know if he learnt anything in those night classes.

Every evening, Chinnasamy would take solace in a bottle of toddy and weep at the state of his life. When Chinnasamy was about twenty-two years old, he had been abducted. He had been on his way to consult a traditional medicine practitioner after his work at the Naval Base that evening. Out of the blue, a few men who were dressed like policemen had jumped out of a jeep while he was walking by the Royal Theatre. They were carrying weapons. They hustled him into their jeep and drove away. It felt like it had happened today. He had struggled with all his might to save himself but to no avail. He was kicked, pushed and stamped upon by the Japanese. The Japanese were going to send him away somewhere. Chinnasamy did not understand what was happening. They put him on a train, and it was only when he entered the carriage and sat down next to several other Tamils who were already there that he learnt about where he was headed. The Japanese were sending him to work on the Siam railway. The train stopped several times that night as more Tamil, Malay and Chinese men were stuffed into the carriage.

By the time they reached Kedah, Chinnasamy was throwing up. He struggled with diarrhoea throughout the trip. Watching him suffer, a Japanese soldier fetched a British doctor to attend to him. The doctor gave him something to ease his ailment. Chinnasamy did not know what the British doctor told the Japanese soldier but, a few minutes after talking to the doctor, the Japanese soldier dragged him by his collar and kicked him out onto the railway station platform. Chinnasamy was barely awake. When he opened his eyes, a elderly Malay man was trying to get him to drink a herbal drink. It took him at least a week to even sit up in bed.

Hearing his story, the Malay man said with a quiet smile, "You're lucky you fell sick. If the Japanese had taken you along, you might have died at the railway." Chinnasamy felt his insides shake.

Somehow, Chinnasamy managed to beg and borrow money from the elderly man and the people he met at the railway platform to buy a train ticket back to Singapore. With great difficulty, he returned but nothing could ever prepare him for the news that awaited him. Not knowing what had happened to her husband who had gone out to buy herbal medicine after work, his heartbroken wife had committed suicide. The female tenants in the house they lived in greeted him with this sombre news. His heart was broken. He never remarried after that. Chinnasamy focused all his energy on raising his only daughter, whom he married off to Machappu. When his daughter died at childbirth and her husband left the infant in his care, he took on the responsibility of raising his grandson. But by now, his heart and body were weary, but the sadness that surrounded that old man's heart and life did not affect his grandson in any way.

"What sort of life is this? I have to study just for the sake of this old man. So, what if I don't study? I just need to get a job, don't I?" reasoned Vellaya.

Luckily, Ramasamy Maama had asked him to help out at his shop. Vellaya spent the whole day at the shop helping him and attending night classes in the evenings. Murugan and Chinnadurai's family were impressed with Vellaya's tenacity.

"Look at Vellaya. Aren't you ashamed? He works the whole day and still goes for night classes."

Vellaya was secretly delighted that anyone would consider him a good role model.

One day, Ramasamy Maama tasked him to take his wife to the gynaecologist. "Can you just take auntie to the gynae and come back?" said Ramasamy Maama.

The clinic was at 14th Mile. Vellaya passed his time watching the pregnant women in the clinic. He enjoyed the outing very much and often asked, "Maama, when should I take auntie to the gynae again?"

Ramasamy Maama was really pleased with Vellaya's earnestness. He allowed Vellaya to handle transactions especially during lunch hour. Vellaya carried out his duties diligently for about a week. The following week, he started putting aside small amounts of money for himself.

Muthuletchimi was returning home from the shop when she saw the elderly Chinnasamy curled up at the veranda of the house next door. Taking Kaali along with her, she brought along a small bowl of porridge for the old man. Kaali could not stay long as she had to finish her household chores. So, she left quite quickly.

Within seconds of Kaali leaving the home, the 'eye-winking Malayalee man' who lived in that home sprung out of his room. He hugged Muthuletchimi in a tight embrace and gave her a rather loud sloppy kiss. Breaking herself free from the embrace, Muthuletchimi ran back to her house. She was fuming mad. But for some unknown reason, she never told Kaali what had transpired next door.

4

A SURPRISE AWAITED Kaali who had just returned from the pasar. There was a small lorry parked in front of her house and several men were moving a bed, a bed frame, cabinets and various household items from the lorry into the room next to Manju's mother.

Kaali peered into the room. She saw an elderly lady checking the items that were being brought into the room. An elderly man with a head full of white hair stood next to her. He seemed to be barking orders at the lady and the movers. Just then, Sethulakshmi Amma called out loudly to her, "Don't you have any household chores to do? Why are you looking at what others are doing?" Kaali hurried away into the *kusini*.

Within a week of Sangkaralingam and Meenatchi Paati arriving, their life became the talk of the town. Sangkaralingam woke up at five every morning. By the time he finished brushing his teeth and got to the breakfast table, he expected to see either idlis or dosa with freshly-made chutney on the table. He did not like leftover curries from the night before. He expected fresh coconut chutney with his breakfast. As there were no refrigerators in each home, Meenatchi Paati had to wake up earlier, grate fresh coconut, fry mustard seeds and hurriedly make the coconut chutney for him. Once or twice, when she brought the freshly-made coconut chutney for his dosa or idlis, she had forgotten to put enough salt or chilli. That was enough to spark off the acid tongue of Sangkaralingam. He would throw the food along with the plate at her. Muthuletchimi had unwittingly witnessed this scene one morning and had run back to the *kusini*.

"How can he scold Paati like this? And how can Paati live with him?" Both Muthuletchimi and Kaali were amazed at Meenatchi Paati's patience with that man.

What was puzzling was that Sangkaralingam's harsh words were only reserved for his wife. He was all smiles and sweet words to the other female tenants in the house.

He expected his wife to cook him non-vegetarian food every day. He wanted either fish curry, chicken curry or *karuvadu* curry — and they must be up to his taste, of course. Once in a while, when Meenatchi Paati made sambar or rasam, he would throw a tantrum and give Meenatchi Paati a hard time. Even when Meenatchi Paati was down with a fever or flu, she had to make sure that she made a delicious meal for her husband. It had often occurred to her that even if Lord Yama arrived with the death rope, it was Meenatchi Paati's fate to cook her husband's meal before she died.

The funny thing was that Sangkaralingam was a huge gossip! He would carry tales about Manju's mother to Muthuletchimi and about Muthuletchimi to Kaali. Once, when Sethulakshmi Amma was a little friendly to him, he told her what the female tenants thought about her. Of course, he added several juicy pieces to the story, with things that the women would never dream of saying or doing. After that, for the next few days, the women in the house could not understand why Sethulakshmi Amma kept picking on them like a scorpion. Sangkaralingam was secretly pleased at the chaos he had caused in the household.

Margaret was the only one who was not taken in by the old man. She made it a point to turn away whenever the man entered the room. She hated the way the old man treated his wife, Meenatchi Paati.

Sangkaralingam made it a point to read every word in magazines and newspapers without fail daily. But he never spoke about politics or global events to anyone. No one had heard him speak about these things. All he spoke about was Tamil cinema news or gossip. He spoke about Saroja Devi who was at the peak of her acting career then.

"Devika has gone on to the next husband. What number do you think this husband is?" he asked with a giggle.

Sangkaralingam was a born storyteller. He knew whom MGR, a Malayalee actor and the leading heart-throb in Tamil cinema, had affairs with and how many women he had been with. Nobody questioned the old man on why he loved to gossip about film stars and people. He would add several juicier details to his stories and make even mundane information sound scandalous.

The strange thing was that both men and women liked him in the Sembawang area.

He also always ensured that he watched the first show of any new movie that was released at Sultan Theatre. The very next day, when the womenfolk finished their household chores, he would gather them and entertain them with the story of the movie. He would provide a scene-by-scene analysis, critiquing the acting and explaining how the audience responded to the actors' expressions. Hearing him narrate and critique the movies, the womenfolk's hearts fluttered like birds and they became eager to watch the movie.

But it was a time when no married woman from 13th Mile would dare to go and watch a movie on her own or with her friends. The only way that one could watch a movie was with one's husband and that too only after Friday, which was the husbands' payday. That meant that they could go on Saturday for the movie. Women with two or three children could not even bring up the topic of going to watch a movie. Asking to be brought to the movie would warrant a sound beating from their husbands. No one wanted to take that risk.

Sangkaralingam had another talent too. He had an encyclopaedic knowledge of homeopathy. Everybody in the house respected his knowledge in natural medicine. He advised men on their stomach problems and backaches. He was a fountain of knowledge when explaining the consumption of which type of fish would result in virility, and which vegetables would control one's cholesterol, as well as what sorts of exercise one should do if one had high blood pressure or what sorts of food one needed to avoid if one had diabetes. He was able to list these things like a real doctor would. It always irritated Meenatchi Paati when he started on one of these long lectures.

This man has high cholesterol, high blood pressure, diabetes and piles! He gives lectures to others on how to live but never for a moment does he follow his own advice. He has no discipline about food, not even for a day. He wants his curries to be tasty and the right mix of salt, tamarind and chilli. In fact, he wants it to be extra tasty and just right but unhealthy.

If the different curries that she had cooked that day did not please him, she would be subjected to his acid tongue. Yet, that hypocrite was a fountain of knowledge for others on what they had to do. Ironically, everyone who heard Sangkaralingam's advice found it useful. They sang his praises especially when they saw their health improve by taking his advice. If Meenatchi Paati was within earshot when they came by to thank him, Sangkaralingam would look at her, smile and twirl his thick moustache with his fingers. He would also give her the look. All Meenatchi Paati wanted to do at that moment was to pick up the broom and hit him.

"Hmm…!" Her thoughts were confined to her heart. Sometimes she felt like laughing. After all, who else can the old man twirl his moustache at and boast of his stature in society? Meenatchi Paati had lost all hope in life.

One day, when Sangkaralingam returned from the polyclinic, he brought along a visitor with him. His name was Maasilamani. Meenatchi Paati gave him a once-over. The quiet man spotted a heavy beard and spoke softly to Sangkaralingam. Despite that, bits of their conversation wafted through the air to Meenatchi Paati's ears. Her heart froze at what she heard. That afternoon, Maasilamani had lunch with Meenatchi Paati and Sangkaralingam. Because it was a rented house, Maasilamani could not linger too long in that house. He left soon after lunch for Kedondong Road, where he shared a room with his friend.

Maasilamani had arrived in Singapore from the Ramanathapuram district in Tamil Nadu, India, in 1958, searching for a job. Within six months of arriving, he fell into the company of a Chinese gang. At first, he did petty crimes with them. In the early days, he even felt guilty about them. But when he saw how much money he was making, he realised that he could never make that sort of money working for someone. That sort of appeased his guilt. The truth was that he did not have the time nor space in his life to weigh in on what was right or wrong.

One day as he was hanging out at a liquor shop with his gang and getting drunk as usual, the police siren shook the building. It all happened in the blink of an eye. There was no way to escape or anyway to get out of there in time. To his credit, he hadn't murdered anyone or burgled any home. But his gang and gang leaders' past were spotted with several unspeakable crimes. Maasilamani was just a henchman and lived off the scraps of the gang leader. Although he had only committed petty crimes, there was no one to defend or argue for him in court. No matter what the crime was, it was still a crime. It didn't matter whether it was a big or small one. They were all crimes, weren't they?

It was during this period of time that a European, a Daniel Stanley Dutton, took charge as the Superintendent of Prisons in Singapore. Prisons were filthy and prisoners died of diseases with no one paying much heed to their fate. Given the sorry state that the prison was in and primarily because of overcrowding, a new prison site on an island called Pulau Senang was selected to house some of the hardcore prisoners. Some of the most notorious prisoners who committed heinous crimes were brought to this prison. Pulau Senang is about fifteen miles south of Singapore. The prison was set up on two hundred and twenty-seven acres of land. In May 1960, a penal reform centre was officially started on this island. The superintendent believed that hardcore criminals could change for the better if they were given a second chance. He believed that he could rehabilitate them with manual labour without bars.

Maasilamani too was put on the list of hardcore criminals and sent to Pulau Senang. Daniel Dutton arrived at the island with fifty criminals and together they built the place up. Soon, thirty more criminals arrived. Within a short span of time, he managed to clear the island, put in roads, a reservoir, workshops, farms and even a sports ground.

The Pulau Senang experiment was a success at the beginning. It was then that another two hundred and fifty prisoners from Changi Prison arrived at Pulau Senang. Within a short period of time, Dutton felt that many of the prisoners had been rehabilitated based on their behaviour. He sent these prisoners back to the mainland after six months. A government agency helped the ex-cons search for suitable jobs. Maasilamani was one of those whom Dutton sent back to the mainland.

By 1963, there were about three hundred prisoners at Pulau Senang. Dutton ordered thirteen of these men to work day and night on the construction of the much-needed jetty. They were ordered to work during low tides. They worked day and night with no rest. The men were fatigued and resentful of Dutton. They hatched a plot to kill him. The good faith that Dutton had in rehabilitating prisoners with kindness was shattered that day.

When Dutton and his prison wardens were resting, a few of the disgruntled prisoners decided to carry out their plan. It had rained heavily that day and the sea was choppy. The prisoners working at the jetty felt that this was the right moment to strike. They brutally chopped and hacked Dutton and his attendants, Arumugam Veerasingham and Tan Kok Hian, to death. About seventy inmates rioted by setting fire to buildings and attacking staff with knives and bottles.

The detainees had taken three years to develop Pulau Senang. It only took the rioters forty minutes to burn the buildings and place to the ground. When Maasilamani heard this news, he couldn't stop crying. He was most disturbed by the death of the kind Superintendent Dutton who had believed in him. His tears continued to flow down his cheeks when memories of Dutton came to him. *What a kind man Superintendent Dutton was! How could they chop him to death? How could I ever have been friends with people who were so cruel and hard-hearted?* Every time these thoughts crossed his mind, his heart burnt with sadness.

After two years of investigation, finally on 18th October 1965, eighteen heartless murderers were sentenced to death for the crime. Hearing the news, Maasilamani resigned from his job and left for Malacca with his friend, Rangan, the next day.

Rangan had run away to Singapore, from his family in Malacca, after a family dispute. As he was not very well-educated, Rangan was only able to land a job as a coolie and he found it difficult to make ends meet on his salary. His heart was heavy whenever thoughts of his family drifted through his mind. It was then that the Pulau Senang murder trial ended leaving his friend, Maasilamani, deeply depressed. Trying to do something to ease his friend's pain, Rangan asked him a simple question.

"Would you like to come with me?"

Without a word, Maasilamani nodded his head. They did not discuss it any further. Maasilamani left for Malacca with Rangan.

The place that they arrived at in Malacca was called Gajah Berang. Rangan's mother always wore a *baju kurung* and his father a lungi and a colourful shirt. Rangan explained that his mother was Malay and his father a Tamil. Rangan had several relatives in both Gajah Berang as well as Bachang. In both these areas, there were many families like Rangan's parents who were called Chetti Melakas. Chetti Melakas were a distinctive group of people with a mixed parentage of Indians and Malays. The area was called Kampong Chetti.

The next day, Maasilamani picked up the farming tools in the home and set out to work in Rangan's father's farm. Rangan knew no way out of his current situation. Rangan had moved to Singapore precisely because he did not want to be a farmer. As fate would have it, he was back where he started. The year that Maasilamani arrived in Malacca was a prosperous one for the family. The land gave the greatest yield they had ever seen in their lifetime. Maasilamani worked extremely hard on the land, day and night, like a possessed man. It was a farm for all seasons. There were brinjal, ladies' fingers, drumsticks, winter melon, yam and many other varieties of green vegetables. There were bananas, coconuts, durians, rambutans, jackfruits, guavas, custard apples and mangoes too. Everything that one's heart would desire was available on the farm. Under Maasilamani's care, they all flourished. They took the flowers, vegetables and fruits and brought them from their farm to the market for sale, filling the van to its brim. They returned with their pockets full of cash. Maasilamani started a savings account at the local bank.

Everyone in that house liked Maasilamani. Rangan's younger sister, Rathinamba, and younger brother, Kumaravel, addressed Maasilamani as Anna. Rangan's family treated Maasilamani as one of their own. The only hurdle in their relationship was language. Rangan's family spoke a combination of Malay and Tamil.

Many of the womenfolk in the village wore the sarong kebaya. Sometimes, they wore saris. In Rangan's father's house, even though they wore lungis in their home, they always wore a dhoti when they went to the temple. They said the daily prayers for Ganesha. Every Friday, they went to the temple for Tamil spiritual classes (*Thevaram*). They ate the temple offerings of *sundal* and *prasadam* with great delight.

It was during one of these visits to the temple that Maasilamani met a woman who taught *Thevaram* and *Thiruvasagam*. Her name was Shanthi. Both Shanthi and he took a vow for Lord Murugan and carried a *kaavadi* for Thaipusam that year. Gradually, they fell in love and tied the knot. Sadly, Shanthi was averse to the idea of having kids. He soon found out why. Six months after their wedding, a visitor arrived at their door, out of the blue, at the break of dawn. He was a middle-aged man with dark skin like the Lord Krishna. He had with him a child who looked about five years old. Within ten minutes of them entering their home, Maasilamani found out that the middle-aged man was Shanthi's first husband and that the child was Shanthi's son. Maasilamani was shocked beyond words.

Are there women like this too who would cheat men? Is this what women are like? Goodness, how she had enticed me! His mind reeled thinking of all the lies she had told him. He couldn't believe that he had been so gullible. He left the house right away and headed straight to the farm where he lay down on the ground.

Hearing the news, Rangan's family ran to the farm to console him. They even blatantly hinted to Maasilamani that, if he wished, he could marry Rangan's sister. But Maasilamani's heart had hardened towards women. He was not able to face the world anymore. Everyone who saw him had a kind word for him. But they also wanted to know all the details of what had transpired. Unable to face their questions anymore, Maasilamani got onto the train one day and headed back to Singapore, without saying goodbye to anyone. Just as he had left for Malacca without telling anyone here, he left Kampong Chetti without bidding goodbye even to Rangan.

Maasilamani returned home to Sembawang as a prodigal
son. He managed to rent a room at the back of Abdul *Kakka*'s
home at 13th Mile along Kedondong Road. He moved in and
took on any odd jobs that came his way.

At 13th Mile, his life ran like an old railway track. But the
two things that never came up again in his life or his path were
marriage and women.

Sᴇᴛʜᴜʟᴀᴋsʜᴍɪ Aᴍᴍᴀ ᴡᴀs unhappy. Her daughter, Prasanna, was turning twenty soon. Now everybody knows that twenty is a marriageable age for a young woman. But there was no sign of a suitable alliance on the horizon. When she was in secondary two, a boy had given her a love letter and Prasanna had promptly replied to the letter. It only took three days for their supposed love affair to spread like wild fire in Sembawang Kechil. A couple of loafers had talked about the budding romance of Prasanna and the boy at the *thongal* shop. The shopkeeper, Madhava Kurup, overheard the conversation and that evening reported what he had overheard to Karunakaran and Sethulakshmi. Prasanna was placed under house arrest.

That was six years ago. But people in that area did not stop gossiping about them. In the beginning, with great difficulty and through their contacts, one or two alliances were found for Prasanna. The prospective groom's families visited them for the traditional bride-viewing. But the response was the same.

"Our son says that he does not intend to get married for now." That was obviously a frivolous excuse. Sethulakshmi Amma was deeply troubled by the situation.

The loafers who hung out in the *thongal* shop were responsible for stopping any alliance from coming to Sethulakshmi's home. In the beginning, there were some eligible men who were interested. Nowadays, nobody seemed to be interested in marrying Prasanna. Prasanna too was frustrated after being put on house arrest for so many years. She took her frustration out on the house tenants by constantly throwing tantrums. In fact, it was Prasanna whom the tenants were frightened of rather than Sethulakshmi or Karunakaran. The womenfolk in the house would go silent when Prasanna walked into the *kusini*.

"Why are the pots' covers on the grindstone? Why is the bathroom so smelly? Don't you people know to pour water down the toilet once you have done your business?"

Prasanna's complaints were loud and clear. As soon as she was out of earshot, the tenants would shake their heads and retort, "Go to hell! Who the hell do you think you are?"

Sethulakshmi knew that her daughter was rude to the tenants. She wasn't blind to what was happening under her nose. She had hoped that she would be able to get Prasanna married off that year. She poured her heart out to Raagavan Anna repeatedly whenever he visited with his wife, Vatsala Akka. They came by to visit Sethulakshmi and Karunakaran frequently at Lorong Maha. But Karunakaran was too proud to ask them for any help with Prasanna's wedding. Despite being relatives, Raagavan and Vatsala had very little respect for Karunakaran.

Karunakaran had little care in the world. *Who cares whether Rama or Raavanan took Sita away?*

The hot springs was a crowd puller. It sat on a mineral-rich land that the Tamils called *kanthaka-bhoomi*. The locals in the area claim that it was Amoy, the daughter of *Apeh*, a Chinese *towkay*, who popularised the curative properties of the water at the hot springs. But historians state that that is not true.

Sembawang residents also recount another story of how in the 1950s a European, WAB Goodall (a Municipal Ranger), was in the area running an errand for his job when his gaze fell on the mineral-rich land. He chanced upon the hot steam and water bubbling out of the ground and watched the hot spring shoot up from the ground for a long time. He visited the place again with his colleagues, armed with four empty bottles. He managed to fill the bottles with water from the hot spring. His friend from London had suggested, "Since you have a constant pain in your knee, see if you can find some mineral-rich water to pour over your knees. The pain in your knee is likely to ease." Goodall collected the water to test his friend's theory.

To the surprise of the locals, in the next week or so, they noticed his manservant, Raamu, collecting several bottles of the water from the hot spring. When Rahuman went to Goodall's home to tend to his garden, he saw Goodall stretched out in the living room, with Raamu dipping a cloth in a pail of hot water and placing it on the Goodall's knees. After a few days of this treatment, the European was able to stretch his legs without any discomfort and walk easily. He was even able to climb up and down the stairs with no difficulty. Raamu could not stop talking about what he described as a near miracle when he visited Rahuman. The womenfolk in Rahuman's house were intrigued.

Although the people heard about this story, this was not the reason that the hot springs became popular among the people of Sembawang. Instead, it is another story that has the credit for making it popular. The daughter of a local sundry shop owner, Amoy, constantly had horrible headaches and she was at her wits' end as to how to alleviate the pain. The headaches were driving her mad. Feeling deeply frustrated, and having heard of the curative powers of the hot springs, she turned to the hot springs as a last resort. There was no taste to the water really. She then took several more gulps and finally managed to drink the whole bottle. Almost like magic, the headaches disappeared. The news spread like wildfire in the village. It was then that people started coming to the hot spring in droves.

If any child in the area fell ill, all the child needed was a bottle of water from the hot springs. When they had a fever, a cloth was drenched in the water from the hot springs and placed on their forehead. The child's body would be wiped down with the water and a hot press would be given too. The child always got better after this.

Menstruating women avoided going to the hot springs as they considered it to be a sacred place. They held a deep-rooted belief that if they visited the hot springs when they were menstruating, they might pollute the water and the environment. They disciplined themselves to stay home during those few days and only ventured to the hot springs once their periods stopped. That too only after they had purified themselves with a head bath. Then they visited the hot springs with their children in their arms. The Indian men and women who lived in Sembawang in the 1960s described a bath at the hot springs to be deeply comforting.

Vellaya saw Mallika for the first time at the hot springs.

Sembakam and her daughter, Mallika, rented a room in Mohan Teacher's house on Bah Tan Road. Mohan Teacher's wife had constant backaches. Mallika came to the hot springs to fetch a bottle of water to administer a hot press to the teacher's wife's back. Her foot hit a stone as she was getting up after filling her bottle with the water. She hadn't noticed the stone in her path. She went sprawling down to the ground, face down. The bottle flew out of her hand and broke. Mallika burst into tears. Vellaya rushed to her rescue and helped her up. Thankfully, she had fallen on the grass and did not get hurt.

"This is a small matter. Don't cry. Here, just take my bottle of water," Vellaya said kindly. Mallika's heart was drenched in happiness at this kind act.

Mallika had stopped studying after failing her primary six examinations. Her father, Raaman, had passed away in an accident when he fell off a high building at the shipyard. What sort of compensation would the company give to the family of a cleaner? Nevertheless, because he had passed away in the course of carrying out his job, he was given a small amount of compensation. The money did not last long. The shipyard also gave Sembakam a low-paying job that helped with the household expenses.

While Mallika might have been really weak in her studies, she was a good-natured girl and of great help to the three tenants in that house. She helped the tenants with their household chores. The prim and proper Mohan Teacher had migrated to Singapore from Sri Lanka. He was also very fair. He ensured that he paid Mallika every month for the chores she did around the house. The tenants in the house too paid Mallika for the help with the household chores whenever they could. That was her pocket money, and she was rather content with her life.

After the chance encounter with Vellaya at the hot springs, Mallika started visiting the hot springs often. She was very appreciative of Vellaya who was attending night school to improve himself and holding down a job at the same time in the day. Once in a while, with the money Vellaya stole from the shop, he would buy her *kway teow goreng* and *yu char kueh*. The only person who knew about their budding romance was her best friend, Jamilah.

Appunni was in bad shape. He did not know what to do. Gurusami's room was locked the whole night. But she could not come to him in the night, could she? Like the starving moon, he gazed at Muthuletchimi's room door with great yearning. His neighbour, Gurusami, worked as a nightwatchman and his room was empty at night. If only Muthuletchimi was available, Gurusami's room would have been their heaven.

Appunni was from a small village from the Kollam district in Kerala. He was the eldest son in a family of eight children. When Veloo Maama asked him, "Do you want to come to Singapore?", his parents had fallen on Maama's feet with gratitude bursting out of them. Carrying just a bag in his hand, he boarded the ship bound for Singapore. He was proud of himself for having done so.

Seventeen years had flown by in a blink of an eye. At first, he joined the Naval Base as an apprentice, cleaning the equipment at the shipyard. After a while, he was promoted to a foreman. But despite several years of hard work, he did not have any savings. He spent all his income paying off his family's debts in Kerala. He had also paid for the wedding of two of his younger sisters. He had helped to find his younger brother a job as a teacher in their village too, with great difficulty. But he still had four younger siblings, who were in school, who needed his support.

Although he was thirty years old, Appunni was in no position to get married. A huge chunk of his salary now went into repaying the debts of repairing his house in Kerala. He wasn't a saint by any chance though. Like all young man, he too had desires. When he could not bear it anymore, he managed to find release in some of the women who worked at his workplace. These women were the low-wage workers at the Naval Base. Sometimes he gave them five dollars for their children's school expenses; other times, he bought them fruits and packets of biscuits to take home to their children or just five dollars which he stuffed into their hands. That's all it took to make these women smile.

Muthuletchimi was different. He wanted her from the first moment he laid eyes on her. He was drawn to her. He could not decide whether it was her enticing eyes or her soft lips. How long could he satisfy himself by just looking at her and winking at her? An irresistible opportunity presented itself like a water to a parched throat one day. Muthuletchimi arrived at his home with porridge in her hands to give to the old man who lived in his house. Appunni lunged at her and hugged her tightly before kissing her briefly. The sweet memory of her soft lips which were like flowers lingered in his heart and his tongue the whole day.

Muthuletchimi's husband, Supramulu, was a foodie but not a fussy one. He had no preference between Muthuletchimi's chicken and fish curry. No matter what she cooked, he found it as delicious as nectar was to a bee. He would eat to his heart's and stomach's content. In fact, he would overeat, sit outside the house and talk to Karunakaran or to the other men and then turn in early for the night. Of course, most days, he would not go to sleep without a bit of a bedroom rodeo with Muthuletchimi.

But it had been four years since they got married! To date, there was no sign of a child in sight. *Wouldn't a husband want to take his wife to a gynaecologist to check it out? Wouldn't a man be worried?* Muthuletchimi's heart was often heavy with the thought that her glutton husband cared more about food than the absence of a child in their arms.

So, although Muthuletchimi was annoyed with Appunni for being inappropriate with her, she was also amazed at how persistent and ardent he was. *Do men like Appunni exist? Am I that beautiful for him to pursue me?*

The bee did not need much coaxing to fall into the trap.

Initially, all Appunni got from her was a slight smile and a shy look. Her head was always bent with her eyes focused on the ground. One day, when he saw Kaali at the market, he decided to take the plunge and asked her a little too boldly, "Didn't Muthu come with you?" Kaali stifled her giggle. *Oh, this guy wants to know more about Muthu. That's why he has been winking at me.*

"I will go and tell her," she said and walked away quickly.

The next day, Appunni boldly stood at the window waiting for her. As soon as he saw Muthuletchimi's head appear at the window, he tried to get her attention. She must have understood what he was trying to tell her for the next instance, her eyes grew wide in shock. She gave him a hard stare. Immediately, he was apologetic.

"*Maapu, maapu,*" he said in Malayalam hitting his cheeks with his hands.

Muthuletchimi was thoroughly embarrassed. It never occurred to her that a man would actually apologise to a woman. *Would a man actually apologise to a woman?* When she gave him a look of sympathy, it was like someone had shaved the horn off the bull to prepare it for what comes next. Appunni decided to take things one step further. He turned his face and pointed his cheek to Muthuletchimi. That startled her. She jumped back from the window and quickly drew the curtains.

Three hours later, as dusk was fast approaching, she switched on the lights in her room again. She passed the window by chance and caught a glimpse of him. There he was, standing exactly where she had seen him a few hours ago, looking completely fallen and heartbroken. Her heart melted at the sight of Appunni who had waited for her for the last few hours. Now it was her turn to say sorry and hit her cheeks with her hands.

That's how, without a soul knowing, their love grew. With each passing day, a different game was played at the two windows. Well, at least that's what they believed.

6

MANJU'S MOTHER COMMENTED that Margaret looked very happy these days.

Margaret wanted to carry Manju all the time but her heavily pregnant body didn't allow her to do so. She was carrying the baby rather low these days. Even the slightest pain might induce childbirth. Unable to bear watching the heavily pregnant Margaret carry a pail of water from the main pipe down the street whenever the water ran out in the home, Kaali, Muthuletchimi and the other tenants carried pails of water for Margaret whenever she needed it. Even Sethulakshmi Amma would set aside a plate of food for Margaret whenever she made something special or delicious. Meenatchi Paati too cooked her herbal food made of winter melon to alleviate the water retention in Margaret's legs. That always worked and, within two days, the water retention would disappear.

One evening, Margaret was in great pain. It looked like she was going into labour. Muthuletchimi wanted to take her to the hospital immediately. But Meenatchi Paati stopped them. "Wait a little while," said Meenatchi Paati who then went into the *kusini* and returned with some heated castor oil. She rubbed the warm castor oil around the stomach and held Margaret for a while. Slowly the pain eased up. When Mathai returned home in the evening, they told him about Margaret's 'false labour' pains. None of them liked how badly Mathai treated his wife.

Mathai was from the Kottayam district in Kerala. His parents worked hard on the farm of Koshy Boss. They had little else except for the only entertainment the poor had — to indulge in the pleasures of the night. It was during one of these intimate moments that their second son, Mathai, was born. One day, soon after his twelfth birthday, Koshy Boss caught Mathai eating a mango that he had stolen from Koshy Boss's farm. The heartless Koshy Boss beat him up like a dog that day. That night, Mathai ran away from his home and boarded a train for Madras. He did several odd jobs in Madras including being a porter who carried luggage from the railway station to the hotel. Once he almost injured his back with the weight he put on his tender twelve-year-old back.

Perhaps, because even Lord Jesus could not watch the young Mathai's sufferings, his hardships came to an end in the form of Abdul Kader (Kader Bhai) from Singapore. Mathai was of great assistance to Kader Bhai in Madras and that really impressed him. *If I could get a boy like this to help out in my shop, it will be very good.* When Kader Bhai found out that Mathai was an orphan, without a second thought, he bought a ticket for Mathai to accompany him to Singapore. The sights and sounds of the *State of Madras* ship was too much for the young boy. He was amazed at the sight of the boys who were his age boldly climbing the ropes up to the ship. He was too scared to even look at the boys. A huge man got off the boat and stood guard, checking the tickets one by one. When it was his turn, Mathai hesitated.

"Don't be scared," whispered the man kindly.

He guided Mathai's hands on the rope ladder. Mathai pressed his legs down on the rope ladder and reached out for the rope above his head. He held onto the rope tightly before he moved onto the next level. Only when he entered the ship did he heave a sigh of relief. His body was drenched in sweat. He had an urgent need to relieve himself.

Kader Bhai had paid for dormitory tickets. When Mathai entered the dormitory room, he realised that there would be two others in the room too. His room-mates looked exhausted.

"If you want, go with them and look around the ship then come back," said Kader Bhai.

He sent Mathai away with a young man who was seated across from him in that room. Everything looked new to him. As Mathai walked around, many new sights awaited him. Holding a canvas-like pillow, many men were lying on the ground in the deck. He wondered why.

"These people bought a cheaper ticket," said the young man who had come along with him.

Mathai was mesmerised at the wide sea that lay ahead of him and he spent the next few days watching it. As soon as they landed in Singapore, Mathai started work at Kader Bhai's *vangsa kadai*. Mathai busied himself with the job. Mathai took a vow that he would only return to the village after he made enough money to be a boss himself. He had been humiliated and had to run away from his family for just a single mango. He wanted Koshy Boss to come to him one day asking for a favour. Kader Bhai taught him the ropes at his shop which was in Chong Pang and provided a space in the shop for the young Mathai to live.

Within two years of Mathai's arrival, the shop expanded. Kader Bhai was able to open another small shop in the market.

Mathai looked after the shop in the market as well. He never took a single cent from the shop for his own expenses. He was meticulous in his accounts. In gratitude for his loyal service, Kader Bhai registered the shop in the market under Mathai's name when he returned to Thenkasi. He also gave Mathai a huge sum of money as a gift on top of four years of salary that Mathai had earned which Kader Bhai had saved on his behalf. Under Mathai's care, the shop prospered and Mathai was able to send money to his family. Within a year of taking ownership of the shop, Mathai was able to return to Kottayam for a visit. He had been sending money back to his family who were now doing well themselves. Given how well he had done for himself in Singapore, Mathai became a hot eligible bachelor in the eyes of the villagers.

To his disappointment, Koshy Boss had passed away. The men in Koshy Boss's family had split the property and wealth and gone in different directions. His only daughter, Margaret, was the only one left in the village. But they were no longer wealthy. Koshy Boss's wife was bedridden. Margaret looked after her with a meagre salary that she made as a teacher. One day, when Mathai chanced upon Margaret returning home from work, he asked her the question directly.

Margaret could not believe her ears. She knew he had run away from the village because of her father. She wondered if he wanted to marry her as a form of revenge. But Mathai convinced her that he really liked her and that was his only motivation for wanting to marry her. Before she could even reply, her bedridden mother gave the approval.

Margaret was over the moon when she first arrived in Singapore. But the euphoria lasted merely three months until she fell pregnant. All she wanted then was to return home to her mother. Mathai refused.

"Which dog is there to take care of you during your pregnancy? Will your bedridden mother hire someone to look after you?"

Margaret felt as though he had thrown a bottle of acid across her face. She cringed at his crude words and cruelty and spent the day curled up in a corner of her room. The news of her mother's death reached her when she was battling nausea and giddiness. The news left her sobbing in bed for several days. Mathai made no attempt to console her. Margaret was merely a body he needed in the darkness of the night. He rarely had a kind word for her. Margaret found herself constantly asking herself why he treated her so badly.

Mathai had his reasons. He had wanted to build a huge house in Kottayam. He was sending money back for this purpose with the help of his father and Mathai's best friend, Michael, who had returned to Kottayam from Singapore. The expenses for the house were rising and were far more than what he had initially calculated. Being unable to send money back in time to complete the building of the house made him resentful and grumpy. He was afraid to ask the moneylender, Mayilvasagam, for a loan. He knew of some of his friends who had borrowed money from Mayilvasagam and, when they were not able to pay the interest in time, they were left in a lurch. He directed all his frustrations towards Margaret and beat her up for no rhyme or reason.

"Isn't it time for you to go to the shop?" she asked him one day. She received a resounding slap across her cheek the next instant.

Once seeing him return really late from work, she asked, "When will you come home tonight?"

"I will come when my job is done. Do you expect me to tell you everything?" His angry words spilt out like fire.

She went silent. *What did I say for him to fly off the handle? Why did he beat me? He stares at me all the time. Why does he do that?* These unanswered questions were her life for now.

Margaret was overcome with the desire to eat a mango. Without a thought, she bought three mangoes from the yogurt lady, Meena Amma, who happened to have mangoes for sale that day. The yogurt lady made house calls with her wares every day. Since a pregnant woman was buying the mangoes, Meena Amma spent a lot of time selecting three of the juiciest mangoes with golden skin for her. Margaret promptly set aside one mango for Mathai. Margaret's mouth drooled as she cut up the other two mangoes for herself. She ate them up with great glee in two gulps. Half an hour later, Mathai came home for lunch. She lovingly cut up the remaining mango for him after he had his meal. But his face darkened at the sight of the mango.

"Where did you get the money from?" he asked.

The next moment, the plate flew from his hand and cut her forehead. The plate fell to the ground.

Manju's father, Kaali, Muthuletchimi and Meenatchi Paati carried her to Ramu's Clinic.

Most Tamils who lived in Sembawang only went to Ramu's Clinic. Dr Raamasamy was a kind man and a Tamil patriot who spoke Tamil to his patients. When some of his Tamil patients attempted to show off their knowledge of English, he would retort, "Why? Don't you know Tamil?" He wasn't rude but his question certainly offended some of his patients.

Dr Raamasamy gave her an injection and sent her home. Margaret was still unconscious.

That night, Mathai did not come home. He slept in his shop. He had not touched a mango since her father, Koshy Boss, had beaten him up for stealing one. Given the circumstances, he could not believe that she had served him the exact same variety of mango that he had stolen years ago. It was the Kilichundan mango. Not only had Margret bought the mangoes, she had eaten them too. *How dare she serve it to me too?*

When he returned, everyone scolded him ceaselessly. After that, no one ever saw Margaret or Mathai engage in chit-chat.

"Get lost! You and your silly reason! What sort of man are you? How dare you beat up a pregnant woman? Now you are trying to justify what you did?"

After that, no one ever saw Margaret talking to him for a long time.

Chinnadurai, who lived on 15th Mile, was furious. His friends, Vellaya who lived at 13th or Murugan on 14th, did not have problems such as his. Chinnadurai had been betrothed to Akhilandam at a young age and now Akhilandam was getting married to someone else. Even his mum and dad had gone to the wedding for the wedding feast. *How could they do this to me! Don't our parents care that we dated? How could her parents marry her off to someone else?* When his parents returned from the wedding, they were greeted by a grumpy Chinnadurai who was sitting outside the house waiting for them to return.

"He didn't study at all! Does he put any effort in the night classes that he is attending? He hangs out with some loafers the whole day and yet this donkey is getting angry about her marrying someone else."

Chinnadurai left his home in a hurry-burry. Murugan caught up with his friend who was walking briskly ahead of him and put his arms around his shoulder.

"I've been calling out your name for such a long time and you've been walking without hearing me!"

Murugan whispered something into his ears in the next few minutes. Without a second thought, Chinnadurai went with him.

Murugan's mother was at first angry that her son had not returned for two days. But, on the third day, she was worried. She did not share her husband's nonchalance.

"He must have gone somewhere. Don't bother about it."

On the fourth day, Murugan returned home. When he arrived, his hands were filled with gifts for the home. He brought a huge fish, a standing fan for their home and a tin of biscuits. His mother was flabbergasted.

"Where did you go for the last four days, dear?" Hearing the concern in his mother's voice only fuelled him further. His arrogance grew a little more that day.

Chinthamani was yelling away at the kampong. Three out of her four chickens had gone missing from the chicken coop at the same time. "Which donkey is stealing my chicken? If you have only one father, come in front of me!" She added a few more curses after that. "Why does your filthy tongue desire stolen food?" The womenfolk standing around Chinthamani could not bear to hear the rest of the offensive words that came spewing out of her mouth and ran for cover in their homes.

Chinnadurai joined the spectacle outside Chinthamani's home with his friend, Maariyappan, whom he had come to visit. Chinthamani was cursing the perpetrators. Later in the evening, when Murugan and Vellaya got together to drink beer, he recounted the story and they laughed uncontrollably. Vellaya had many other ideas on what they could do next. He planned the next few escapades without any issue.

One evening, when Chinnasamy saw a cigarette packet fall out of Vellaya's pocket, he yelled out, "*Dei! Dei!* What is this?" Vellaya dashed out of his house.

Vellaya headed straight to Ramasamy Maama's shop. "This month you need to take Auntie to the gynae," said Ramasamy.

Feeling the need to assert himself, Vellaya responded, "No problem, I will take her, Maama. But please speak to Fisherman Rahim. He hasn't settled his old debt yet. I think you should ask him for it."

Ramasamy was pleased. *How responsible this boy is! This month onwards, I will pay him five dollars more.* He had no way of knowing that Vellaya was well-versed in the art of theft. Only God knew that it was the trio — Vellaya, Murugan and Chinnadurai — who were responsible for the frequent theft of chickens in Sembawang.

The womenfolk too shared with one another as they walked to the market in the morning, that they had lost the money that they had set aside for 'marketing'. What was far more surprising was that money went missing even from the home of a high-ranking officer at Naval Base, Kuttan Pillai.

Kuttan Pillai's wife, Omana, often packed her husband's lunch in a tiffin carrier for him whenever he was not able to come home for the afternoon meal. During those occasions,

Kuttan Pillai would ask Chinnadurai's father to go home and pick up his meal for him. The task inevitably fell on the rather lazy Chinnadurai. Chinnadurai had no sense of initiative and waited for his father to tell him explicitly what was needed before he would grudgingly do it. But Chinnadurai's father was hoping that Kuttan Pillai would arrange for a job for his son. He just needed to ask him at the right moment. He certainly did not want his son to be a road sweeper like him.

Chinnadurai could never forget the first experience of bringing the food from Kuttan Pillai *Krani*'s home. In the fifteen minutes that Omana Amma took to pack the food for her husband, his eyes fell on the pair of earrings on the coffee table. At first, he could not believe what he had seen. The next moment, a thought struck him. He then picked up the tiffin carrier with lunch from the *Krani*'s wife, Omana. Two hours later, Omana realised that the earrings, which she had taken out before her oil bath, were missing.

When Kuttan Pillai returned home that day, he found his wife's eyes swollen from crying the whole day. He was furious. Even the wife of the welder, who worked under him, was rather careful with her jewellery. *How could this woman have been so careless?* The next day, he took out his anger on his colleagues and barked at them for every little thing.

The thieves struck again. Omana lost twenty dollars that she had kept aside for her 'marketing'. Foreman Gabriel's wife too reported that she had lost her nose ring.

No one suspected Chinnadurai, Vellaya and Murugan.

7

Unbearable sadness overwhelmed Kaali.

There was not a grain of rice in the house. Twice Kaali had already asked for a loan from Kurup's shop which was across the house. She had told him that she would return on Friday which was Chandran's payday. But that was three Fridays ago. She was embarrassed to walk by the shop. What if Shopkeeper Kurup asked for the money or insulted her? She might have to pull out her tongue to kill herself. What else could she do? The thought of that happening made her stomach churn.

These days, Chandran did not return home on time. He had started drinking after work. Kaali was worried at this new-found habit. The truth was that Chandran already had a drinking problem before he met her. He had just had his tail curled between his legs for a short while in front of Kaali whom he had brought along with him. But now that he was not as enamoured with her anymore, he found pleasure in having a drink or two with his colleagues after work.

Some days, he would even have dinner with his friends before he returned home. Whenever he returned drunk, Kaali was afraid to ask him anything. She had a reason to be afraid. The first time he had returned home in that state, she had said something rather inconsequential which made him leap out and yank her hair. He had dragged her down to the ground and stamped on her repeatedly before hitting her face with his fists.

Kaali had been astounded by his actions. For the next few days, she was even afraid to look at her face in the mirror. The irony was that she hated her former husband because he had a drinking habit. That was what had driven her to fall in love with a Singaporean whom she thought was a dream man with clean habits. That was what had prompted her to elope with Chandran. How could she be in the same situation even here in Singapore?

Chandran's erratic behaviour only lasted till dawn broke. When he sobered up, he fell at her feet and asked for forgiveness. He got Kaali to lie on his lap as he wept. He did not let her move or go out of the room. He told her how remorseful he was. Kaali was just a simple woman. She melted in his arms. "Just leave it," she consoled him before asking him for money to buy groceries so that she could cook lunch.

"I had to repay the loan I took from my office, Kaali. I only have a little bit of money left for the next three or four days of daily expenses, dear," he cajoled.

For the first time since she had eloped from the estate, she took out a small gold chain that she had brought with her and gave it to Chandran so that he could pawn it. That day, Chandran lay in her like a bee drowned in honey. When payday arrived the next Friday, it was the same story all over again.

But when Friday came, Chandran returned home completely drunk again. Kaali did not have any strength in her body to be beaten again so she wept quietly in a corner. This time, another piece of gold found its way to the pawnshop. Chandran made no attempt to retrieve her gold from the pawnshop. After thinking long and hard about what was going on, Kaali came to a decision.

She had gotten to know the vegetable store owner, Chinnasami Anna, rather well. It was he who came to her rescue by giving her a job as an assistant. She learnt how to weigh vegetables, when to give a few extra vegetables to those who bought a lot of vegetables, how to add a handful of curry leaves and coriander leaves that were essential for cooking for everyone who bought vegetables from them. She was a quick learner and learnt how to run the shop in a month. The person who was most happy with this turn of events was Muthuletchimi, who was happy that her friend had found a way out of the problems in her life. Everyone in Sethulakshmi Amma's home started to buy vegetables from the shop Kaali worked in.

Chandran showed no signs of mending his ways. Now that Kaali had a steady stream of income, he felt free to do what his heart pleased. He only treated Kaali badly when he was drunk. On other days, he did not give her any trouble. Once when Kaali was not well for two days, he even took time off from work and stayed home to look after her. He cooked and washed their clothes. Kaali's heart melted at his kindness.

Out of the blue, Karunakaran and Sethulakshmi Amma decided to leave for Kerala. What was more surprising was that they were taking a rather reluctant Prasanna to Kerala as well. Initially, Prasanna kicked up a fuss but, as the day grew closer, she seemed to have come to terms with what lay ahead of her. Her relatives, Bhaskara Anna from 15th Mile, Vidyatharan Anna from 14th Mile, as well as a second uncle, Kochappu Maama, all came to say goodbye. They brought her gold jewellery and saris according to their earning capacities. The tenants too gave Prasanna gifts.

Only Kaali was in a dire state as she had no money on her hands. How could she ask her fellow tenants for money anymore? She had even borrowed money from Meenatchi Paati and struggled to pay her back. Kaali did not know that Meenatchi Paati had given her own savings. Every time Kaali saw Sangkaralingam and heard him make fun of someone, she thought it was targeted at her and that made her feel really small. As soon as she could, she returned the five dollars to Meenatchi Paati. It was only then that she could heave a sigh of relief in that house.

The only person she could now turn to was the shopkeeper, Chinnasami Anna, whom she called *Annachi*. He gave her ten dollars to buy Prasanna a sari. In return, he asked her to come by in the evening to unload the vegetables and sort them out into different containers. She did not question him on why he was making her do extra work when he planned on deducting ten dollars from her salary. After all, when she was in need, it was Chinnasami Anna who helped her.

Sethulakshmi Amma was particularly kind to her that day when she saw Kaali at the pasar. "Tonight, don't cook. I have arranged for a feast in our house. Please have dinner with us. Come home early!" Sethulakshmi Amma then bought lots of vegetables for the feast she was preparing which brought a huge smile to Chinnasami's face. As she was leaving, he gave Kaali a few slices of jackfruit to take back with her.

When she got to Sethulakshmi Amma's home, she found the place teeming with people for the grand feast that she had arranged. Sethulakshmi Amma, her husband and Prasanna were going to leave for Kerala in two weeks. Prasanna wore a lovely Kerala sari with a huge gold border and a matching silk sari blouse. She had jasmine flowers in her hair. She wore traditional jewellery from Kerala, a chariot (*chakkara*) necklace and a coin necklace in the shape of grapes (*kaasu-maala*). She looked divine.

Sangkaralingam gave Prasanna a hundred dollars as a wedding gift. Relatives stood around Prasanna and Sethulakshmi Amma and were laughing away. The air was joyful. Kaali's eyes searched for her friend, Muthuletchimi.

"Hey, you haven't eaten yet! Come! Come and sit here," said Sethulakshmi Amma, reaching out to hold her hand and guiding her to the long mat on the floor, where the other guests were seated. Kaali had no other choice but to go with her.

Kaali enjoyed every bit of the sumptuous meal of *aviyal, pulisseri, thoran*, as well as Kaali's favourite Kerala dish — fish curry — along with pappadam and payasam. Margaret, who was seated next to her, too seemed to be enjoying her meal. Neither of the women said a word to each other during the meal as they focused on the wide spread of food in front of them. What was surprising was that Sangkaralingam *Ayya* himself was walking around with the vessel filled with sambar and serving the guests. Meenatchi Paati was nowhere in sight. Manju's mother said that Meenatchi Paati had a severe headache and was resting in her room.

Sangkaralingam *Ayya* behaved as though it was his family function. Sethulakshmi Amma was clearly touched at his gesture. When the guests finished their meal and got up, Sangkaralingam *Ayya* sent them off home personally. He distributed the laddus from the huge tray that Sethulakshmi Amma had prepared and handed it to each guest in their hands.

Just then Muthuletchimi entered the house hurriedly. She had a parcel in her hand which she handed over to Prasanna.

Kaali managed to grab hold of her friend and ask her, "Where did you go, Muthu?"

Her face turned red for some reason. "Let's talk about that later. Let me have dinner first," she said as she sat down on the mat to eat.

What happened to Muthuletchimi? Why was she blushing? But Kaali did not have the luxury to worry herself with this small matter. It was getting late. *If only Chandran would be home on time that day to partake in the feast.* She stood at the doorway, watching out for him on the road. But that night, even after midnight, Chandran did not come home. *It wasn't payday so where could he have gone? Could he have gone with his friends and gotten drunk and fallen somewhere on the streets?* A million thoughts raced through her mind but she could not stifle her yawns or stop her eyes from closing. She retired to the room but found herself drifting in and out of sleep when she saw a shadow by her window. She jolted out of the bed, pulled the curtains aside and looked out. There was someone there. She rubbed her eyes and looked again and was surprised at what she saw.

It was none other than Muthuletchimi. *What! Why is she walking at the back of the house at this time of the night?* Kaali hurried to the *kusini* to look for her. *Hey! Where did she go? Has she gone into her room so quickly and fallen asleep?*

"Hmm!" Kaali's thoughts returned to Chandran. She was worried sick. She went back to the entrance of the house and looked out at the main road. There was not a soul in sight in the middle of the night. Everyone was asleep. *Where has this man gone? No matter how late it gets, he always eventually comes home. What happened today? Did something happen to him?* Just as dawn was breaking at about 6 a.m., a completely drunk Chandran walked unsteadily into the home.

Meanwhile, Vellaya, Murugan and Chinnadurai were walking towards the Maternal and Child Health Clinic at 14th Mile. They did not know then that that day would be a red-letter day in the history of Sembawang. They were completely drunk when they arrived at the clinic.

8

Manju's mother was bewildered.

These days, Muthuletchimi often came by and asked Manju's mother to teach her how to cook 'Kerala food'. Muthuletchimi's husband, Supramulu, was not a fussy eater. No matter what Muthuletchimi cooked for him, he would eat it without a word of complaint. Manju's mother was surprised at Muthuletchimi's new-found interest in learning how to cook *aviyal, pulisseri* and other traditional dishes from Kerala. Manju's mother taught Muthuletchimi how to make traditional coconut Kerala fish curry. Muthuletchimi put in a lot of effort to get the dish just right. She thought the curry turned out splendid and tasted like what nectar would be to a bee. "Mmmmm, delicious." That day too, Supramulu came. He ate, he belched and he left the dining table without a word or praise about her curry. There was nothing unusual about his behaviour but, today, his behaviour irritated Muthuletchimi. She did not have time to dwell on her emotions because in the next half hour, the whole house turned topsy-turvy.

Mathai was running around like a mad man. Margaret's water bag had burst and she was in great pain. Unable to bear the pain, Margaret's crying kept getting louder. It was only when Mathai heard his quiet wife wail in pain that the reality sank in. He didn't know how to comfort his pregnant wife nor did he have any kind words. He had never been kind to her especially since it had been cold war between them for such a long time. What was he supposed to do now?

Manju's father barked instructions at everyone. Meenatchi Paati brought some herbs that she quickly ground in the *kusini* then asked Margaret to swallow them. Margaret wailed even louder. Within the next ten minutes, Manju's father arrived with a taxi. Muthuletchimi and Meenatchi Paati managed to carry Margaret into the back seat of the taxi. Mathai got into the front seat. They left for the hospital.

Ten minutes after they arrived at the hospital, the baby was born. It was a good-looking boy. Meenatchi Paati took the packet of sugar that she had brought with her and asked the Tamil nurse in the room if she could have some water. She mixed the sugar in the water and gave the cup to Mathai. When Mathai fed a spoon of sugared water to his son, his heart was bursting with joy and he kissed Margaret on her lips in front of everyone.

Muthuletchimi carried the child in her arms, not wanting to put him down in the cradle. Mathai hurried to the post office to send a telegram to his family in Kerala with the good news. As soon as they got home, Muthuletchimi spoke to Manju's mother and made a list of all the things a newborn would need. She gave the list to Mathai and told him to buy the items. Meenatchi Paati gave the baby his daily bath. Muthuletchimi and Manju's mother took care of the cooking. Kamatchi Paati from next door came every day to give Margaret a traditional bath. Their warmth made Margaret feel like she was near her family. She did not miss her family after childbirth as she had feared. Nevertheless, she found herself crying quietly often.

Kamatchi Paati was an expert in taking care of mothers who had just given birth. She was well-known in the Sembawang area for her post-natal care services. The bath for a new mum involved mixing turmeric in a pail of warm water, tying up the hair of the mother in a bun and slowly pouring the warm turmeric water all over the body. The water would be splashed on the stomach area of the mother several times. Then, she would take some hot oil and massage the stomach and the whole body. The massage would take place for a while. Oil would also be put on the hair and a head massage would be given. When Margaret was brought into the room after her daily bath by Kamatchi Paati, she looked like she could almost sparkle.

Muthuletchimi cooked Margaret's meals every day, with the herbs as Manju's mother had instructed her. Only after she finished the cooking would she retire to her room. Her quiet moments were punctured by an unexplainable longing in her heart. She found it unbearable that her whole body smelled like the baby. Unable to hold her tears back, she found herself crying whenever she was alone.

Mathai was a changed man these days. With his child's birth, he was no longer gruff to Margaret. In fact, he took exceptionally good care of his wife. He met all her whims and fancies so much so that he left tongues wagging on how a man changes when he becomes a father.

Kaali was in a dire state. These days, the sight of Chandran disgusted Kaali. Chandran continued to return home in a drunken state and in a bad mood every night. Both her heart and her body were weary. *What sort of life is this? Why did I leave my village for this man!* It was only now that she had frequent thoughts about her son, Raasu, and she began to pine for him. Her thoughts lingered over Munusamy too. Several times she wondered if she should return to her husband but the thought of facing Munusamy's wrath stopped her. She wondered if he would even accept her again. It was a possibility that was too frightening to even imagine. To make matters worse, the jewellery on her ears and her neck had all been pawned off. It didn't look like Chandran would retrieve them for her.

She made ends meet with the money she made at Chinnasami Anna's vegetable shop. Sometimes she had to ask Muthuletchimi for a loan. Unable to return the loans she had taken from her friend, she had no choice but to ask Chinnasami Anna for a loan once again. He might have given her a loan right away, but Chinnasami was no saint or saviour.

One morning when Muthuletchimi came to the vegetable shop, Kaali could not believe her eyes. Muthuletchimi, who always had her hair tightly wrapped up in a bun or tied up in a single plait, looked different. Muthuletchimi's hair was untied. She had a tiny knot at the bottom of her hair. She had lined her eyes with kohl heavily too, like the Malayalees do. On her forehead, her usual huge kumkum dot was missing today. Instead, in its place was a strip of sandalwood. For a moment Kaali did not recognise her friend.

"What is this? Everything looks new?"

Muthuletchimi gave a slight smile and busied herself by picking vegetables and putting them into her basket.

"Ahh, Kaali, I forgot to tell you. When you come back in the evening, can you buy me some *nendra pazham*? Don't forget. The fruit seller said that the fruits will only come after 10 a.m.

Here's the money for it."

Kaali nodded her head. *What a kind soul Muthu is.* She always lent a helping hand to all her friends. *It is because of good souls like her that I too am able to live.* Kaali returned home that evening with the fruits in hand that Muthuletchimi had asked for. Muthuletchimi entered her room with a covered plate in hand. She removed the cover to reveal what was under it.

Kaali exclaimed, "Wow! It's *puttu!*"

Looking at the snow-white *puttu* with a generous shaving of coconut on top, Kaali drooled.

"Here, these bananas go well with *puttu,*" said Muthuletchimi handing her two pieces of banana that Kaali had brought. Muthuletchimi left her room soon after.

What is this? Muthu has become well-versed in cooking Kerala food. Mmmm... mmmm... I wish I had the time. Sadly, I don't have time to go and learn how to cook. But Muthu's hands are able to do what her eyes see right away. She is a great cook. But where did she get the container to make puttu*? I thought she didn't have it. When did she find the time to learn? Muthu's husband is a lucky man.* With many questions in her mind, she mixed the brown sugar and banana into the coconut-filled *puttu,* rolling it into little balls and putting it into her mouth.

Meenatchi Paati was really busy these days. She had the additional duty of giving Margaret's baby a bath as well as dispensing herbal medicine to the baby before and after meals in a small spoon. After that, she would hurry into the *kusini* and get started on her cooking. Sangkaralingam looked rather grumpy these days.

When Chandran did not return home that night too, Kaali tried to reassure herself that he would return sometime before dawn. She wasn't successful in calming her heart. Tossing and turning in her bed, she felt an urge to relieve herself. As she was walking out of her room to head to the bathroom, she noticed Muthuletchimi walking into her room rather stealthily and locking her bedroom door. Kaali wasn't sure if Muthuletchimi had seen her before she went into her room. But what struck Kaali as strange was that Muthuletchimi was wearing a brand-new sari in the middle of the night. She knew it was new as she had never seen it before. *Why would Muthuletchimi go out in the middle of the night in a brand new sari? Where did she go?*

"*Aye!*" There was a loud noise in front of the house, followed by a loud retching noise. Kaali rushed to the entrance of the house. Unknowingly she let out a yelp, "Ayyo!" and tried to stifle her screams the next moment with her hand.

She found Chandran being held up by Maasilamani. *Who is this man? Is he one of the men that Chandran goes drinking with?*

"I found him lying on the floor of Jalan Kadai when I was returning home from my night shift. He wasn't able to walk on his own so I brought him with me."

"Sir!" said Kaali as she brought her hands together in gratitude. Words failed her.

"Don't cry, please. First, take him to your room."

She held onto Chandran and tried to bring him to their room. But he mustered all his strength and gave her a kick instead which sent her flying across into the cement *aluru* nearby, injuring her badly. Within a few minutes, everyone gathered around them. Maasilamani explained what had happened. Sangkaralingam slapped Chandran across his cheeks.

"How could you… how could you… do this to me?" He wasn't able to say anything else. Chandran vomited all over himself.

Everyone in that house was mad enough at him to want to slap and kill him. They managed to drag him into the bathroom and pour buckets of water over his head. He kept muttering vulgarities at Kaali when he came out of the bathroom. Thankfully, he did not have enough strength to lift his hand to hit her. His hangover, retching and the cold bath finally took a toll on his body. All he wanted to do next was to curl up in bed.

The next day, Sethulakshmi Amma told both of them firmly to leave the house. Where could they go at such short notice? Kaali wept uncontrollably.

When he got over his hangover the next morning, no one spoke to Chandran in that house. In the past whenever he had gotten drunk and misbehaved, he would go out of his way to talk to everyone in the house as though nothing had happened. This time, no one budged. No one made eye contact with him. Even the old man, Sangkaralingam, spat on the ground outside the house at the sight of Chandran. Chandran was insulted. What irritated him more was that Kaali would not stop crying as she sat in the corner of the room.

How dare this filthy dog look down on me as well? The day I eloped with this awful woman was the day I lost my freedom and started having bad luck. I have to get rid of this woman who brings me bad luck.

He wasn't able to take their stares for too long. He stayed there for two days more and saw that everyone looked at him as though he was a lowly worm. He could not live with people who looked down on him. He gathered his clothes in a bag and left without a word — even to Kaali.

He never came back.

Except for Muthuletchimi, no one else in that house spoke

to Kaali either. Chinnasami Anna suggested a way out of her predicament.

"If you want, you can sleep in the tiny room at the back of the shop. But no one should know about this arrangement."

Soon after that, Sethulakshmi Amma left for Kerala. Prasanna bade goodbye to everyone. No one said goodbye to Kaali. That day, Kaali vacated that house and moved into Chinnasami Anna's shop.

9

VELLAYA WAS A carefree man. Unlike his friends, Murugan and Chinnadurai, there was no one to question him. His only relative, his grandpa Chinnasamy, was easy to fool. All he had to do was pretend to study and have his books open in front of him whenever the old man came into the room. As soon as he was out of sight, Vellaya would lie on his bed and smoke a cigarette. He hung out with his friends the rest of the time. Life was good. He even gave Mallika ten dollars when they met one day.

"Today, my boss gave me my salary. I want to buy you a dress with ten dollars but I don't know your size."

Mallika was moved to tears. No one had treated her with so much kindness and affection before. After her father's death, her mother's complete focus was on work. Vellaya's love for her and his gesture touched her in a way that nothing else could. She was very proud of Vellaya who held a day job and, at the same time, studied in the evenings. On top of that, he always made time for her too and worried about her well-being. What else could a woman ask for?

The next day, she decided to cook the chicken curry that Chinnamma Akka had taught her. To make it tastier, Chinnamma Akka had told her to grind cashew and *kasha kasha* into a dry paste, roast it well in a pan before soaking the chicken in it. She then fried the chicken in that paste with fresh oil and tossed it into the curry she had spent a long time cooking over the stove. When she brought the curry to him, Vellaya melted.

In all his memories, at least the ones that he could recall, he had only been insulted and called a lazy bum or a useless fellow. No woman had treated him with so much kindness nor cooked anything with love. This was the first. He locked his eyes with Mallika, pulled her towards him and whispered into her ears.

"Thank you, darling. I love you." He had managed to show off his command of the English language too.

Vellaya had failed his primary six examinations. How could he — a failed product of the primary school system — speak proper English? But Mallika was oblivious to that and too gullible to know any better.

Mallika was floating on air after hearing him utter those three words. "It is because he attends night classes that he is able to speak English beautifully. No matter what, how can I be as smart as him?"

Vellaya, on the other hand, was thrilled that he had finally met a woman who was in love with him.

"The chicken curry was very tasty," he said grabbing her hand and pulling her towards him once again.

"I am going to buy a gold bangle for the hands that cooked this meal for me!"

Mallika was convinced that she was floating in the sky. "I don't want all that. In front of your pure love, the bangle is just dust," she added dramatically before running off.

The next day, Murugan gathered his friends to join him in their usual drinking routine at their favourite spot. Chinnadurai's contribution for that day was three bottles of beer. He was already seated there when the other two arrived. They had packed a packet of spicy fried fish from the shop close by. Opening up the packet, they dived into the fish and the beer.

These days, all their meetings revolved around alcohol. When they could not afford beer, they bought themselves *samsu*. It was not what they wanted but they acquired a taste for it after a while. They often set out to Newton to drink toddy which made them happy. But on the days that they were flushed with stolen money in their hands, they set out to Sungei Road to drink.

It was not just Chinnadurai. All three of them preferred the food at the toddy shop. More than the toddy, it was the food that enticed them the most. The toddy shop had spicy fried fish, mutton fry, sambal chicken, piping hot idli, string hoppers, dosa, prata and many varieties of food that the men loved. Once the alcohol got to their heads, one or the other would exclaim, "Money is not the most important thing in the world. If we want, we can make the money in one night." Their boasts were reserved for their ears alone.

After a while, they got restless as they listened to Murugan revealing the juicy details of his own sexual encounters with the Malay neighbour. Vellaya's jaw naturally dropped with a wanton need. He listened intently. No matter how much Vellaya wanted Mallika, nothing had happened between them as they had just met. She was his first girlfriend. He had never felt the pleasure of a woman. The thought of a woman's body made his body rise with desire. One could easily blame that on his age.

The talk went late into the night and they found themselves hatching a way to meet their needs. Chinnadurai cautioned them.

"Okay, let's think this through and look for the right time before we make a decision."

The three of them parted ways on that note. Murugan arrived home past midnight and surreptitiously went into his room. No one noticed him coming in that night. It was the same for Chinnadurai too. But Vellaya's grandfather was awake. He hit Vellaya with his soiled slippers for coming home drunk and that too in the wee hours of the night.

"At this age, you're coming home drunk, you bloody dog! Dog!"

"You are no better than me. You too drink!"

"*Dei*! I am an old man. I have gone through life. I drink to forget my pain. What's wrong with you? I bought you everything that you wanted. Why would you pick up this filthy habit?"

It did not look like the old man was going to cease hitting Vellaya any time soon. Partly in anger, partly to escape, he shoved his grandpa hard and ran out of the house.

Kaali's heart was bitter and filled with a deep-rooted loathing. The room that she stayed in at the back of the vegetable shop was tiny. All it had was a single small bed. Every evening after they closed the shop, she would go to the Chinese shop next door to take a quick shower, return to the room, lie in bed and inevitably cry herself to sleep. The man that she had built her dreams on and eloped with had deserted her with no warning. Her heart was shattered.

On the third day after she arrived to stay in the shop, Chinnasami joined her in her bed. Well, as the saying goes, there may be snow on the rooftop but there is fire in the furnace. Once he got his much-needed release, he left for his room at 15th Mile. Truth be told, he already had a long-term secret liaison with a married woman in 15th Mile. It was not a daily affair. They only got together whenever the woman's husband had to work the night shift. During those nights, she was his. Their relationship was an open secret in that area.

But no matter what he did or whom he did it with every day, he never forgot his responsibilities to his family in India. He never failed to remit his earnings home to his wife every month. He had married off his eldest daughter well. His son was now studying in a university. He had bought land and built his own house in the Tripur district, where his wife lived with all the material comforts she needed and desired.

It was then that Prema Akka, who came to the shop, brought Kaali a piece of good news. A family that Prema Akka knew needed a live-in domestic helper. The daughter-in-law at Paarukutty Amma's home was about to deliver. They were looking for someone to help out in the house during the delivery. The person had to live with the family and take care of all the household chores as well. There was no doubt in Kaali's mind about what she needed to do. She readily agreed to work at Paarukutty Amma's home. The next day, ignoring Chinnasami's sullen look, she packed her belongings and headed off to Paarukutty Amma's house. The house was in 13th Mile Lorong Maha. It was a huge house with five spacious rooms and a smaller room. There were three daughters-in-law in that home. All three of them were from Kerala. The second daughter-in-law was pregnant. The family gave Kaali space to sleep in the smaller room across from the *kusini*. After a long time, that night, Kaali slept peacefully.

At Paarukutty Amma's home, everything was made from scratch. All the spices were ground by hand in the grindstone for the various curries. They soaked the rice grains and ground it to make *puttu*. They pound it all using a rod on a pounding stone. The rod helped to grind the rice into powder. This was despite the fact that they had a mill near their home. Not once did anyone in Paarukutty Amma's house go to the mill.

"Are the daughters-in-law staying at home to eat, sleep and become fat?"

That was Paarukutty Amma's question. From dawn to dusk, all three daughters-in-law had household chores to do until it was time for bed. In the morning, the womenfolk had to stretch out their hands in front of Paarukutty Amma for her to give them their daily ration of onions. Paarukutty Amma kept the onions, garlic and other main food items in her room. Only when Paarukutty Amma had handed out the essentials for the day to each daughter-in-law were they able to cook.

The daughters-in-law welcomed Kaali's arrival into their household as it gave them some reprieve from their household chores. Paarukutty Amma herself did not do any chores around the house. She would not even pick up anything on the floor that was in the way to put it away. What was even more surprising was that even when the babies in the house cried, Paarukutty Amma would not pick them up to soothe them. She expected her daughters-in-law to stop their chores midway through grinding spices on the grindstone and rush to attend to the child.

Nor did Paarukutty Amma help out in the *kusini* to even peel an onion. That required too much effort. But whenever she had the chance, she complained about her daughters-in-law to her sons. The fact that the sons did not believe anything

Paarukutty Amma said about their wives was another matter. Paarukutty Amma spent most of her days gossiping with the neighbours, making the lives of her daughters-in-law miserable and getting as much work out them as she possibly could.

It only took Kaali three whole days to learn the chores in the home and the ways of the family members. She also learnt to prepare the *arishtam*, a herbal medicine from Kerala, for the expectant second daughter-in-law. She learnt to bathe the pregnant second daughter-in-law as Meenatchi Paati had done for Margaret. She bonded far more closely with the second daughter-in-law as a result of this. When she wasn't sure about what to do, she asked Paarukutty Amma and learnt it quickly. She also learnt to cook the special *pathiya samayal* for the expectant mother. She was tasked to bathe the children in the house and pass them to their mothers to be breastfed. This was all on top of the help that she gave to the daughters-in-law with the household chores. It was back-breaking work but she was at peace when she slept at night. The family only knew that Chandran had abandoned her without a word. That was the version of the story that she had told them. She had not told anyone in the house about what had happened prior to that. For now, that kept her honour intact.

It was at this time that their neighbour, Mageswari, registered her marriage with a Chinese man without the knowledge of her family. She had met him on her daily route to the factory where she worked. He was a bus driver on her daily route and they fell in love. In those days, there was very strong opposition to such mixed marriages. That's what happened in Mageswari's house too. As no one accepted them in her home, Mageswari and her new husband rented one of the rooms at Paarukutty Amma's home. Mageswari and Kaali became fast friends.

Now, every fortnight, Kaali had to get her passport 'chopped' (stamped) at the customs office. She always had to beg and plead with someone to accompany her during these outings so that she could extend her stay in Singapore. One day, as she returned with Jameela Akka after getting her passport 'chopped', she found out that the eldest son in that house worked as a customs officer. She was relieved. Somehow after that, she did not have any difficulty getting her passport stamped anymore. The eldest son's wife spoke to her husband and asked him to help Kaali with her predicament. Whenever she needed to go to the customs office after that, he took her in his car.

The next day, at the pasar, she chanced upon Manju and her mother. Manju immediately jumped into Kaali's arms. Manju's mother told her that Sethulakshmi Amma had returned from Kerala. Prasanna was married and living in Kerala with her husband and his family. Sethulakshmi Amma had become more domineering these days. The news did not sit well with Kaali.

"How is Muthu?" she asked.

"Why? Don't you see your friend these days at all?" replied Manju's mother with a smile and left without answering her question.

Kaali felt uneasy. She couldn't understand why Sethulakshmi Amma was so set in her ways. She really wanted to see Muthuletchimi by any means. But Kaali was snowed under with household chores at Paarukutty Amma's home that day, as usual.

Kaali felt really sorry for Paarukutty Amma's daughters-in-law who were frightened of her. 'Thrifty, thrifty, thrifty' — that was the motto that Paarukutty Amma governed her home with.

Kaali was surprised at how thrifty they were. Only when it was absolutely necessary would they spend money in that home. But all the women had plenty of gold. The three daughters-in-law were always decked out in beautiful jewellery on their ears and necks. Kaali had never seen such beautiful bangle designs as those worn by Paarukutty Amma.

That evening, when they ran out of wheat flour, Kaali rushed out to the shop in front of Jalan Kadai. As she was walking there, she caught a glimpse of a familiar figure. For a moment, her heart skipped a beat when it dawned on her who it was. She stopped in her tracks.

"What is this? You seem to have gotten really wealthy in that Malayalee house." The disdain in his voice was revolting. She wanted to spit in his face. Instead she retorted.

"How dare you ask me such a question? I can't believe I left my home for a rogue like you. How could I have believed you?" She screeched out at him in her unsteady voice before briskly walking away.

He yelled out behind her, "Ehe! Ehe!"

She did not turn around to respond to Chandran. While she walked away with her head held high, she could not contain the tears that welled up in her throat and came up in her mouth.

Mageswari was always the last one to go to bed in that house as she waited for her Chinese husband to return home. Kaali would keep her company while she waited. With both women trading stories about their lives, time went by quickly. Mageswari's husband only returned home after he had dropped off all the factory workers at their homes. He was often bone-weary by the time he walked through the door. As soon as he returned, Mageswari too would retire for the night leaving just Kaali awake in the home. But that was not for long, as her day would start shortly after that at 4.30 a.m. Once she was up, she would not have even a moment to breathe.

One day, at the break of dawn, there was a frantic knocking on the *kusini* door. Kaali could not guess for the life of her who that could be. *Why would anyone be knocking on the door at this time of the night? Who could it be?* She found a distraught Muthuletchimi standing outside the door. Her hair was in a mess. She fell into Kaali's arms sobbing.

10

FOR ONE SECOND, Kaali could not believe the sight in front of her.

Muthuletchimi was a good-spirited soul who loved a good laugh. She only had kind words for everyone. She was always well-dressed. Her hair was always tied in a single plait and had beautiful hairclips on both sides. Her face would be evenly powdered and her sari neatly tied. She had a wide range of beautiful saris too. There was no doubt that Muthuletchimi was a stylish, elegant and graceful damsel.

But why did she look so dishevelled today? For one second, Kaali's heart sank.

"What happened, Muthu? Your husband is not the sort to say anything harsh to you? Did someone say something to upset you?"

Hearing Kaali's question, Muthuletchimi was even more disheartened. She held onto Kaali's hands tightly and sobbed. Kaali knew something was terribly wrong.

"Hang on a second. Let me make you a hot cup of tea," said Kaali, turning to go into the *kusini*.

"No, Kaali," said Muthuletchimi as she pulled Kaali's hand towards her. She brought Kaali outside the house.

"Here, you take this from now on." Muthuletchimi placed a curved gold (*neli*) ring into Kaali's palm. Muthuletchimi started crying again, "I have been cheated, Kaali."

"What happened, Muthu? Why are you crying like this? Tell me what the matter is. Did someone do something to you?"

Just then, a loud shrill voice called out in Malayalam, "Where did this Kaali go? She is missing."

It was Paarukutty Amma's voice. Seeing how agitated the voice made Kaali, Muthuletchimi quickly added before disappearing into the dark, "Don't forget me, Kaali."

As usual, Kaali did not have a moment to rest or worry about her friend once the day started. She had to look after the new mother, make breakfast for everyone at home, cook the meals, sweep the house and take care of many other jobs. She was a spinning top in Paarukutty Amma's home. She placed the baby on her legs to bathe him. She had to nimbly turn him over twice before the bath was complete and then hand over the baby to his mother to be fed. Then the chores in the *kusini* beckoned her. She had meals to cook. For some reason, it seemed like more jobs kept piling onto her usual routine. Her burden was slightly alleviated by the other two daughters-in-law who worked in tandem alongside her.

When everyone had had their meals in the afternoon and retired for their afternoon nap, Kaali was tasked to go to the store. She thought that this was the opportunity she had been waiting for to slip away for a short while. She had to see Muthuletchimi. As soon as Sethulakshmi Amma saw Kaali's face, she frowned and walked back into her room. Muthuletchimi hurriedly pulled Kaali and walked towards the hot springs.

It was the middle of a hot afternoon and there were a few Indian women at the hot springs washing their clothes.

There were no Malays or Chinese anywhere to be seen that afternoon. Both of them sat in the corner of the hot springs. Almost immediately, the next moment, tears rolled down Muthuletchimi's face uncontrollably like a water pot had broken in her eyes. It didn't look like anything at all could be done to comfort her. Rather hesitantly, she told Kaali what had transpired over the last few months.

Appunni managed to stop Muthuletchimi in the pasar, at the back alley behind the Chinese shop one morning. Understandably, Muthuletchimi was both angry and embarrassed at his action. To contain her emotions, she used one foot to squeeze the toes of the other foot.

"What?" she had asked him, perhaps too boldly.

In response, Appunni took her hands in his, drew her close to him and whispered, in his heavily Malayalam-accented Tamil, "You must come to me tonight."

He had shown no hesitation in asking her that question. For a moment, she did feel like slapping him. But before she could react, he gathered her in his arms and held her tight to his chest. They were at the back of a small shop at the end of the lane that sold incense sticks. The shop was manned by an old Chinese lady who always looked very sleepy. The shop only drew Chinese customers, so even if anyone were to see them embrace, it would have been someone who didn't know them. Furthermore, there was hardly anyone around during those hours of the morning. They must have stayed in the embrace a little longer than they should have. Appunni could not bear to contain his emotions anymore. With tears in his eyes, he mustered enough strength to pour his heart out to her, cupping her face in his hands.

"I can't forget you. It's a torture to watch you every day. I am dying. I can't take it anymore that you are so near and yet so far... too far for me to touch or hold. I want you, *Sundari*. I want you!"

Muthuletchimi had never been held so tightly as though a man's life depended on her consent. This was a novel experience. His feather-like kiss left her breathless. More than that, she could not believe that he had gazed into her eyes and called her *Sundari*, the beautiful one. She found it hard to believe that a man found her beautiful.

Overwhelmed by guilt, in the next moment, she pushed him aside and ran away, ignoring his cries behind her. "*Sundari... Sundari...*" His voice followed her home as she ran all the way back to her room. *How affectionate he is and how strong....!* She was heady with the masculine power he exuded. She could not get past how masculine his strong arms felt around her. That day, she put an extra effort into making a delicious chicken curry for her husband. As usual, Supramulu licked the plate clean without saying a word of praise or complaint and promptly went to sleep.

To her chagrin, Appunni was nowhere to be seen for the next three days. His window panes remained closed. She wanted to pretend that she didn't care but she could not escape from thoughts of him that plagued her. Out of the blue, that night, Supramulu drew her close to him in bed and placed his legs over her.

The next evening, Supramulu was tasked to personally check on the pipes that had to be delivered from Pasir Gudang to the shipyard as there were some concerns regarding them. Supramulu worked at the Naval Base as an apprentice who repaired pipes. He played an important role in checking the pipes of the ships before they sailed.

"Today, I have to go to Johor to check the pipes. Will you be okay in the night to be on your own, Muthu?" He was worried about leaving her alone. She could not hide her irritation. *Even if he was sleeping next to me, what does he do?* Without a word, she got out of bed.

Fortuitously, that evening, Appunni appeared at his window sporting a two-day-old beard and forlorn eyes. When she finally caught a glimpse of him at the window across from her home, her heart melted a little. Instinctively, she brought her hands to her cheeks, and slapped them asking for his forgiveness.

At 1 a.m. that night, she walked over to Appunni's room. Both houses lay still with its inhabitants fast asleep. As soon as she entered the house, Appunni jumped out from behind the door and held her tight. Everything that happened afterwards in his embrace brought her sheer pleasure. At about 4 a.m., she reluctantly peeled herself from his warm embrace and tiptoed as quietly as she could to the *kusini* door at the back of the house. The latch of the back entrance was rusty and it did not take her long to push it aside slowly without creating a ruckus to enter Sethulakshmi Amma's *kusini*. Although the houses were right next to each other, she needed to ensure that nobody saw her. She didn't dare breathe when she crept into the house like a cat past the first room, which was Sethulakshmi Amma's room. As soon as she got to her room, she locked the door behind her. It was only then that she felt a gush of joy rush all over her from her head to toe.

The next time they met at a different location. His friend, Vellappan, who lived in Teo Lee Road, had gone to India with his family. Before leaving, he had entrusted Appunni with his house keys and told him to keep an eye on the house while they were away. Seizing the opportunity, Appunni took a half-day leave from work and went to his friend's house to wait for her. Muthuletchimi found it hard to return home that day. Her heart lay in their embrace. Appunni drowned in her like a bee in a bed of nectar. She had to muster all of her willpower to leave him that evening.

She started wearing saris in Appunni's favourite colour. She did not tie up her hair and instead let it flow like Malayalee women did. It was how he liked seeing her. She got into the habit of putting on thick eyeliner. No one seemed to comment about the sudden changes to her attire. Only Sethulakshmi Amma thought it was unusual. *She was such a nice girl! Why is she doing all these? Maybe, after living amongst so many Malayalees for so long, she too desires to dress like us. Never mind. Why does it matter what she does?*

Appunni bought her a curved gold or *neli* ring as a sign of his affection. Muthuletchimi bought him a watch from the Chinese shop. Supramulu noticed the ring on her finger but he did not suspect anything. He was always proud of his wife's ability to scrimp and save. No matter how little he gave her, she found a way to save part of it. *No one is Muthuletchimi's equal when it comes to saving money.* Muthuletchimi handled all the household expenses and grocery bills at home. His job was to be the sole breadwinner.

Throughout the day, Muthuletchimi's gaze constantly fell on her finger, where the *neli* ring lay. The sight of the ring always brought a smile to her face. She even started putting on weight.

On her lean frame, the extra pounds only made her look more beautiful than ever.

In between all these shenanigans in the household, nobody paid much attention to the arguments that were occurring in Meenatchi Paati's room. Sangkaralingam often scolded Meenatchi Paati. On most days, Meenatchi Paati did not even come out of her room. Maasilamani was a frequent visitor to their home. Whenever he came by, Sangkaralingam would leave the house with Maasilamani right away.

One early morning, Meenatchi Paati left for the Holy Tree Sri Balasubramaniar Temple in Sembawang. She did not return till late afternoon. Sangkaralingam paced up and down the living room like a cat who had just delivered her babies, waiting for her to return. He muttered under his breath but did not say anything aloud. How could he say anything to his wife who returned from the temple with *prasadam* for him? He made his displeasure known with just a hard stare. The only reason he did not fight with her was because he knew that his neighbours would laugh at him for getting angry at his wife because she had spent a few hours at the temple. Within a week, this became a regular occurrence. Meenatchi Paati would wake up early, cook for Sangkaralingam and hasten to the temple.

But the old man's attention was diverted from his affairs at home. On 9 August 1965, Singapore and Malaysia parted ways. Sangkaralingam could not stop discussing the turn of events. He had many relatives in Malaysia so he was very happy that Singapore and Malaysia had separated.

The reason was simple. His relatives dropped in at all times of the year with no prior notice. As soon as they arrived, they would demand to be taken all around. He could not say no to them. But he did not take them too far or to any of the important or historical sites like the Sir Stamford Raffles statue in the city. Instead, he would take them to the zoo and the hot springs that were close by. The visitors would drink the water and pretend to be amazed. When they left, without fail they would take four or five bottles of water from the hot springs back with them. By the time they left, the expenses would have chalked up to a sizeable amount.

Appunni and Muthuletchimi's love for one another increased every day like an untamed wild river. They were prisoners of their desire for one another. The difficulties that they faced in getting together every day or every other day left Appunni in frustration quite often. She had to pacify him with a long hug and a promise to find a way to be with him often. She spent all her energy consoling and reassuring him of her love for him. Both of them were not able to bear being separated from each other much longer. One day, nature found a way to help them.

Muthuletchimi found herself giddy all the time. She could not stop throwing up either. Supramulu stood next to her for a short while and watched her without saying a word. He did not eat that day. He did not eat the lunch that she had packed for him the next day either. The food was brought back intact. He seemed lost in his thoughts when he walked through the door. He did not draw Muthuletchimi close to him as he usually did. He remained silent in the room too. Only then did it occur to Muthuletchimi that something was amiss. Her body was in shock — head to toe — about what would be bothering Supramulu. She needed to do something.

Appunni was taken aback.

"What did you say? Marriage? You want to elope? Where can we go? No matter where we go, someone will find us and bring us back, won't they? What's more, no matter where we go, I have to come to Sembawang Shipyard for a job. Who is going to give someone like me a job other than the shipyard?"

Muthuletchimi was crestfallen and could not stop the tears from dripping down her face. She could not bear to see Supramulu's dejected face at home either. Supramulu looked like he had lost everything in his life. He tossed and turned in his bed and somehow fell asleep unknowingly.

At dawn the next day, everyone in that house ran into his room to wake him up. Margaret was the first to start crying and screaming out, *"Ayyo!"*

"Dei, sinner!" said the houseowner, shaking his shoulders. Supramulu woke up in a daze, not knowing what had happened or what he had done wrong. Mathai dragged him to the *kusini*.

In the middle of the *kusini* with urine flowing down her legs, her eyes wide open, her tongue hanging over her chin in a grotesque manner, hung Muthuletchimi on a rope from the ceiling.

11

Vellaya had an urgent need to see Mallika.

Vellaya's boss trusted him to look after the shop on his own and left him to run things in the shop whenever he had to run an errand. That was the secret to Vellaya's full pockets that were never short of money.

But Mallika had a lot of household chores to take care of that day and could not leave her home. The teacher's wife had a fever. Mallika had to look after their child as well as the household chores. She could not move an inch out of the house that day.

Vellaya came by her house on Bah Tan Road and he paced up and down on the streets in front of her house hoping to catch a glimpse of her face. After a long wait, he saw Mallika walking out of the house with a child in her arms. Mallika was a little embarrassed but at the same time touched that Vellaya had made the effort to come by her home. *Goodness, he must really be in love with me to do this!*

"Could you come out of the house with me for a little while?"

"Ayo! Until, the teacher comes home in the evening, I have to look after the baby. The teacher's wife has a fever. I can't carry the baby and come out there."

"Okay! Let's see. If you can get away in the evening, come to that side, okay?" he said placing a five-dollar note in her hand. After he left, Mallika was filled with anxiety. She could not wait to leave the home to meet her Vellaya. At about 4.30 p.m., the teacher returned home, relieving her of her child-minding duties. In a hurry-burry, she quickly scrubbed and washed her face, put on some talcum powder, tied up her hair and left the house. She walked briskly to their usual spot — the *kway teow* shop near the Jalan Kadai.

She waited for a half hour but Vellaya was nowhere in sight. *Wasn't this the spot he told me to come to? Why is he making me wait for so long?* She waited a little while longer in front of the bakery. Later, she walked to Sukumar's clothing store and pretended to check out the clothes. She then walked back to the *kway teow goreng* shop. By now, she had waited close to two hours but there was still no sight of him. If she waited any longer, her mother would come looking for her and for some godforsaken reason, if her mother discovered her loitering around the shops, she would hit Mallika's head with her knuckles. Fearing an altercation in public, Mallika decided to head back home.

The next morning, the Sembawang area was embroiled in a flurry of activity. A few police jeeps entered Sembawang Kechil, Lorong Maha, Teo Lee Road and the surrounding kampongs. The policemen were specifically looking for Indian youths. They hit and dragged away any Indian youth they were suspicious of.

"My child did not break any law. What on earth is wrong with the policemen these days? Why are they misusing their power these days?" protested the parents.

About two in the afternoon, Mallika's mother returned home unexpectedly, having taken sick leave from her work that day. No sooner had her mother returned home than she tore into Mallika and started to beat her senselessly.

"Tell me, are you pregnant? Has he made you pregnant? Do I have to take you to the hospital for an abortion? Couldn't you have found someone else to fall in love with? Why do you need to fall in love?"

Despite the pain that was being inflicted on her, Mallika was shocked. *Someone must have told her about my love affair. What does it matter if I am in love with Vellaya? He is a good man.* Mallika was furious with her mother for making the senseless accusations.

"He's not a bad man. He loves me with all his heart!"

Before she could finish her sentence, her mother slapped her mouth. Mallika's lips started bleeding.

"He doesn't love you with all his life. He wants every woman that he sees. He is a dog that wants sex. Those poor women! Those midwives work the night shift with no sleep to save pregnant women and help them with childbirth. These animals raped those nurses! Do you know that the nurses had begged them to let them go! But these men beat them up. The first one to get caught for the crime was the dog that you have been hanging around with!"

With that, her mother yanked her thick hair and stamped on her back several times. She had no fight left in her after that nor did she feel any pain. She lay on the ground without moving. Soon she could not cry anymore. *How could this be true? Even yesterday, he had come over to see me. How could he, of all the people, do this? That, too, to the nurses who looked after the pregnant women.*

By noon the next day, Chinnadurai was picked up by the police. Murugan was the police informant. It was he who revealed the events of the night. The events that transpired became the talk of the town at 13th Mile and the tongues that wagged in Sembawang showed no sign of abating any time soon.

The second son of Paarukutty Amma, who was a policeman, came home with insider news of the crime every night. Apparently, in the middle of the night, when the town was asleep, the three men had broken the gate of the clinic using a metal rod. They had discarded the lock, dashed into the room, grabbed the two midwives and raped them. When the women put up a fight, they were beaten till they could not protest anymore. Their mouths were stuffed with cloths to muffle their screams as they were raped brutally. Of the two women, one was a prison officer's wife. The other was an unmarried young lady.

When dawn broke, the policemen started searching for the criminals. Even young men who had done nothing wrong were beaten up and questioned. It was an unspeakable crime. In the first line-up that the police put together, it was Vellaya's blood-stained shirt that gave him away. He was the first to be caught like a winter melon who could not be hidden away. The nurses were not able to identify the other two men. They said it was too dark to identify the men. One of the midwives had fainted after giving her testimony. Both the women had been taken to the hospital immediately.

Chinnadurai was caught in front of Sultan Theatre, between the laksa store and the laundry shop, as he lay on the ground nursing a bad hangover. It was a tiny lane that divided the two stores. The policeman carried him, put him in the jeep and drove away.

The men were rounded up and sent to Sembawang police station where they were beaten continuously. "Who? Who?

Who did this? We will beat you up until you tell us the truth!" roared the nameless police officer. Murugan too had been caught and not having the strength to get beaten up any further, Murugan told the truth as blood filled his mouth.

It didn't matter that it was Murugan who had given them the idea in the first place. Both Vellaya and Chinnadurai were a little afraid of getting caught or committing the act. But Murugan continued to ply them with stories about his experience with women in graphic detail that aroused them to no end. It was what Murugan had wanted. In the end, it was ironical that it was Murugan who became the police informant that led to their conviction. The police continued beating Murugan for more details. Murugan gave a detailed description of what had transpired at the crime scene. That led to a three-hour manhunt for the other two accomplices.

No amount of description could capture how badly the three men were beaten over the next few days. The Chinese policemen spat at them. Even Murugan who was the government informant was beaten periodically. Unable to even stand up after a severe beating they had endured, Chinnadurai retaliated one day by shouting a profanity at one of the police officers. For that, he received a sound punishment that he never forgot in his lifetime. Chinnadurai did not speak a word after that. Not just Chinnadurai. None of them ever spoke up against the police officers in their cell. One week later, when Chinnadurai saw the same officer, he was frightened to the core. He had been beaten to a pulp, leaving him looking like a deranged man.

For the first time in his life, Vellaya thought of his grandfather and berated himself for the state he was in. *After mum died and dad eloped with that nameless woman, Thaatha must have gone through so many difficulties to raise me. He must have had many dreams about me. But not a single day have I respected that old man.*

He also remembered an incident that was etched in his memory. Once, when his grandfather had refused to give him money for his unnecessary expenses, Vellaya had cut up his grandfather's khaki work *seluar.* The next morning, his grandfather tried to salvage the pants by using several safety pins to hold up the two severed pieces. But he was not able to hide the damage done to his pants. Left with no other choice, he had dug out his dirty pants from the night before and worn it to work.

There were so many such instances when Vellaya had misbehaved. When he started working in the *vangsa kadai*, he had used his earnings to shower Mallika with presents but it had never once occurred to him to buy his grandfather a packet of *mee goreng.* Despite all that he had done, not once had the old man hated him or treated him badly. Vellaya bent over in remorse and cried uncontrollably.

Whenever the prison officers walked into a room, the prisoners had to stand up. The prisoners had to do all the work that the Chinese officers told them to do. The policemen's unflinching gaze burrowed into their souls.

"Thaatha, I made a mistake… Thaatha, I should have listened to you. I made a huge mistake." He meant these words from the bottom of his heart. But his grandpa never came to visit him nor heard these words. Chinnadurai's younger sister and mother came once and stood there by the cell crying. Murugan's family too came once. But not a soul came from Vellaya's side.

In between all these events, the case came to court. During a heated exchange, Chinnadurai threw his shoe at a police witness in court. His sentence was increased immediately. Each time they were given a stroke of the cane, they waited for the area to heal before administering the next stroke. The affected area would turn green and all blood would die. The searing pain was far more painful than anything one could have felt in hell. When the pain subsided, the next rattan stroke would fall on their buttocks. It was a life worse than a dog's and Vellaya did not know why he was still alive. The others faced the same fate. Vellaya beat himself up for going along with the plan. If only he had walked away that night.

Even the other prisoners did not respect the three of them. Suicidal thoughts plagued them constantly but they did not know how to take their lives when they were constantly being watched. The only thing that they could do was cry. That they did every day for a long time.

It was then that another unspeakable incident took place at 13th Mile.

12

WHEN KAALI HEARD the news, she was preparing breakfast for the family.

"Ayyo!!' she screamed. Her scream woke the whole family up. "Ayyoo! Ayyoo! My darling!"

Watching Kaali crying her heart out, the daughters-in-law in the house told her to go to Sethulakshmi Amma's house immediately. Only Paarukutty Amma was annoyed that she was leaving without completing her tasks.

"If she goes now, who will do the household chores? Finish the household chores and then you can go."

I am just a maid in this house. I have to wait for permission to go. Kaali finished her chores as quickly as she could, stifling her tears with no avail. As soon as she was done, she rushed out to Sethulakshmi Amma's house. She arrived just as they brought Muthuletchimi's body down and lay it on the ground. They had to wait for clearance from the policemen before moving the body. Kaali screamed in agony.

"Muthu! My darling! My darling, what happened? Why did you do this? Why, Muthu, why?" Kaali held onto Muthuletchimi's feet.

"Although you came to me, darling, I was not able to save you. I am a sinner. Why, Muthu, why? My darling, Muthu!"

Her cries and her pleas to the dead Muthuletchimi broke the dam of restraint that the others had around them. Everyone standing around the two women started crying. The body was not brought back to the house after the post-mortem at the hospital.

"Why should we trouble the houseowner? It's not my house, is it? Let's take the body to the crematorium from here."

Those were the only words Supramulu uttered that day. Not a drop of tear fell from his eyes. His face looked hardened which frightened everyone around them. *How could he be so strong?*

Supramulu was a man who did not even know how to speak harshly. He had married a woman from his hometown in Andhra. There was a ten-year age gap between them. Both family members were happy about the alliance and had celebrated the wedding with great pomp. He had returned to Singapore with his new bride. From the day that he married her, he never hurt her or misbehaved with her in any way. He even handed over his salary to her as soon as he received it. He would ask her for money that he needed for his daily expenses. She managed the household finances. It was only during the recent few months that he had felt her distancing herself away from him. But even then, he had not suspected anything.

One day, when he wasn't well, he had taken a half-day off and come home without any notice at 2 p.m. Uncharacteristically, Muthuletchimi was not at home. As he was sick, he fell asleep right away. Even when he woke up, she was nowhere to be found. She only returned at about five-thirty in the late afternoon.

"Where did you go, Muthu? I came home at 2 p.m."

"Oh, that. A friend of mine from the pasar, Revathi, isn't well. So, I went to see her."

She had walked away from him while answering him and disappeared into the *kusini*. She made mouth-watering *kaara kuzhampu* and chapatti for him that day. Supramulu ate to his heart's content.

Another day, he ran into Muthuletchimi at Teo Lee Road. He had gone to see his friend, Kunjuraman, that day. He was surprised to see her walking towards him in that area.

"Someone said that a lady was selling banana flowers here. That's why I came here. But I couldn't find her house."

It was the same day that she had complained that her stomach was churning when they had returned home. Soon she started vomiting. Supramulu was distressed to watch her suffer.

"What happened, darling? Did you eat something that did not agree with you, sweetie?"

Supramulu brought her a glass of water, held her as he rubbed her back and chest gently. He managed to bring her back to their room slowly. But no sooner had she reached their room, she broke free from his embrace to run back to the *aluru* outside the *kusini*, where she bent over and continued retching. At some point that night, he finally managed to bring her back to the room. She wasn't even able to stand up straight or sit down.

"Lie down, darling. I will come soon." He told her before running out to her favourite *thongal kadai* run by a Chinese man and bought her a packet of *kway teow goreng*.

"Here, eat this when it is hot, darling."

He opened the packet up for her. As soon as the waft of the *kway teow goreng* hit her nose, she started vomiting again. Supramulu was taken aback that even the smell of her favourite food was not enough to squelch her vomiting spell. Throughout the night, she continued retching. Her eyes were turning white. He had never seen Muthuletchimi so ill or so weak.

Supramulu was struck speechless when Mathai's wife and Manju's mother told him the cause of Muthuletchimi's vomiting. He could not breathe. His body shivered.

"What? Aiye, you are speechless with happiness, aren't you!"

The womenfolk in the house took Muthuletchimi to the bedroom and coerced her to lie down. He left the house immediately. *Do such things happen in life too?* That night when he walked into their room, he saw her eating porridge and mango pickle. He watched her enjoy the meal.

As she placed the mango pickle on her tongue, she turned to him and said, "Manju's mother made this food for me."

Her voice was weak and she looked dreadfully pitiful. He realised that she had forgotten to even ask him if he had eaten. He could not bear to look at her.

Muthuletchimi did not seem too perturbed by his reaction. Supramulu rolled out the mat in the corner on the floor and lay down. This continued for a week. To be honest, Muthuletchimi was relieved. Her body was aching and all she wanted was to be left alone to sleep on the bed. She did not realise then that something was amiss. Within a week, Supramulu lost a lot of weight. He stopped eating at home.

It was payday that day. As usual, he brought his pay cheque home and handed it to her. Again, he took out the mat and spread it on the floor. It was then that it occurred to her that something was wrong.

"What happened to you? This is when we are supposed to be happy and you're keeping mum!"

She reached out to touch his shoulder. He pushed her hand away. She pulled him towards her to hug him. He actually let out a yelp as though he had been struck. "Hmm!" he grunted as he pushed her away, got up and left.

She thought he would return at dawn to change his clothes and leave for work. But sand fell onto her wishes. Supramulu did not return home that day. She did not see him much for the next two days as he worked non-stop. After two days of throwing himself into work, Supramulu found that there were no pipes left at the shipyard that required his attention. There was also a strict policy in place that dictated that no one was allowed to sleep in the office.

For those two days, his lunch was just a slice of bread and ginger tea from a *Kakka* shop. But he really could not bring himself to swallow anything. His head felt like bursting. The mere thought of it made his heart burn. He held his head with his hands and sat in the corner of Jalan Kadai. When he finally returned home one afternoon, she was nowhere to be found again. She returned at about six in the evening. He did not ask her where she had gone.

Something jolted him from his sleep that night. When he looked around, he realised that she was not in bed. She walked into the room after a while and crawled into bed. In the dark, he could not see her crying, but he could hear her quiet sobs. Unable to bear her pain, he reached out to her and held her head close to his heart for a fleeting moment. She jerked away from his embrace and moved to the far end of the bed and curled her body up into a foetal pose.

Supramulu felt guilty. His conscience pricked him as he was reminded of the secret that he carried in his heart. Two years ago, when his mother was not well, his *machan* had sent him a telegram urging him to return to the village immediately. Just as his *machan* had feared, his mother passed away three days after he arrived. At least, she got to see him. A relative of his who had come to his mother's funeral told him about a famous doctor who specialised in fertility treatments. Supramulu went to see the doctor. After running extensive tests on Supramulu, the doctor explained the diagnosis to him. While Supramulu did not understand many of the things that the doctor said, he understood one thing rather clearly — he would never be able to father a child.

Supramulu took a vow that day that Muthuletchimi would never have any want that would go unfulfilled in this world. He would take very good care of her till death pulled them apart. She would be as treasured as the pupil of his eye and, to the best of his knowledge, that's how he treated her. If she laughed, he laughed. If she got angry, that whole day he followed her around the house like a lost puppy. Only when she calmed down and her face was relaxed would he let out a sigh of relief and feel his heartbeat slow down.

What he did not realise or know was that for some time, she had been oblivious of his presence. He did not know that she saw him as a glutton with very little interest in anything else. He did not know then that she despised him.

The more he thought of it, the more his body burnt. He was just a layman, not a saint to say, "It's okay; whatever has happened, has happened." He was filled with rage and misery at the same time. He did not know what to do. He chose to return home as late as he could. That day, as he walked through the door, he found Muthuletchimi weeping in bed. As soon as she saw him, she threw herself at him and clutched his feet.

"For two days, you did not come home at all. Where were you? What will I do without you?"

He removed her hands from his legs, picked out the towel from the rack and went to the bathroom to shower. When he came out of the shower, she served him piping hot rice and *udang* curry. She must have cooked the curry hurriedly when he was in the shower. She was a fabulous cook and the smell of the food tickled his nose. But Supramulu had no appetite. He did not even glance at the food.

Without even drying his wet hair, he went to sleep. He didn't know how to wipe his hair properly. Whenever he claimed that he had wiped his hair after having a bath, it was Muthuletchimi who would have to do it because his hair would be soaking wet. But that day, she was frightened to reach out to him or even go near him.

Every gesture of his frightened her. She felt like a blazing ball of fire had burst in her stomach. She wished that the volcano of fire would melt under her tears. It was the wish of a simple woman and all the simple woman could do at this point was to cry her heart out in the bathroom that night. The thought of Appunni made her heart burn with fire. *How could he have showed so much interest in me only to disappear at the sight of the first problem? Why did I trust this man?* She returned to the room with puffy eyes and a swollen face. Supramulu did not even turn around to look at her. Sometime in the middle of the night, after tossing and turning and not being able to sleep, Muthuletchimi reached out to Supramulu. She placed her face on his feet. The hot tears that flowed like a broken dam woke him up. For some reason, her action angered him. *Who is she trying to trick with her tears?* He curled his legs away from her reach.

Sometime in the wee hours of the morning, Mathai needed the washroom. He stumbled out of his room unsteadily with his eyes still half-shut. That's when his head hit something. Instinctively, he opened his eyes and looked up. The next minute, he screamed.

The houseowner, Sethulakshmi Amma, was stunned.

As Supramulu had decided that they should take the body directly to the cemetery rather than bringing it to the house for a wake, none of the womenfolk was able to participate in it. In the evening, when the men returned home from the funeral, none of them came out to the veranda to enjoy the breeze or to chat. The whole house was eerily silent.

One month after Muthuletchimi was found hanging on the rope, Supramulu found a room within the Naval Base compound which housed two other single men. After negotiating the rent of the room, he decided that it was for the best. He prepared to move out of 13th Mile. He threw out all the things that he no longer needed.

When he opened the almirah, it struck him how neat it was. Muthuletchimi had a way of folding the clothes that would put any clothing shop to shame. When he took out her saris one by one, he felt as though someone had slapped his heart. It was only then that the gravity of what had happened hit him. *Why on earth did she do that? How could she pretend to be virtuous after all that she did?*

He had promised Subramaniam *Krani* that he would send all her clothes to an ashram in the *krani*'s hometown. As he gingerly packed up her saris and tied them up in a bundle, something caught his attention. At the bottom of the pile lay a new sari. Without much thought, he took it too to add to the pile of the saris. That's when his eyes fell on a photograph that fell out of the sari. He picked it up and looked at it. The next moment, his eyes grew wide and he fell to the ground. He didn't know how long he had been unconscious. When he woke up, all he could cry out was "Adiye! Adiye! Adiye!" He repeated the words clutching his heart with his hands. He collapsed onto his knees and banged his head on the ground.

Of all the men in the world, why did you fall for this Malayalee man? Of all the men in the world, how could you think this... this... fellow was good-looking? Why? Why? Why did you allow yourself to be cheated by this man?

He did not move for half an hour. Then he slowly made his way to the house next door. He went to the fourth room and knocked. The door opened right away. But the man he was looking for was not there.

"He left last week for his village in Kerala."

"Thuuuu!" he spat at the closed door before turning away. Nobody saw Supramulu in Sembawang Kechil area ever again after that.

THE NEWS ABOUT a temple in Malaysia where wishes were granted was spreading like wildfire amongst the womenfolk in Sembawang and Kaali was the first to bring the news home to the daughters-in-law.

Apparently, womenfolk were heading in droves towards the Sri Maha Siva Muniswarar Temple in a town called Tampoi in Johor. Many reported that they had applied for a Singapore Restricted Passport just for this purpose. Unmarried girls went to the temple and lit oil lamps as they prayed for a good alliance. When their marriage was fixed, they returned to the temple to give their thanks to the deity.

Paarukutty Amma's second son had an unbearable stomach ache that would not go away. Kaali gently suggested once to his wife that they take him to the temple. His wife clutched onto the thought as nothing else seemed to help her husband. They had gone to the doctor several times with no sign of the pain abating. Paarukutty Amma thought it was ridiculous for her sick son to travel such a long distance. His wife won the battle that day. Even when he was moaning in pain in the night, his mother never woke up to check on him nor was she flustered. It was his wife who stayed up with him, comforted him and watched him suffer.

His mother was always unperturbed even to the cries of her grandchildren. Once one of the daughters-in-law had to pick up her child after pounding chilli in the *kusini* as no one seemed to be attending to the wailing child. In her haste, she didn't realise that she had not washed her hands properly. She had picked up her child and given it a bath. Afterwards, no matter how much she washed her baby, she wasn't able to calm the crying baby whose skin was clearly inflamed from the chilli padi that had touched its soft skin during the bath. Watching the baby cry made Kaali really sad. *How could Amma do that? Why doesn't she carry her crying grandchild? She certainly has the time to go to the neighbour's house to gossip. How can she be in the neighbour's house for hours?* Kaali did not articulate these thoughts aloud when the daughter-in-law came back into the *kusini*. Instead, both women worked in silence next to each other. The daughter-in-law clutched the child to her chest as she breastfed it.

Goodness, she has the patience of a saint, thought Kaali.

Kaali's main chore in the home was to help the daughters-in-law complete their tasks. She was well-loved by them as they found her agreeable and hard-working. So, when Kaali suggested going to the temple in Tampoi, they decided to go along with her suggestion.

They had heard that Maayilvaganam *Ayya*, who was from Sri Lanka, had found an alliance for his son soon after visiting the temple. He had been really worried about his son as all the alliances that kept coming their way did not materialise for one reason or the other. Hearing about the temple in Tampoi, his wife had convinced him to visit the temple for nine weeks and light an oil lamp for the deity. Before they could complete their nine weeks of prayers, a good alliance came by in the eighth week. Their son's marriage was fixed. His gratitude to the

Muniswarar deity who had cleared the path for his son was unwavering. Maayilvaganam donated a *Thoondamani vilakku* as a gift to the temple. The news of Maayilvaganam's vow being fulfilled appeased Paarukutty Amma a little. The family made the necessary arrangements for her son with the stomach ache, his wife, child and Kaali to go to the Tampoi temple in Johor.

First, they had to go to the Singapore customs and get their passports 'chopped'. Then they had to find a car that would get them across to Johor customs. Upon reaching the Johor customs, they had to join another long queue. After a long and tiring journey, they managed to cross the border into Johor Bahru town. As soon as they reached Johor Bahru, they stopped the car so that the daughter-in-law could feed the child. The journey from Johor Bahru town to Tampoi was short and they got there in no time. They stopped their car in a corner and went into the temple. The daughter-in-law took the child from Kaali. The temple priest came out of the temple to greet them, probably sensing that they were foreigners. Hearing about his persistent stomach ache, the priest said, "Go and buy an *archanai* and come back to me with the receipt."

They returned with the receipts and milk packets to pour into the snake pit at the back of the temple. With great faith that her vow would be fulfilled, the daughter-in-law poured the milk into the snake pit. They also bought a packet of milk for Kaali and *archanai* receipts for her. The *archanai* receipts were tokens taken to pay for their prayers to be read out by the priest. Generally, one *archanai* receipt would be needed for each person or family. Devotees would include their names and astrological signs on these receipts, which they handed over to the priests.

If they had come to the temple expecting a fierce-looking Muniswarar, they were mistaken. The daughter-in-law felt her heart grow warm at the sight of Muniswarar staring down at her. Kaali, on the other hand, started crying. Thoughts of the three people whom she had loved and lost overwhelmed her. She thought of the husband she had left behind. She thought of her son, Raasu Boy, who had constantly followed her around the house, calling her '*Yemma*'. She thought of her friend, Muthuletchimi, who was gone too soon.

Why have you made me a woman in this lifetime, God?

After the *pooja*, the priest brought the plate with the small fire on camphor. They placed their hands over the fire and brought the palms to their eyes. They put a sizeable amount on the plate as an offering. After that, the priest took the blessed *vibuthi* and spread it over the child's stomach as the child too had a stomach ache. He spread the *vibuthi* generously over the father's forehead and stomach as well. The priest took the string from the Muniswarar's feet and tied it on Paarukutty Amma's son's wrist. As the couple walked away from the sanctum, Kaali turned around to look at Muniswarar's face one last time. In a stage whisper, she said "Muniswara! *Ayya*! God! My God! Please look after everyone, my God!" With those words, she left the building.

Perhaps because they had travelled a long distance, the baby fell ill with a fever the next day. That was it! Paarukutty Amma was furious. Kaali had never seen this side of Paarukutty Amma.

"Is this all necessary? Who is putting ideas into your head? Why are you bringing new practices into this house! I want to know why now! Why? Aren't there any temples in Singapore?"

Kaali was shocked. *Does one need permission to go to a temple?* She had never seen Paarukutty Amma pray ever. In fact, there was no designated prayer room in that house. So no one even

knew when the womenfolk in this house had their periods.
Generally, Hindu women abstained from many things during
their periods and avoided the prayer room. No one seemed to
get their periods in this household. Kaali thought it was strange.
What she didn't know was that even when the daughters-in-law
and Paarukutty Amma had their periods, they had the unusual
habit of putting the *vibuthi* on their foreheads.

They took the baby and went to Ramu's Clinic. Two days
later, the baby started smiling again. Kaali and the daughter-
in-law heaved a sigh of relief.

That evening, when all the household chores were done,
their neighbour, Manohari, came by to invite the family to the
Holy Tree Sri Balasubramaniar Temple's nine-day Navarathri
prayer. Manohari's daughter was performing a dance that night
at the temple. Rather nonchalantly, Paarukutty Amma pointed
to Kaali, "If you wish, you can take her with you." Kaali was
secretly pleased that she was allowed to attend the prayers and
left right away with Manohari.

Worshipping at a temple in Singapore was a novel experience.
She had never seen such a beautiful sight or such a temple in the
rubber estate that she had grown up in. There were huge grand
oil lamps that were lit with a dozen or so wicks. Everyone was
dressed to the nines. The womenfolk wore silk saris and the
men wore white dhotis. Kaali was mesmerised by the beauty
of the temple under the moonlight. Ambaal looked stunning
that day.

Several groups of young girls performed in front of the deity.
It was then that she heard someone spitting 'thu!' behind her.
Puzzled, she turned around to see what the commotion was
about. Chandran's mother was openly staring at her in disgust.
If looks could kill, Kaali would have died in that crowded

temple. Thankfully, no one seemed to have noticed Chandran's mother spitting at Kaali as they were standing at the entrance of the temple. There weren't that many people around her. *Nevertheless, it is still a temple. How could someone spit in a temple? What sort of degraded soul does that?* Very quickly, Kaali elbowed her way through the crowd to get closer to Manohari. She did not leave her side for the rest of the evening.

Long after she returned home that night, Kaali was troubled by the evening's events and could not fall asleep. She had an early day the next morning. It was time for her to get her passport 'chopped' again. She would have to leave early with Paarukutty Amma's son and head to the customs office. It was then that she heard an unusual noise outside her room. She bolted out of bed wondering if someone was in trouble.

She slowly opened the door, not wanting to startle whoever it was outside the door, and peered out. Paarukutty Amma's eldest son was throwing up near the *kusini*. His wife was standing next to him and gently rubbing his chest. Sensing that something was wrong, Kaali threw caution to the wind and hurried towards them. But she was taken aback when her favourite daughter-in-law and the eldest son's wife snapped at her in a loud hiss.

"Shut your mouth and get lost! Who called you here? Don't poke your nose into other people's business."

Dawn broke. Kaali continued her chores like a robot. She didn't feel like talking to anyone after what had happened last night. *No matter what, we're just the household help. How will we know when they will laugh or when they will get angry?* She consoled herself. But something was amiss that day in the house.

For a start, Paarukutty Amma was in an unusually bad mood that morning. Her daughters-in-law always did her bidding to avoid her wrath. Kaali never understood why they were so afraid of their mother-in-law or why the mother-in-law kept onions, tamarind and other important items for cooking in her dark room. Seeing these women stand before their mother-in-law with their outstretched hands for essential ingredients, like beggars asking for alms, made Kaali sad. The daughters-in-law looked pitiful. It might have been understandable if it was a home where they struggled to make ends meet. But this was a wealthy home in Sembawang. *Why does Paarukutty Amma behave this way?*

The baby started crying suddenly and almost on cue, Paarukutty Amma's screeching voice followed.

"Can't you hear the baby screaming? Take the baby, go to your room, lock the door and give milk to your baby!"

The daughter-in-law was embarrassed. With a downcast face, she ran into the room carrying her baby. *What gave her the right to yell at me to feed my child? Just because she is my mother-in-law doesn't mean that she has the right to announce to everyone at home that I need to breastfeed my child! Why is that woman angry all the time?*

As soon as his wife entered the room with the baby in arms, Paarukutty Amma's son walked out of the room and sat in the sofa in the living room. He did not go into the room until his wife was done.

Kaali was puzzled. It was unusual to see the eldest son at home on a weekday. *Why didn't he go to work today? Maybe it's because he was throwing up so much last night. I wonder if he is ill.* Sometime past noon, after everyone had gone to sleep, Kaali finally sat down to eat. That's when she overheard the conversation between the mother and her pleading son.

"Please listen to me. I swear I will not drink again. Please trust me, please trust me,"

At first, Kaali got up to move away. Then she sat down quietly not wanting to draw attention to herself. *Oh! That's what the drama last night was. So Paarukutty Amma was angry that her son had returned home drunk last night. How could a grown man be afraid of his mother?* For the first time, Kaali felt a new-found respect for Paarukutty Amma. It was only because Paarukutty Amma was such a strict disciplinarian that the men in the home had turned out to be such good people. There is a time and place for everything. She was reminded of the saying: "Even during a flood, you still have to sow the crops in the valley."

As far as Kaali was concerned, all men who did not drink were good men.

14

THAT MORNING, A surprise waited at the pasar. Prasanna was at the market with her mother.

"Prasanna! How are you? Are you well? When did you come back from India?"

Kaali rushed to Prasanna's side, brimming with affection. For a moment Prasanna did not react. She wondered if she should talk to Kaali. After a few seconds, she nodded at her with a lifeless smile. Sethulakshmi Amma's face did not seem to be clouded with the usual irritation or anger.

"Seer fish is being sold quite cheaply on that side. Go to that Chinese shop, Amma," Kaali bravely initiated the conversation.

"If you can, you come home in the evening, Kaali," said Sethulakshmi Amma in a lifeless voice.

"Today, I can't, Amma. I will come tomorrow."

The next day, after she had finished all her household chores and the daughters-in-laws as well as Paarukutty Amma had gone into their rooms for their afternoon siesta, Kaali arrived at Sembawang Kechil.

Sethulakshmi Amma had spread out what looked like two sacks of anchovies in the middle of the living room. Manju's mother, Margaret and the new tenant were seated around in a circle, cleaning the anchovies. They made space for Kaali and signalled for her to join them. This was the usual practice in that house. The womenfolk would sit in a circle chatting away as they cleaned the anchovies together. Then they would divide it up according to their pre-arranged share and store it away. Sitting together to do an otherwise mundane task ensured that the job got done without anyone feeling tired.

But something was amiss that afternoon in that house. There was no small talk. At most, they said a few words to each other when needed. Halfway through the task, Sethulakshmi Amma retired to her room.

"I will go and lie down for a bit. Let me know when you leave, Kaali."

With those words, she headed off to her room. The next minute, Prasanna too got up and left. Only after both women had left the room did things return to normal and the conversation start. Apparently, the tenants had known that something was amiss when Manju's mother was severely scolded by Sethulakshmi Amma for brushing her teeth behind the *kusini*. For two days, Manju's mother was too embarrassed to look at anyone in the house after that incident. *What gave the houseowner the right to tell tenants where they should stand or shouldn't stand*, thought Manju's mother.

Then Sethulakshmi Amma went on to attack Manju's father next. She spied Manju's father the next day helping his wife to wash their dirty linen. Sethulakshmi Amma teased him and called him an *ull paavadai*, referring to the petticoat that women wore under their saris. It was a roundabout way of calling him henpecked. All hell broke loose that day.

Manju's father confronted her and asked, "How does it concern you if I help my wife with her household chores? What is your problem really?"

Sethulakshmi Amma must have been taken aback as she stopped making fun of her tenants or hurting their feelings for a short while after that incident.

Then the news about Prasanna came to light. Kaali's heart was heavy listening to what had transpired.

"How could this have happened especially when you marry your daughter off to someone in India? Is this how men in India treat their women?"

Sasidharan had a dark complexion but pleasant features. He had no reservations about marrying the Singapore-born Prasanna particularly since he received a hefty dowry from her family. Sethulakshmi Amma gave a fifty-pound sovereign as well as her house in Kerala to Sasidharan. She renovated and painted the house before gifting it to them. Both her husband and she furnished the home with all the household items that a newly-wed couple would need. The wedding too was a grand affair. As Prasanna was from Singapore, her mother-in-law initially didn't complain about Prasanna not doing any household chores. But once Prasanna fell pregnant and took to her bed all day out of sheer exhaustion, the mother-in-law could not bear to hold her tongue much longer. Prasanna had her meals in bed too and expected someone to bring them to her. As soon as she had her meal, she plopped back down onto the bed and promptly went to sleep. Which mother-in-law could bear such behaviour from a daughter-in-law?

Sasidharan had other issues with her behaviour. Whenever his friends came to visit him, he did not like Prasanna joining them in the conversation, nor did he like her wearing the maxi or any long frock rather shamelessly in front of his friends. He detested her giggling in front of his friends as well. In fact, he was truly embarrassed at her behaviour. It was a time when villages in Kerala weren't as progressive as they are today, and to make matters worse, Prasanna was living in a small village. Sasidharan's sisters too started talking about Prasanna's inappropriate behaviour to him rather blatantly. Unable to bear it any longer, Sasidharan decided to address the elephant in the room when he started the conversation with Prasanna. She could not believe her ears. *Was it wrong to even speak to guests?*

"Fine! Let's talk about the other things you do. Is it so wrong for you to help Amma with the household chores? Why don't you ever help out in the house?"

Should I be doing household chores when I am pregnant? What a heartless man. How could he be so calculative?

Prasanna spent the day in bed crying her eyes out. Her face swelled up. When her mother had left for Singapore, she had given Prasanna money for her own expenses. Sasidharan's mother often asked her to use a part of this money. She hadn't taken it too seriously because it was for the household expenses after all. But what troubled Prasanna and upset her the most was that Sasidharan's younger sister would often take the new saris that she brought from Singapore and wear them to the university as though they were hers. She could not bear that at all!

The following day, Sasidharan told her that the family was going to the Attukal Bhagavathi Temple for the Pongala festival. The Pongala festival in Kerala was a prayer done only by women, where they would boil sweet rice as an offering to the goddess. Sasidharan wanted to take her there so that she could offer Pongala to the goddess with his mother and sisters. Prasanna refused but Sasidharan was relentless. He held her hands and pleaded with her. His voice threatened to break into sobs at any moment. Watching him break down calmed her down a little and she agreed to attend the Pongala festival after all.

This was the beginning of the tiny cracks in their marriage. Prasanna's letters to her family contained detailed descriptions of these disputes. She exaggerated some of the details and blamed her mother for her fate in life. "How could you throw me into such an old well?" Her parents were deeply troubled.

Out of the blue, a telegram from Kerala arrived. It read: 'If you do not come immediately, the next news you will get is of my death.' Sethulakshmi Amma's husband left for Kerala right away with a heavy heart. No one knew what happened in Kerala but when he returned, he had Prasanna in tow. For a week, there were fights between mother and daughter or the husband and wife. There was a lot of commotion in the house.

Finally, Sethulakshmi Amma and her husband decided that after Prasanna delivered her baby, they would take her and her child back to Kerala to her husband. Prasanna was now five months pregnant.

Exactly at three-thirty in the afternoon, Kaali got up. Before leaving, she went to Sethulakshmi Amma's room and knocked on the door. "Come in," said a firm voice. When Kaali entered the room, she was shocked to find Sethulakshmi Amma in tears.

"Here, I fried some banana chips yesterday. Take it with you. It's fresh," she said handing over a stuffed packet which Kaali accepted gladly.

"Whenever you have time, please do visit us, Kaali." said Sethulakshmi Amma. Kaali walked out of the room with a heavy heart. As she turned around to leave the house, she walked past Muthuletchimi's old room. Her heart felt like it had dropped. *Sinner girl! In one second, she destroyed her life.*

It was then that Kaali heard a voice. "Come here, *ma*." Meenatchi Paati called out to her as she reached out to hold Kaali's hands and brought her to her room. It had been some time since Kaali heard Tamil spoken in the house.

"Can you spread this ointment on my legs and massage them please?" asked Meenatchi Paati in a quivering voice. Asking her to lie down, Kaali massaged Meenatchi Paati's legs with the ointment. As soon as Meenatchi Paati felt a little bit of relief from the pain, she got up.

"Thank you so much, *thaayi*."

"It's okay, Paati," said Kaali as she went off to wash her hands. By the time she returned, Meenatchi Paati had made her a cup of coffee and placed a few pieces of *murukku* on a plate for her. Kaali felt an instant affinity to Meenatchi Paati.

Thaipusam was fast approaching in three months. Many Hindu families everywhere around her were preparing the *kaavadis* in their homes in Sembawang. They only consumed vegetarian meals and some even cut that down to one meal a day. They also hosted bhajan-singing sessions in their homes every day. The day finally arrived.

That morning, Paarukutty Amma's second daughter-in-law told the family that she had taken a vow that she would go to the Muniswarar Temple in Johor Bahru to offer milk to Lord Murugan on Thaipusam. Paarukutty Amma was furious. Kaali had never once seen Paarukutty Amma pray at the altar. *Obviously, Paarukutty Amma would be upset, wouldn't she?*

"Of all the places in the world, do you have to go to Johor Bahru to offer milk to Lord Murugan? What's more, do you have to do it today?"

The daughter-in-law did not budge. "Only when I prayed at that temple did your son's stomach ache start abating. We are going."

With great difficulty, the both of them managed to convince Paarukutty Amma to let them make the trip. They hired a car to drive them across the Singapore-Malaysia causeway to the temple in Tampoi. They took Kaali along with them. Kaali had never seen such a crowd before. There were vendors selling *ice kachang*, drinks of different colours, hot *goreng pisang, jemput-jemput*, different types of *vadais* and *kuehs*. The sights took away the weariness Kaali's body felt after the long car ride. They bought Kaali a cup of piping hot tea and a *vadai* but they did not eat anything until the *pooja* was over.

The daughter-in-law managed to cut through the bustling crowd to carry out the rituals. While doing the rituals, she handed the baby over to Kaali, who duly placed the baby on her hips. The daughter-in-law first made an offering to the guardian snakes by pouring a packet of milk into the milk pit. She then filled a small pot with milk and went around the temple. The milk was then offered to Lord Murugan. They were focusing on the deity in front of them and the *pooja* when she felt someone scratching her from behind slowly.

At first, she thought she was mistaken or that she was imagining it. She continued to gaze at Lord Murugan. Then it occurred again. She felt someone's hands on her back scratching her a little more firmly this time. This time, a little more firmly. She was understandably annoyed. *How could anyone do this in a temple, especially on Thaipusam?*

"Which dog is molesting me now?" In anger, she spun around a little too quickly to face her perpetrator.

"Amma!" said the little voice who hugged her. It was Raasu Boy. She also saw a man further away staring at her. It was the man who had married her — her husband, Munusamy!

15

In the 1960s, Sembawang was a small village.

It was a rainy and windy day. Three drunk ruffians roamed the streets of Sembawang Village. The men were believed to have been high on drugs too — for it is said that that drugs were available to anyone who knew how to procure them. The intoxicated men created a ruckus on the streets as they headed towards the 24-hour Maternal and Child Health Clinic in 14th Mile. Their goal was to rob and rape the midwives at the clinic. One of their victims was a married lady and the other a young unmarried one. They first took whatever the two women had on them and then the brutality began. They raped and abused them for several hours until dawn broke.

The next day, this matter was reported to the Chong Pang Police Station in the village prompting a massive manhunt in the surrounding Naval Base and Sembawang areas. The police left no corner unturned in their pursuit. All the young men who fitted the description were called up for questioning.

The residents of Sembawang and all of Singapore were devastated and angry at what had happened. It was just unbelievable that such a crime could have taken place. After great difficulty, the policemen nabbed the criminals. There were no DNA kits in those days so the onus was on the police to gather indisputable evidence against the criminals and to build a strong case. Finally, the men were presented in court and were charged with gang rape. The trial was lengthy and was filled with twists and turns. One of the accused even took out his shoe and threw it at a police witness. It was one of those cases that sparked a lot of interest amongst the public.

When reading his judgement, Justice Choor Singh commented "You behave like docile lambs in this court, but on the night in question, you behaved like lions." The men were sentenced to a few ten-year sentences to be served out concurrently and several lashes of the brutal cane. It was a night that no one could forget, especially not the two young midwives who had their innocence stolen from them.

Kaali turned around quickly causing great discomfort to the baby in her arms. The next minute, the baby cried out in pain. The daughter-in-law quickly snatched the baby off Kaali's arms. Once she had handed over the baby, Kaali reached out to hold Raasu Boy's hands as she walked out of the temple. She got as far away from the crowd as she could before she leaned forward to hug him tightly to her chest.

"My darling... my precious... my sweetie... my prince."

Words that had been at the tip of her tongue and buried in her heart came flowing out as she kissed her son repeatedly. Raasu Boy did not want to let go of his mother either. He too held her tightly. Kaali could not hold back the tears that rose up in her throat and exploded in her eyes. Tears flowed continuously from her eyes as she ran her hands over Raasu

Boy's head, face, stomach and his whole body searching for any change since she had last seen him.

"Enough! Enough of your drama! I can't believe we saw you when we are here to pray. *Oodukali*! I guess it's just fate! Come, Thambi!" Munusamy released a few more cuss words in Tamil at her as he yanked his son's hands and dragged him away.

"*Yeppo*! It's Amma! It's our Amma!" cried the desolate child trying to get his father to release his hands. Kaali fell to the ground and held onto Munusamy's legs to stop him from leaving.

"Just because he left you, you suddenly remember your child? You suddenly miss your child? You shameless thing! Don't you know that desire only lasts sixty days and lust thirty days? How could you run away leaving this helpless boy behind? Shameless woman! Your disgusting story has spread across the estate. How can you call yourself a woman? Filthy scum, let go of my child!"

He stopped short of using more vulgarity as it hit him that he was standing outside a temple. He grabbed Raasu Boy once more like a thorn out of a wounded flesh and disappeared into the crowd.

"What happened, Kaali? You didn't even take the blessed water from the temple. Why are you standing here outside the temple?" It was the daughter-in-law calling out to her. Kaali stood there not moving and staring into a distant spot. She slowly turned around to address the daughter-in-law.

"Ohh that… my head was spinning. I was worried that I would fall in the temple. So, I came out to get some fresh air."

"Why are you crying then?"

"I don't know, Amma." With that, she took the child back into her arms again. Kaali did not speak during the car journey back to Singapore. She handed over the child briefly once to the daughter-in-law to be fed, before putting the child on her lap and patting the child to sleep. *Life is strange in so many ways. What an irony that my child is growing up like an orphan while someone else's child has a place on my lap?* Kaali's heart was heavy.

Two days later, it was time for Kaali to get her passport 'chopped'. As always, the eldest son took Kaali to the customs office. When they got there, they found the place filled with policemen. Paarukutty Amma's son went inside the office to find out what had happened. He then came out and took Kaali to another counter.

It was quite a serious matter. Each month, Malaysians who lived in Singapore had to get their passports 'chopped' to continue to reside in Singapore. There was a loophole in the system. If one were not to come in person, all one needed to do was to pay ten dollars to a particular customs officer who would take the necessary actions. But today, that officer was caught in the act and the policemen had arrived to arrest him. They handcuffed the customs officer and took him away in their jeep.

"The guy who got caught is a Tamil," said Paarukutty Amma's eldest son.

Hearing that, Kaali turned around to look at him. His posture and downcast eyes arose sympathy in her. *I wonder if he was going through a bad patch. Why would anyone commit a crime intentionally? Why did he destroy his life like this?* She felt sorry for him.

Vellaya was surprised. He had just heard that he had a visitor. *Someone is here to see me? Who could it be?* That sight that greeted him of the visitor standing on the other side of the metal bars broke his heart.

He shuffled forward towards the visitor, flanked by two prison officers on each side of him. They had handcuffed him, following their protocol. His grandfather must have come to give him a piece of his mind or to ask him hard questions that would make him wish he could commit suicide by pulling out his tongue. Perhaps then he need not answer the question in his grandfather's eyes. But when their eyes met, that was not what happened. His grandfather's heart was heavy with grief and all the old man could do was to yell out at the sight of Vellaya in handcuffs.

"*Yellai! Yellai!* Was it all for this? Was it all for this? Was it just for this I am still living? What did I do wrong? How...? Why? The midwives... we look at them as mothers... guardians. How could you destroy their lives? Is that how I raised you?"

Thaatha could not speak anymore. Tears welled up in his throat. Vellaya watched rapid tears roll down his grandfather's wrinkled face. He thought that his grandfather's lips looked dry. He stared at his grandfather, not wanting to look away. The man who stood in front of him looked like he had lost everything in his life. Vellaya could not peel his eyes away from him.

After a long while, his grandfather stopped crying briefly. He reached out to unfold the top of his dhoti, to fish out a few crumpled notes which he pressed into Vellaya's hands. His grandfather's hands were shaking.

"Here take this. I wasn't able to buy anything when I was coming. Come... take this. Keep this. Come," insisted the old man in a soft voice.

For the first time, Vellaya opened his mouth. "No, Thaatha. I don't want it. Don't come here again, please." Vellaya got up and walked away with the prison officers. He did not turn around even once to look at the frail figure who stood there watching his back.

That evening, a few prison officers came to their cell. They stood outside the cell staring at the men without a word. There was something in that hard gaze that Vellaya could not comprehend. The prisoners were brought out of the cell one by one in handcuffs. The officers slapped and punched them repeatedly. There was nothing unusual about the encounter. But, today, it didn't hurt as much as it usually did. Vellaya's mind and body had gotten accustomed to the pain by now.

But, this time, he could not ignore the nagging doubt that something was different. It was the tall prison officer's gaze that he found most disconcerting. He was the only one who did not raise his hands to the prisoners. He did not spit at them either like the others did when they walked by his cell. But even a worm would have cringed in shame at the menacing glare that he gave them whenever they were in sight.

Vellaya could not forget that day. It was the day that the three men were scheduled to get their next round of caning. The caning sessions always brought them to their knees. It felt like they had died and returned from hell to suffer more on earth when the officers were done with them. For some reason, the look the prison officer gave them was far more troubling than the pain any cane could inflict on them.

The tall Chinese prison officer walked out of the room where the men were being caned. He slumped into his chair in the office, placing his head on both his hands as he leaned against a table. Officer Ibrahim, who was on duty that night, walked around to him to pat his shoulder. Both men sat there in silence. How could he ever console him? There were no words in any language that could accomplish that.

Sinners! What an honest man he is! How could a prison officer's wife face such a situation? Why will anyone trust the police force when there is no protection for an officer's wife or family? How cruel fate is that he has to face the man who abused his wife every day? There is nothing worse in this world than this. He is such an honest officer! How could they have done such a thing to his family? Thankfully, no one could hear Officer Ibrahim muttering away under his breath.

The officer had just returned from the hospital after seeing his wife. It was his downcast eyes and slumped body on the table that riled up Ibrahim. *I will whack those three fellas this evening.*

Vellaya could never forget the day he was sentenced. All three of them had been restless. None of them had slept the night before nor had they eaten anything that day. Needless to say, they were worried. The other two men spent the night talking about the impending outcome ad nauseam. Vellaya was quiet. He did not respond to his friends repeated questions and worries. The officers were surprised at his behaviour. "What an arrogant bastard he is!" grunted the Tamil officer, Muthaya. Muthaya constantly scolded them in Tamil whenever he laid his eyes on them.

That day, Vellaya did not drop to the ground writhing in pain when he was caned. He did not scream out, "Ayyo!" like he had in the past. Vellaya stood firm and held on to the metal bar as he was caned. The prison officers were taken aback that Vellaya seemed unaffected by the caning. That was unusual even for them who prided themselves in having seen it all. *Not just this, I deserve even more than this. No matter how much you hit me, I deserve this.* His body was ready for the pain. Vellaya wanted the punishment to hurt.

16

TELUK INTAN WAS founded on the river bank of Perak River. It is believed to have been established by Sultan Mahmud Shah's eldest son, Raja Muzaffar Shah, who had escaped from the Portuguese invasion into Malacca in 1511. It was first called 'Teluk Mak Intan'.

In the 19th century, Sir Archibald Anson drew up a plan to bring together the three surrounding villages into one town. In his honour, the town's name was changed to Teluk Anson. A hundred years later, in 1982, the name was changed to Teluk Intan. In the Malay language, *teluk* means 'bay' and *intan* means 'diamond'. It was a flourishing trading area which exported coconut, rubber and tin.

The Karaikudi Chettiars established a moneylending business in Teluk Intan. Business was brisk as they charged a dollar's interest for every hundred dollars that they loaned. It was a time where the Chettiars would sit cross-legged at their low wooden table and write their accounts for the day. Not a cent was left unaccounted for as they were careful accountants. It is often said that they were the first Tamils to buy several acres of rubber plantations and build massive homes in Malaya.

But from the 1990s, things slowed down and there were fewer job opportunities in that town. Several people left for

Shah Alam and other places seeking work. The remaining folks depended on the rubber plantations and the fishing trade to make a living. The preferential treatment for the locals meant that, for several years, government jobs and tenders were primarily awarded to the Malays. Indian students found it hard to obtain a seat of their choice at educational institutions. That prompted many Tamil families to migrate to Tamil Nadu.

Teluk Intan is also famous for its Leaning Clock Tower. The Chettiar communities' *kittangi* or warehouse where they did their accounts was located near this tower. Apart from the moneylending business, one would also learn the most important skill in life, which was how to keep track of the expenses. All one needed to do was to watch the manner in which the accountants kept track of each and every single five-cent coin that they spent. Record-keeping was a way of life and one that helped them to progress in life.

Chithamparam grew up in a place near Trichy, which was neither a village nor a city. When he turned nine, his mother sent him off to Teluk Anson to join his father. It was hoped that he would learn their traditional moneylending trade there.

But his idyllic life at Teluk Anson threatened to come to an end all too soon before he could finish his Bachelor of Science degree. Chithamparam was irritated at the interruption this upheaval caused in his life. His father had just sold a hundred acres of rubber estate, his moneylending businesses, five houses and taken all their money out of the bank in a single day. Preparations were being made for them to leave for Tamil Nadu on a ship. It was not that he didn't know or understand his father's rationale. The racial riots had resulted in several deaths. The curfew placed a lot of families in great difficulty. What he did not want was for his life to turn around overnight.

In 1969, Malaysia's general elections in the Selangor district saw both the ruling party and the opposition party winning the same number of seats. The opposition party called for the ruling party to step down and protested publicly with a procession. In retaliation, the ruling party too had processions. In two days, the processions escalated into a protest on 13th May. As the ruling party had more Malays while the opposition party had more Chinese members, many viewed it as a racial riot. The riots spread across to many states killing several people in its wake. The government had to call on the army to bring the situation under control.

The then prime minister, Abdul Rahman, stepped down from his post. Parliamentary sessions were stalled. An Emergency was declared. Under Deputy Prime Minister Abdul Razak, a new party was formed. The ruling party implemented many new rules. One of which was that those who had red identity cards and were permanent residents needed a permit in order to work in Malaysia. This affected many Indians.

There were stricter rules about land ownership as well. This was an impetus for many Indians to hurriedly dispose of their land, gather their possessions and head back to India with their families in tow. There was a constant underlying fear that they might be treated like the Indians in Burma. One of the many Indians who returned was Chithamparam's father, who packed his bags and bade goodbye to his life in Malaysia for good.

Thankfully, fate intervened once more in Chithamparam's life. No matter how hard he searched, he was not able to land a job after his graduation in India. Against his father's wishes, Chithamparam returned to Malaysia. What awaited him was the moneylending family business of his father and his ancestors. But as a graduate, that was the last job he wanted to take up. It was not that he was ungrateful. He was thankful for the business that had fed his family and helped to educate him. But it was not what he wanted. He was steadfast about refusing all offers to return to his family's ancestral job.

Finally, upon the recommendation of his mother's brother, he found a job in a company as an accountant. The job barely lasted three months. Business was hit by the bad economic times. The small company soon closed down, unable to take more financial beating.

Exactly forty days later, another friend showed him a job advertisement in the Singapore English newspapers. The opportunity and a chance to move to a different location piqued Chithamparam's interest. Without a second thought, he sent out the job application with his educational certificates.

While Chithamparam was searching for a job in Malaya, his mother was busy searching for a wife for him. Her letter informing him of her search irked him to no end. But he could not reply harshly to his mother. The thought of her kind face crossed his mind several times as he debated on how he should respond. He had never disobeyed her.

Meanwhile, he travelled to Singapore for the face-to-face interview. He was hopeful that he would land the job. With God's grace, his hopes were not dashed. Within two weeks, he received a letter of offer from the company. It was an important job at an English magazine's news section. He could not contain his happiness on the first day at work. It was only later that he realised how onerous the job was.

At first, he stayed at his father's relative's home while he searched for a suitable room to rent. Without much difficulty, he found a room in the Sembawang area at 13th Mile. Although the place was a little far from the office, he liked the kampong house very much. The neighbours were kind. When he wasn't well one day, they made him *pathiyam* food and checked in on him often.

One day, when he returned home late after working overtime, he found the houseowner Amma and her daughter waiting for him to have their dinner. He was a little embarrassed at their attention at first. But gradually, he warmed up to their affection that day, sensing their sincerity in waiting for him so that the family could have dinner together. He did not have the heart to tell them not to do so.

In no time, his neighbours started coming to him for advice on any official matters pertaining to documents or government-related matters. They followed his advice to the tee and his words were treated as holy words. Sometimes, he was tasked to read and respond to official letters on behalf of his neighbours.

Chithamparam's room was the second room in the four-bedroom kampong house. The houseowners and their only daughter, Vaani, stayed in two rooms. A Malayalee family with a baby stayed in the fourth room. Vaani was often spotted playing with the child. Sometimes when the parents were not around, the baby would crawl into his room. Once, looking at the drool dripping from the baby's mouth and its innocent smile made him want to carry the baby. But just as he was about to pick up the baby, a voice called out to him in Malayalam.

"Ayyo! Sorry, Chetta," said the baby's mother.

Chithamparam giggled. He didn't know many Malayalees

nor was he familiar with their ways. It was only at Sembawang 13th Mile that he encountered so many Malayalee faces around him.

The next day, a Chinese man joined his department at the office. The first thing the man asked him was, "Where are you staying?"

"In the Sembawang area."

"Yeah, where in Sembawang?"

"A place called Jalan Ulu Sembawang."

"Hey! That's the 13th Mile area, right?"

Chithamparam nodded his head.

"Last year, I stayed in that area for two months. It's a really nice place."

Within a week, his Chinese friend, Chua, moved into Ambusam's house and became Chithamparam's neighbour. As Chua had a motorbike, he gave Chithamparam a ride every morning to the office.

How could Chithamparam have known that his cursed seven-and-a-half-years of bad luck was about to start with the arrival of Chua next door?

One evening, Vaani brought a woman to the house. The woman wanted to know whether she could get her passport 'chopped' every six months instead of every two weeks. She wanted Chithamparam to write the letter on her behalf.

Chithamparam did not know whether to laugh or to snap at her for the silly question. The woman was from an estate in Malaya and worked as a maid in Singapore. She had to get her passport 'chopped' every two weeks at the immigration office to stay in Singapore. She was dependent on her employer to help her. She was worried about troubling the employer's family for fear that they found it a hassle and might tell her off in the near future. She did not lift her head to look at him when she spoke. Chithamparam did not know how to explain the law to her in a way that she would understand.

In those days, even those who were born in Malaysia but raised in Singapore their whole lives found it difficult to obtain permanent residency in Singapore. It was quite unlikely that someone who worked as a maid for several years in Singapore was going to be granted a long-term visa.

"You won't get it," he said patiently. But as soon as the words rolled out of his mouth, the lady started sobbing.

"Why are you crying? The person who helps you now lives in your house, right? If he is a customs officer and you live in his house, there should be no problem getting it renewed. Just stay in their house and continue to work for them. You won't face any problems". It didn't look like the woman was going to stop sobbing any time soon. Chithamparam felt sorry for her.

As she turned to leave, he asked her, "Hey, what's your name?"

"Kaali… Kaali, sir," came a faint reply.

CHITHAMPARAM WAS SURPRISED beyond words. *How is she able to move at the speed of lightning?* After a couple of days of moving in, his friend, Chua, hired Kaali to clean his room. She came by every day. She swept Chua's room, then wiped it down by hand using a cloth before proceeding to wash and iron his clothes. She did all that in a short span of time.

Sometimes, Kaali picked up dinner for him too. Usually, it was *mee goreng* and tea. She took on these additional cleaning jobs with the permission of her employer, of course. She only came to Chua's room after she finished all the household chores at Paarukutty Amma's home.

"Let her work and make at least two cents. Otherwise she will stretch her hands out to us for soap, comb and other essentials. We don't want her to be a burden, do we? Just ask her to finish the household chores first before she goes to other houses," decreed Paarukutty Amma to her daughters-in-law.

Chithamparam, too, hired Kaali to help him with his household chores. That meant that when he returned home from work, he could lie in his bed and rest. Of late, he had been asked to work overtime rather often.

His idyllic days were broken by the arrival of his father. It was still dark. Dawn was just breaking when he heard someone knocking softly on his door. Wondering who it could be at this hour, he got up and went to the door. He did not expect to see his father there. "Appa!" That was the only word he could muster for the moment. He had never really spoken much to his father all his life.

"You go to work. I will take care of things here," said his father rather firmly.

Not wanting to argue, Chithamparam quietly completed his morning duties and left on time for work. Before he left, he introduced his father to the houseowner and his wife. But Chithamparam wasn't able to accomplish much at work that day as his mind was preoccupied with thoughts of his father's unannounced arrival. *Why did he come without any notice?* Feeling anxious, he reached home a little earlier that day. The sight that greeted him was Kaali seated on the floor having an earnest conversation with his father. As usual, the room was clean and bright whenever Kaali visited. What was unusual was watching his father and Kaali laughing.

"Sir! You know, *Ayya* is asking me which part of India I am from. I have never seen India! I was born and raised in Anjarai Kattai. I got married in Anjarai Kattai and lived in Anjarai Kattai all my life until I came here. I have never been to India."

Kaali left soon after that. Chithamparam took a quick shower and got ready to take his father to the mess close by that was run by Malayalees.

"Clerk Thambi is here."

Everyone in Sembawang addressed him as 'Clerk Thambi'. When the mess owners realised that it was his father from India, they paid extra attention to him. His father seemed to enjoy the fish curry very much. He took a bite of the *aviyal* but did not finish it. He did not even try the rest of the vegetables on the banana leaf in front of him.

"These Malayalees use too much coconut in their cooking."

"Don't you like the food, Appa?"

"Not that I don't like their food. It is okay, I suppose. But I don't think it's good for my body."

Food was their main point of discussion until Saturday. On Saturday evening, when he took his father out for dinner once again, his father broached the topic rather pointedly.

"Amma keeps thinking about you and worries about you. She worries about who is taking care of your meals. She wonders if there is anyone who is looking after you. She worries that you might fall ill. She talks about you all the time. She is worried all the time. You know, there is this alliance from Chithambaram Pillai for his granddaughter. Why don't you come to India with me now? We can fix the marriage once you see the girl. Then you can come back to Singapore after that."

What could he say? *I am just twenty-three years old. How can I even toy with the idea of marriage now?* But Chithamparam had never spoken his mind to his father nor was he about to start now. He remained silent.

"I will leave in two days. If you don't want to come with me now, it's okay. Let me know when it will be convenient for you to come so that it is easy to make the arrangements."

Not once did his father ask him what his plans for marriage were. It looked as though his father had made the decision for him and was merely asking him for appearances' sake. Chithamparam's heart was weighed down with his parents' expectations. They did not say anything else to each other for the rest of the evening. They ate their meal in silence.

The next day, when his father was in the shower, the houseowner's wife came into the room to talk to him.

"I asked your father to have breakfast with us twice. But he said no. Please tell your father to at least have a cup of coffee and a dosa for breakfast. Go. Bring your father to breakfast."

Hearing the houseowner's wife's pleading voice embarrassed Chithamparam to no end. When he told his father that the houseowner's wife was insisting that they had their breakfast together, his father thought about it for a few minutes before nodding his head to give his consent. Vaani and the houseowner *Amma* bent over backwards to serve his father. Not wanting to be rude, his father thanked them but said very little else before retiring to the room to lie in bed for a bit. When it was time for his father to leave for India, Chithamparam tried to press some money into his hands rather unsuccessfully.

"Never mind, you have expenses too. You keep it. We are okay in India."

Chithamparam's father received the letter exactly ten days after he had left for India. His wife was devastated when she read it. He had to read the letter several times before it hit him. This was the gist of the letter: "I have just started working. I barely make enough for one person. If I were to get married, I would have to feed my wife. I don't have money to feed two mouths. So, I will let you know when the time is right. I will write to you again. Be patient until then. Please forgive me."

That was it.

Chithamparam felt that he deserved a pat on his back for mustering enough courage to stand up to his father for the first time in his life.

One morning, Vaani came into his room crying, with a letter in her hands. It was a love letter from Chua. Chithamparam tried hard to stifle the giggle that arose in him. But he was also irritated with Chua for distressing Vaani. Without a second thought, he went over to Chua's room and grabbed his friend by the collar.

"What is this?" Chua looked amused.

"You know that I stay in that house. How could you do such a thing? How could you have the heart to do such a thing?"

"Oooi, you are not interested in her, are you? What does it matter to you if I go after her?"

"That's not the point! I want you to vacate this house tomorrow."

"Sure!"

But Chua showed no signs of moving out. Three days to the end of the month, Chithamparam raised the matter again.

"Now, I am not doing anything, right? So, what's your problem?" retorted Chua, putting an end to the conversation.

When Chithamparam saw that Vaani too was not too perturbed by Chua's continued presence in the neighbourhood, he decided to let the matter rest. In fact, Vaani looked happy these days as she was always humming a song under her breath. She even seemed to take greater pride in how she dressed.

That day, when Kaali went to Unnithan's shop to grind coriander and chilli into a paste to use in curries, she had a surprise waiting for her. Clerk Thambi's houseowner's daughter, Vaani, was at the shop waiting to grind spices into a masala paste.

"Why did you come here, *paapa*? I can help you with these things. Why didn't you tell me? You don't have to come to the shop."

"Aiyoh, Kaali, I don't like staying at home all the time. It's so boring at home. I want to do something too."

By then, the mill owner, Unnithan *Ayya*, noticed Kaali in the shop.

"How are you, Kaali?" he asked.

Unnithan *Ayya* always had a kind word for her and everyone who came by to his shop. Seeing the queue to grind the spices grow behind her, Kaali took the packet of masala that Unnithan *Ayya* had handed to her and offered to help serve the customers.

Unnithan *Ayya* was from Kerala. He started his business with packets of masala that was ground at home by his wife. At first, he distributed these packets as samples to the families in the neighbourhood. His wife's masala recipes were a hit and soon he had orders for more. He started a small shop and hired someone to help in the store. As the business grew, he hired one more person.

His customers claimed that once you had tasted the ground spices in their shop, the taste lingered on your tongue. Through word of mouth, the customer pool grew. Standing orders came gushing through for Unnithan's masala from the mess owners in Sembawang and the small shops that catered for the workers at the Sembawang Shipyard.

The customers were also drawn to Unnithan *Ayya*'s kind demeanour. He had a way about him that made his customers feel at home in his shop. He was often invited to his customers' homes for gatherings and important events. For his customers, he was part of their family as he often lent a helping hand to those in financial need. For that and for many other reasons, the mill owner, Unnithan *Ayya*, was well loved by everyone.

Kaali, too, was fond of him. Whenever she went by his store, she would take it upon herself to sweep the floor of the scattered spices. Sometimes, she even helped to sort out the coriander seeds, chilli and dal for Unnithan. Unnithan *Ayya* did not know about Kaali's story. All he knew was that she worked as a maid in several houses. He made it a point to pay her generously for her help in the shop.

Sethulakshmi Amma came by to see Unnithan *Ayya* that day. Prasanna had given birth and Sethulakshmi Amma wanted him to check the almanac for an auspicious day to send both Prasanna and her baby back to India. Unnithan *Ayya* was known in the neighbourhood for selecting auspicious dates for all good occasions. More than his ability to read the almanac, the Sembawang folk considered him lucky. Sensing Sethulakshmi Amma's distress, Unnithan *Ayya* enquired about the child's well-being.

"Prasanna insists that she will not go back to India. I don't know what to say to her. What can I do?"

Unnithan *Ayya* listened patiently before giving her advice on how to deal with Prasanna. What Sethulakshmi Amma did not tell Unnithan *Ayya* was that she was also worried about another impending volatile situation that was likely to erupt at any time in her home. Her second son, Rajan, was dating Mottai, whose mother worked in Ibrahim *Ayya*'s house.

Chithamparam woke up from his slumber in shock. For a moment he thought he had been dreaming. But it wasn't a dream. Someone was crying outside his door. When he hurried out of his room, he found Vaani's mother wailing away right outside his room door.

"Ayyoyoo! Clerk Thambi! The girl has dashed all our dreams for her and run away with some man!"

Vaani's mother started hitting her stomach with her hands as she cried. Her husband was seated on the floor at the other end of the living room, holding a cloth over his mouth to muffle his anguished cries.

Chithamparam could not believe his ears. *What? Vaani has eloped in the middle of the night? That girl who screams her lungs out at the sight of cockroaches? Didn't she kick a big fuss when Chua had given her a love letter? When did she fall in love? And how did she have the guts to run away in the middle of the night when ghosts wandered around?*

"Whom did she elope with?"

"We don't know whom she ran away with, Thambi. Ayooo, Thambi!"

He picked up the letter that Vaani had left behind for her parents:

"I am eloping with someone who has captured my heart.
Please do not search for me.
Vaani"

Chithamparam was shocked.

CHITHAMPARAM COULD NOT figure out whom Vaani could have eloped with. He was not in a position to take the day off that day to help the family with the search.

"I need to go in for a short while. I will take half-day leave and come home after lunch hour. Please don't cry and let the neighbours know, Amma. If word gets out, it will become the talk of the town."

As Chua had applied for leave that day, Chithamparam had to take the public transport to work. He had forgotten what a hassle that was. He had to take two buses and barely made it in time. Once he got to his desk, he worked briskly to complete the tasks at hand so that he could rush home after lunch.

Little did he know that a surprise awaited him at home. He spent the day racking his brains on how to comfort the houseowner's wife. All the way home, he worried how he was going to comfort her. The houseowner's wife turned around and walked out of the living room as soon as she saw him at the entrance of the home. In fact, she banged her bedroom door with great force behind her. Chithamparam was puzzled. Why was Vaani's father scowling at him?

"What happened, *Ayya*? Did…"

Before Chithamparam could complete the sentence, the houseowner started yelling at him at the top of his voice.

"Get out! I want you to vacate the house today! Scoundrel. You snake, how could you bite the hand that feeds you? I didn't know I had a snake under my own roof."

"Just get out! I am trying to be polite here. If you don't leave, I don't know what I will do to you!

Chithamparam was annoyed.

"Why? Why should I vacate the house? What did I do? Why are you yelling at me?"

"You want to know why? You scoundrel!"

The houseowner went to his room and dragged out a limp figure. Chithamparam was speechless.

"Vaani! You are back? What happened?"

It was Vaani's mother who answered him in between sobs.

"You… you… you… you dare ask? You don't know who took her away? Enough! We've paid the price of trusting you. We treated you like our own son. We didn't know you were a scoundrel…"

They were interrupted by a young man who worked at Unnithan *Ayya*'s shop.

"Here… your *paapa's* bag. *Ayya* told me to bring it to you. You left it behind in a hurry."

Not wanting to stand there any longer, Chithamparam left the house to chase down the young man. The young man didn't need any cajoling to spill the beans.

Unnithan *Ayya* had seen Chua and Vaani at the railway station in the wee hours of the morning. The look in both Chua's and Vaani's eyes gave them away. It was obvious to Unnithan *Ayya* what was happening. Without a second thought, he went right up to the couple and confronted Chua. He would have beaten him up if he had to. He had his son, Jagadeeshan, right next to them. But Chua did not put up any resistance when he saw Unnithan *Ayya*. But he restrained himself as he did not want to cause a scene and risk people finding out that Vaani had eloped. Unnithaan *Ayya* left with Vaani in tow. Vaani did not protest either. One could not tell if she was relieved or embarrassed at being found out. Her downcast eyes did not meet Unnithan *Ayya*'s eyes. Chua and Vaani had not thought they would get caught so quickly.

Fortuitously, Unnithan *Ayya* had gone to the railway station to send relatives off to Kuala Lumpur. Chithamparam could not imagine what would have happened if Unnithan *Ayya* had not been at the railway station that morning.

All Chithamparam had done was to invite Chua over to his room a couple of times. After all, they were friends. *How can they punish me for that? How would I know that Chua and Vaani were in love or planning to elope? Vaani had even cried and complained when Chua had given her a love letter. When did she fall in love with him! What a rascal!* Chithamparam was disgusted.

To make matters worse, Chua was Chinese and Vaani was from a Tamil family with roots in Thanjavur. Her people were averse to marrying anyone who did not belong to their caste — what more to someone of a different race! *How could Vaani have the guts to fall in love with a Chinese man?*

Even Tamils and Malayalees did not marry one another. On the face of it, they were friendly with one another and supportive of each other. But there were deep-rooted prejudices hidden from the naked eye in Sembawang. It was only when it came to matters of the heart that neither family would give their blessing to a couple if they chose to marry outside their community. Those who fell in love had to elope and face the consequences of their bold action. The couple in question would face a lot of difficulties from the community. There are so many stories about such couples who were not allowed to live in peace after having defied their parents. This was the case even if they married someone from the same religion. The Hindus had an additional caveat. The couple had to be from the same caste.

What was Vaani thinking when she fell for Chua? Surely, she didn't expect parental approval or support?

Chithamparam finally understood Vaani's parents and why they were directing their wrath at him. He could not forgive Chua either for what he had tried to pull off. Left with few options, Chithamparam packed up his things quickly and left the house in two hours. His colleague, Mustafa, had kindly agreed to allow him to stay with him for one or two days while he searched for another place. The houseowners did not bid him goodbye. They had been good to him all this time. Now he had to pay for his friend's indiscretion. He had to face the wrath of the family. Chithamparam's heart was heavy.

Thankfully, he heard about a vacant room at Malabari Rahim Bhai's home the next day. But by the time he went over to enquire about the room, news about him had reached the ears of Rahim Bhai.

"There are girls in this home too. There is no space for men like you in this house," said Rahim Bhai rather curtly.

Chithamparam was shaken. He could not fathom why they were accusing him of breaking his houseowner's trust. All he had done was to trust his friend. Here he was being punished for that trust. He left the home quickly and went to Kedondong Road to meet a friend who might have some leads on vacant rooms. But his friend was not there and it was time for lunch. His stomach was growling. Instead of going to the usual mess, he went to one of the shops in that area. The food was incredibly spicy. He wasn't able to finish the food. He just ate a small portion to ease his hunger. He did not know what to do next. He stood outside the mess, staring at the street.

"*Saar*," said a familiar voice.

It was Kaali.

"*Ada*! I just dropped off the Maadi-veedu Amma's grandson at school. Where are you going, sir? Why are you standing here?"

The concern in her voice broke his resolve. In a halting voice, Chithamparam narrated what had transpired.

"*Ada*! Why are you upset about this? There's a vacant room in the goldsmith's house in Lorong Maha. The *paapa* in the house told me about it this morning. Just go there, *Saar*."

Chithamparam moved into the goldsmith's house the next day. Kaali continued to do his household chores in his new residence. She swept his room, washed his clothes and had them ironed before he returned home.

Kaali woke up with a sense of foreboding that morning. There was nothing unusual about that morning. The daughters-in-law were waiting outside Paarukutty Amma's room for their daily ration of garlic, onion and ginger.

They cooked either sardine or mackerel almost every day in that household. Sometimes they cooked a store-bought chicken. Side dishes were usually stir-fried cabbage or long beans with coconut. When Paarukutty Amma's friends returned from iguana hunts, they cooked them too. But Kerala coconut *udang* curry was everyone's favourite dish.

Kaali did not like their cooking in the beginning. Having grown up in a rubber estate, her comfort food would always be a dried salted fish curry with dried beans. The Kerala dishes covered in grated coconut did not sit well with her in the beginning. But beggars can't be choosers. In about a year, she had got used to the Kerala dishes. Living in Paarukutty Amma's household, she even learnt how to cook food that suited lactating mothers really well — so much so that she was often called upon by families with newborns to help out in their homes and cook for the mothers.

That's when the buttermilk seller, Anjalai, arrived at the doorstep looking for Kaali. Kaali was at the grindstone, grinding the spices for that day's meal. When Paarukutty Amma found out what the matter was, she hurried into the *kusini* and gruffly yelled out, "Hmm. Go!", almost chasing Kaali to the door.

The sight that awaited Kaali left her dizzy. Munusamy stood at the door with his downcast face.

"Amma!"

Raasu Boy ran towards her and hugged Kaali tightly. *Why did Munusamy come here with the boy? Why did Munusamy have to leave the estate?* Kaali could not stop the tears that burst out of her eyes that cascaded down her face. She hesitated for a moment before explaining who Munusamy and Raasu were to the daughters-in-law. But that took all her energy. In an act of kindness, Paarukutty Amma invited Munusamy and Raasu Boy to stay for lunch.

But Kaali's mind was racing. She didn't know where she could put Munusamy and Raasu Boy up that night. They certainly could not stay with her. She was too frightened to ask Munusamy anything. When it was time for the Clerk Thambi from India to return home from work, she took her husband and her child to him. At Chithamparam's invitation, Munusamy squatted on the floor and narrated his story. Chithamparam racked his brains on where and what sort of job he could find for Munusamy. That night, Raasu Boy and Munusamy stayed in Chithamparam's room.

Munusamy had done many odd jobs at Anjarai Kattai. He had been a gardener at Periya Durai's house. He had done odd jobs at the small *Krani* Mathews' house. He had even washed the toilets at *Poonai Kannu Krani*'s house. He knew all the *kranis* well.

One day, when *Poonai Kannu Krani* had fallen asleep on the floor after his usual round of beer, Munusamy made the mistake of finishing the remaining beer in the bottle in one gulp. The alcohol went straight to his head and he dropped off to sleep. When the *krani* woke up, he found Munusamy's leg on him. In his drunken stupor, Munusamy was snoring away. The *krani* was offended. *How dare Mumusamy — a lowly worker — put his leg on me!* But deep down he knew he was partly to be blamed. He should have never sat down to drink with a coolie.

Munusamy found himself at the brunt of the *krani*'s anger. The next day, when Munusamy reported to the *peratu* as usual, Lingam *Krani* did not look at him or even signal to him to join the crowd of men waiting there.

"Which lorry should I go into, *Ayya*?"

The *krani* pretended to not hear the question. Munusamy inched his way close to the *krani*. That seemed to irk the *krani*.

"What do you want, you bloody dog?"

Munusamy's body cowered in shame. None of the *kranis* had ever insulted him with the derogatory Tamil words that they used on others like dog or a ghost. They had always been fond of him. They sought him out to buy them alcohol in the evenings. He also fried eggs or crispy anchovies to go with their drinks. He was their right-hand man. But, after the unfortunate incident with *Poonai Kannu Krani*, nobody wanted him near them. Day after day, he stood in front of them, shedding aside his pride with his head hung down without meeting their eyes. They had chased him away as though he was a stray dog yelling out, "*Poda*!"

Munusamy did not know what to do without a way to make ends meet. The *kranis* found fault with everything that he did. They claimed that not even the *lallang* died when he sprayed insecticide on them. He was a broken man. Nothing he did after that pleased the *kranis*. He briefly wondered if he should go to the estate — where his Maama's son worked — to look for a job. But as luck would have it, his Maama's son, Thangarasu, turned up at his doorstep one day, looking for a job. Thangarasu had lost his job in the estate that he worked at and did not have anyone else but Munusamy to turn to. Thangarasu's tears rendered Munusamy helpless.

With great difficulty, Munusamy managed to find a job in the city at a Chinese man's shop which sold *chendol*. The salary was low and he found it hard to make ends meet. Despite that, he persevered until he was slapped for breaking a glass by accident. The Chinese man slapped him on his cheek in public. That night, Munusamy left for Singapore with Raasu Boy in tow.

It was only then that Kaali got to know what had prompted this visit. Munusamy had not come looking for her because he missed her or that he wanted her back in their lives. Kaali was slightly disappointed. But she knew deep down in her heart that what she had done was unforgivable. She consoled herself

CHAPTER 18   183

with the thought that it was to her that he had turned to in times of need. *What right do I have to question him? At least now, I am near my child.*

Chithamparam found Munusamy a temporary position as a cleaner in his office.

Within a week, Paarukutty Amma made the decision for Kaali.

"Why are you still living here now that your husband and child are back? Just come in the day to do the household chores. Don't stay here anymore. Go! Go and live with your husband and child. Leave today. Just go and rent a room for all of you."

If only matters were as straightforward as that. Kaali did not know where to go or whom to turn to for help. She was stranded.

19

JAIL SENTENCES WERE usually reduced when they deducted public holidays and the good conduct of the prisoners. The three men, Vellaya, Chinnadurai and Murugan, were released from prison after serving out their time. There was no welcome party waiting for them when they stepped out of the prison. The men had been gone for many years.

Chinnadurai's mother pleaded with her elder daughter's husband to give Chinnadurai a job. Feeling sorry for him, his Akka's husband found him an errand boy's job at the sundry shop that he owned. It was a low-paying job but Chinnadurai was deeply grateful for the opportunity. He started work at the store right away.

Vellaya had nowhere to go. His father had passed away some time ago. His grandfather passed away partly because of old age and partly because he was drinking excessively for three years after Vellaya was imprisoned. Chinnadurai's mother had come by the prison with news of his grandfather's demise. Vellaya could not bring himself to eat anything the whole day. He threw himself at the jobs he was assigned to in the prison with gusto. He worked till he dropped with exhaustion. Despite working himself to the bone, he just wasn't hungry. Fellow prisoners wondered how he could sustain himself without food for so long. Late in the night when everyone had gone to bed, Vellaya let his guard down and allowed the tears that had welled up in his eyes to escape into small cries of "Thaatha, Thaatha". His grandfather had raised him against all odds. But Vellaya had not been around to provide his grandfather with even one meal in his old age. The thought left him sobbing uncontrollably.

Something changed within him when he lost his grandfather. Vellaya threw himself into his studies and completed his Senior Cambridge examination while he was in jail. He fared better than all his friends in jail. The warden had advised him to further his studies by learning a trade. He applied himself to learning carpentry at the jail workshop. He learnt the art of cutting down the right trees and transforming them into doors and beds. But his newly acquired trade skills did not land him a job right away when he came out of prison. Instead, society still viewed him as a rapist and treated him as an outcast.

While his friends had families to return to, Vellaya had no one. But he did not let that bring him down. The difficulties that he faced in the prison had taught him to be tolerant. He had matured by leaps and bounds over the years. He was now slow to anger and knew when to hold his tongue.

Over the years, Sembawang too had changed a lot. After searching high and low, he finally landed a job as an apprentice in a Chinese man's carpentry shop at 15th Mile.

"You just give me what you think I deserve. If you like my work, then let me have the job. If not, you can let me go."

Despite those words, the Chinese store owner was not taken in by him. *This fellow looks like a ruffian. What sort of skill set would he have? Furthermore, he is an ex-con.* Despite his misgivings, something compelled him to hire Vellaya. In lieu of payment, he provided Vellaya with two meagre meals a day and boarding. The job was his lifeline and Vellaya gave it his all. He returned to work even after his dinner. When an order for a bed came in that had to be completed by the next day, he stayed up all night to complete the job. His boss was over the moon. Vellaya received his first salary of one month that day. In fact, he paid Vellaya more than what they had agreed upon. Vellaya brought the money in his hands to his eyes, in gratitude. He could finally move out of the carpentry shop.

Vellaya knew it wasn't going to be easy for him to rent a room in Sembawang. He finally found a room in Jalan Ulu Sembawang which was quite a distance from his workplace at 15th Mile. He offered forty dollars a month for the room in a rental market where people only paid eighteen dollars a month at the most. The houseowner told him that he could move in the next day. In the face of the potential high rental yield, it did not occur to the houseowner to ask too many questions. The houseowners, Usman and his wife, were childless. They ran a small food stall in the pasar, selling *jemput-jemput*, prata, *dalcha*, fried fish and fried chicken.

One day, Murugan came by to his shop to see him. Vellaya did not even ask him to sit down or engage in a conversation. Seeing Vellaya's hardened stare rest on him, Murugan turned around to leave right away. But Vellaya stopped him.

"Come after 5 p.m. later today. This is my place of work. My boss will not like me talking during my work hours."

Exactly at five-thirty in the afternoon, Murugan returned. He was visibly in a bad shape. Vellaya took him to the food store close by and bought him dinner. Watching Murugan gobble down the food brought tears to Vellaya's eyes. Murugan opened up. No one respected him in his home. Apart from his mother, no one even spoke to him or asked him if he had eaten.

"I feel like dying. I don't know what to do."

Murugan started crying with no inhibition — like a woman, his chest heaving up and down. Vellaya took thirty dollars out of his wallet and slipped it into Murugan's pocket.

"I will look for a job for you too. Don't lose hope. Let me ask around."

With those words, Vellaya sent him away.

A few days later, Vellaya's boss gave him an ang pow, a box of *char siew* and a set of new clothes as it was the eve of Chinese New Year. The gesture brought suppressed memories of his grandfather flooding back into his mind. They closed their shop at noon that day. In fact, all Chinese shops would remain closed for the next three days. This left him in a lurch. For once, he did not have anywhere to go.

The womenfolk generally stocked up on groceries, fish, chicken and vegetables from the pasar to last them for at least three days. The streets would be empty but the messes run by Malayalees remained open, of course.

Vellaya had never returned to his room in the middle of the day before. It just wasn't something he did. After thinking about it for a while, he decided to head to the Sembawang beach at 15th Mile. The beach was a popular destination for Sembawang residents. The beach was forgiving — she welcomed both the poor and rich alike. They mingled at the beach during the evening walks. There were several Europeans too, out for a walk with their dogs in the evenings.

It was only noon and it didn't occur to him that he would be under the scorching sun at the beach. He hurried to sit at a bench on the beach. In the distance, a few Malay and Indian women were gathered together and were digging the ground. They picked up something and put it in their bags. Wanting to know what they were doing, he moved closer to them. They were digging live snails from the ground near the beach and were engaged in an animated conversation on how to cook the snails. Apparently, if you dropped live snails into boiling water, the shells would come apart and it would be cooked. One could then fry the snails or soak the meat in soy sauce.

"It's so tasty, lah," said a woman. He did not recognise her when she glanced at him before walking away.

The beach was quiet and calming in the middle of the day. The waves were not rushing to the shore. Instead, they gently caressed the shores. But he wasn't able to lie on the bench with his hands to support his head for too long. The bench started getting too hot for him. He got up and left for home.

As he walked in, he heard soft sobbing coming from the houseowner's room. Then a door banged shut as someone hurried out of the house. Vellaya did not pay too much heed to it. He was exhausted from having roamed around under the hot sun and hanging out at the beach. He fell into a deep slumber as though someone had beaten him to a pulp. When he finally woke up, it was already past nine at night. *Where will I go now to eat? Never mind. I won't die if I don't eat one day.* All he needed was a good bath. A sight that greeted him near the washroom shocked the living daylights out of him.

Although there was running water in the washroom, they also had a well. The water in the well came in handy for watering the durian and rambutan trees as well as the other plants around the area. Vellaya spotted a woman balancing herself at the ledge of the well with her leg raised and ready to jump into the well. Without a second thought, he ran towards the woman and pulled her away from the well. Only then did he notice that it was none other than the houseowner's wife, Mumtaj. It was the first time that he had a good look at Mumtaj's face which was otherwise always covered by the pallu of her saree. Vellaya was furious. *No matter what had happened, how could she resort to suicide?* Mumtaj wept as she narrated what had transpired. Her story melted his heart. *Was the houseowner such a cruel man? Was he just pretending to be a saint in front of others?* In fact, he was rather critical of Vellaya because of Vellaya's criminal past. Vellaya reached out to hold Mumtaj who was now curled up in a foetal position on the ground. He lifted her gently by her shoulders.

"Don't cry. Go to your room. Let me see how this man will beat you again!"

People were strange. Vellaya felt like laughing at the irony. He had been uneducated, foolish and young when he made a mistake. The houseowner, Usman, on the other hand was a mature man of fifty years, with a stable marriage and four children. Yet, he had coveted a twenty-three-year-old woman. How unfair is this world!

Usman had worked at Dawood Maraikkayar's butcher shop. When Dawood Maraikkayar passed away one day, of a heart attack, out of the blue, Usman took over the running of the shop. He started exerting control over Dawood Maraikkayar's daughter as well in subtle ways. Mumtaj was a sheltered young lady who rarely left the house except in exceptional circumstances. She soon found herself married to a man twice her age. No one understood how such a conservative young lady as Mumtaj fell in love with Usman. But the age difference did not bother Mumtaj nor were there any issues in the marriage in the early days. When six months had passed, Usman brought his wife and family over from Malaysia and put them up at Bah Tan Road. He started staying away from home rather frequently. That's when their problems started.

She didn't know that anything was amiss until she found her *karimani maala*, a gold chain with dozens of small black beads, missing from her jewellery box. She found a pair of pearl-studded bangles and her eight-stone ring missing too. Her *Vaappa* had commissioned the bangles for her mum specially. Mumtaj had never tried on those bangles even once. *How could they have gone missing?*

"I gave them to my wife," came a rather nonchalant reply from Usman.

"In that case, who am I to you? I want my jewellery back tomorrow. Bring it back to me!"

"What will you do if I don't bring it back? I took pity on you when you were orphaned and married you. How dare you question me?"

That was the first time that he beat her up. He only returned three days later. When he did, he knelt in front of Mumtaj and begged her for forgiveness.

"Please don't blow up this matter. I can't leave her on the street either. Please understand."

This was how he started milking her for money. When Mumtaj did not conceive after two years of marriage, he started criticising and torturing her with spiteful words. One day, he arrived home with legal documents to transfer the home that was under Mumtaj's name to his name.

"Absolutely not!" Mumtaj held firm.

He beat her up badly again, yelling out vulgarities as he struck each blow. The filth spewing from his mouth made her ears melt. He left the home soon after without getting her signature. Feeling completely broken and having no solution in sight, Mumtaj walked to the well, wanting to end it all that day. That was when Vellaya rescued her.

"You please go and sleep peacefully. I want to see how he will beat you from now on."

For the first time, it occurred to Mumtaj to lift her head and look at Vellaya's face.

20

KAALI RENTED A room in Sembawang Kechil at the house of the buttermilk seller, Anjalai Amma. Munusamy took on the job as a cleaner at a company, upon the recommendation of Chithamparam *Ayya*. But he wasn't able to hold onto the job for too long. The Chinese employees in the company treated him well but one of the higher officials, who was a Tamil man, was rather abrasive and once insulted him in the washroom.

"I scrubbed and cleaned the toilet floor, *Saar.*"

The officer was in no mood to listen to Munusamy's pleas.

"Can't you be honest and work at least for the money that we pay you?"

Munusamy was depressed at the officer's hurtful words. He wanted to talk to Chithamparam *Ayya* about being unfairly accused. But the senior officer was Chithamparam *Ayya*'s close friend. He swallowed his pride and carried on with the job. But for the next six months, he was treading on thin ice at work. It was then that he learnt about a job at the moneylender Seeni Chettiar's shop.

The job was to chase down loan defaulters at their home and to collect payment. Munusamy's rambunctious form must have impressed the Chettiar who told him to report to work the next day. The job suited Munusamy very much. In no time, he was a permanent employee of the shop. The Chettiar required Munusamy to dress well and arrive at work in clean and well-ironed shirts and *seluars*. He showered twice a day and always looked fresh and neat. Watching him get ready for work, Kaali wondered if this was the same man who worked as an estate worker a lifetime ago.

His job with the Chettiar also helped him to obtain temporary residency in Singapore. Kaali too now only needed to go once in every three months to get her passport 'chopped' rather than every fortnight because she worked as a maid at an immigration officer's home. Soon, she needed to go only once every six months. Later, she applied for a long-term re-entry visa upon the advice of Paarukutty Amma's son. But that was only a temporary solution.

She did not have the guts to speak to Munusamy so she approached Chithamparam *Ayya* on this matter. Chithamparam *Ayya* summoned Munusamy the next day to discuss the matter. Munusamy did not commit to anything. He nodded his head and left the room. He did not bring up the matter to Kaali either. After a couple of days, it was apparent to Kaali that she had to take matters into her own hands. When Munusamy left to meet loan defaulters, she headed out to meet his boss, the Chettiar. She was in tears when she spoke to the Chettiar. That did the trick. Two days later, Munusamy took Kaali to the Singapore Registry of Marriages Office to legally register their marriage. It took another two months before they received their certificate of marriage. With that, Kaali too was granted a long-term re-entry visa.

Kaali went with Paarukutty Amma's daughter-in-law to the Sri Muniswaran Temple in Johor and poured milk into the snake pit to fulfil her vow. It wasn't just women from 13th Mile

at Sembawang who went to the Sri Muniswaran Temple at
Tampoi. It was common for the residents of the Naval Base —
those who lived at 14th and 15th Mile — to head to the temple
to pray. The temple priest was particularly fond of the women
from Sembawang who made the long journey from Singapore.

With her prayers fulfilled, Kaali now applied for permanent
residency in Singapore and was hoping to receive positive
news from the government. The passing of time did nothing
to change things between Munusamy and Kaali. He did not
have an iota of respect for her. He never made eye contact with
her nor talked to her. If he had something to say to her, he did
so through his son. They shared the same living quarters but
she slept in the corner of the room on the floor, curling up in a
foetal position each night. Raasu Boy and Munusamy slept on
the bed. Munusamy paid the rent for the room and for their
meals promptly. He gave her an allowance and provided for all
of them.

Despite being sad at his rejection, Kaali's heart was filled
with pride at the thought of how far Munusamy had come
from their time in Anjarai Kattai. He had basic primary school
education as he had stopped schooling in grade six. She knew
he was literate but it had not been his nature to pick up a book
to read ever. In the evenings, he would frequent toddy shops.
When he returned, his feet were never steady and his body
slumped onto the bed the moment he walked through the
door. He was always too drunk to even know if a lorry were
to run over him. All that had changed. Now he was constantly
seen with a book in hand, writing accounts and making notes
about loan defaulters. She could not believe it was the same
man. Munusamy had made a hundred-and-eighty degree turn.
The people in Sembawang called him Vatti Kadai Thambi or

the man who works at the moneylender shop. Others tried to court him with sweet words. Kaali too felt a new-found respect for him that she never had when they lived in Anjarai Kattai. Everyone treated them as husband and wife and, for now, that was enough for her.

Munusamy had not stopped drinking though and did so in the company of the Chinese and Malay men from the shop next to his. He was careful to stop drinking before he got drunk. Despite that, once or twice, he went overboard and drank more than he should have which inevitably led to a scene. When his boss got wind of it, all hell broke loose.

"Look here. I am well-respected in 13th Mile. If you want to drink and create a scene, stop working in my shop today! Everyone respects the people working in my shop. Don't destroy the goodwill I have in this community. I don't want anyone who does that in my shop."

Munusamy was shaken. He promptly fell at the Chettiar's feet and asked for forgiveness.

"You have my word, *Ayya*. From now on, nothing like this will happen again."

He could not imagine the fate that awaited him if he lost this job. He realised that people were just beginning to respect him as an equal in the community. He would have to return to cleaning toilets if this job fell through. He did not have any other skills either.

The Chettiar had no reason to have the conversation with Munusamy ever again. Whenever Munusamy felt like drinking, he drank in the privacy of his home. Whenever he opened a beer bottle, Kaali would go to the *kusini* and fry an egg or chicken for him to have with his drinks and place it in front of him. Even when his friends who worked in the shops next to his invited him to parties where alcohol was being served, he learnt to limit himself to one or two drinks. But when he was home, he sometimes drank too much. When he was sufficiently drunk, there was no way to stop his venom-spewing tongue. He would use all the expletives that he could think of on Kaali. But that too ceased when Munusamy realised that Raasu Boy was older and was beginning to understand the words coming out of his father's mouth. Kaali wasn't too perturbed by his words. She was just happy at how well her son was doing in school.

Raasu Boy was an intelligent young boy. He had completed his secondary education at the Naval Base Secondary School and was studying for his Senior Cambridge examinations. He did well in all his examinations and joined the Ministry of Education as a teacher. Both Kaali and Munusamy spoke about their son with great affection and pride.

Kaali continued to work as a maid in several homes. Raasu tried to dissuade her constantly.

"I am working now, Amma. We have enough. You don't need to work anymore."

"No, darling. I will work as long as I have strength. Anyway, it is only for half a day. After that, I am home the rest of the day."

Munusamy bought the Chinese man's shop that was next to the *thongal* shop. He got the shop painted and soon he was in business. He had learnt the nuts and bolts of the moneylending business from the Chettiar and was ready to run his own business. It was all due to the blessings of Seeni Chettiar who was not upset with him for wanting to branch out. In fact, it was Seeni Chettiar who had told him that he should consider starting a business of his own, now that he had worked for fifteen years under his guidance. The truth of the matter was that Seeni Chettiar was migrating to India the following month. Despite parting on a positive note, Munusamy was a tad sad that the Chettiar had not consented to selling Munusamy his shop. Munusamy consoled himself with the knowledge that the Chettiar was superstitious and truly believed that, if he had sold the shop to Munusamy, all of his luck would pass on to Munusamy, leaving the Chettiar desolate.

Munusamy hired two people to work in his moneylending shop. It was a shophouse. The front room was where the business took place. At the back, there were two rooms and a compact *kusini*. It was set up like a house with a squatting toilet too at the back of the house, hidden away from prying eyes. Kaali managed to hide the sadness that overwhelmed her heart at the housewarming prayers for the shophouse. Munusamy did not allow Kaali to touch any of the auspicious items for the prayers. When the priest arrived, she was not allowed to partake in the prayer session. Instead, she was tasked to make coffee and sweetmeats for the guests, whom she served. She circulated amongst the guests and served them continuously. He did not object to her handling the glasses, spoons and plates or to spreading the mat on the floor for the guests. That was all that he used her for. Other than that, she did not get to stand next to her husband to welcome the guests nor did they stand together as husband and wife during the prayers. It was Raasu who took her place next to his father in her place. Kaali consoled herself that at least her son was blessed to be able to stand in for her.

But when the prayers ended, Kaali did not know what to do. She had no idea if Munusamy would allow her to stay in the shophouse. He had his usual grouchy expression whenever he laid his eyes on her. Given that he hardly spoke to her, she did not know how to broach the topic with him. After everyone had left, Kaali swept the house, used a cloth to wipe the floor and cleaned the walls in the *kusini*, scrubbing off the food stains on the wall. She put away the things in the room in their rightful places. She did not pause for a moment to rest. But there was still work to be done. Munusamy watched her patiently while she went about the chores. Munusamy had second thoughts about sending her away. Finally, when Raasu returned to the house, Munusamy handed over some money to him and, as usual, gave her instructions through their son.

"Tell her to go and give this money to the houseowner. Tell her to also collect the advance that we paid for the room."

It was only then that Kaali could breathe in peace. Maybe he needed someone to do the household chores. Whatever the reason might be, she was happy.

Kaali's days started at four-thirty in the wee hours of the morning every day. Her first task for the day was to make Munusamy and Raasu Boy breakfast. She would then iron Munusamy's and Raasu's shirts and *seluar* for the day. She would then place Munusamy's medicine for the morning on the side table next to his bed with a glass of water. Making as little noise as possible, she would then leave for Paarukutty Amma's home. The three sons and daughters-in-law still lived under one roof with Paarukutty Amma and her husband. Kaali was amazed that they were able to co-exist harmoniously together after all these years. *Aren't there problems in all homes? How is it that the women in this household were able to get along so well or were they just really good at hiding their feelings? How could they be steadfast like a rock?*

Over the years that Kaali had worked as a maid in several households in 13th Mile, there were tiny problems and unresolved issues hiding in every *kusini* in these homes. There was a mother-in-law who would spread out her mat at the entrance of the *kusini* when she napped in the afternoon, knowing that her pregnant daughter-in-law would return from the gynaecologist's visit and head straight for the *kusini* to have a second round of lunch. Pregnant women were always hungry and when the daughter-in-law returned home with a growling stomach, she found her mother-in-law guarding the *kusini*. There was no consideration for her daughter-in-law who was carrying her son's child nor any sympathy for the daughter-in-law. Kaali had unfortunately been a witness to this act of cruelty.

In contrast, the road sweeper in her rubber estate whom everyone called Kuruvi Paati never allowed her daughter-in-law to do any household chores or go hungry. Kuruvi Paati was poor but that did not stop her from being generous with her pregnant daughter-in-law.

When she was done with all the chores at Paarukutty Amma's home, Kaali would head to Sethulakshmi Amma's home. Sethulakshmi Amma had changed a lot over the years. She had married off her only daughter, Prasanna, with a huge dowry of money, jewellery and two acres of land. But the groom's family had betrayed them. Sethulakshmi Amma could never bring herself to forgive them. Never even in her wildest dreams did she imagine that Sasidharan's family would cheat them of the land that Sethulakshmi Amma had bought for her sons.

Sasidharan was a college-educated graduate but he never went to work. He lived off his family's wealth. By the time Sethulaksmi Amma's family realised this, it was too late. To make matters worse, Sasidharan secretly sold off one acre of land that they had bought in the name of their son, Rajan. He had not asked for their permission to do so. Rajan was taken aback that his sister had also not stopped the sale from going through nor kicked up a ruckus about her husband siphoning off Rajan's property. When questioned, Sasidharan reasoned that those who lived in Singapore did not need the land or money in Kerala. He wasn't ashamed of what he had done and had even retorted rudely to his mother-in-law when he was queried about siphoning off his brother-in-law's land. When her daughter, Prasanna, too did not see the folly in her husband's deed, Sethulakshmi Amma's heart sank. The ten years in Kerala had changed Prasanna. She spoke and behaved like Sasidharan who did not cease demanding money from her family.

"Amma, when you come to visit me from Singapore, don't just buy me talcum powder, sardines, sour plum and clothes. My husband has been asking you guys for a camera and a radio. How many times should I ask you? Can't you ask my Annas and buy them?"

When her older brothers heard what she had said and what had transpired in her home, they stopped sending their mother to Kerala after that. They found it strange that Sasidharan stayed home the whole day, hanging out at the veranda of his massive *tharavad*. The idea of a male graduate who refused to work puzzled Prasanna's brothers in Singapore. Having grown up in Singapore, they were used to a life where one made a living by working.

Sethulakshmi Amma, however, understood that Sasidharan did not need to work given his family's wealth and land that he managed from home. There was more than enough to last them for several generations. But what troubled Sethulakshmi Amma was that he neglected his ancestral land as well. He would not lift a finger to harvest any vegetable on his land. The land lay in shambles around the house. The only movement that his body received was when he ate. He was a lazy man who bossed everyone at home. Watching him strut around pompously made Sethulakshmi Amma feel like spitting on his face. To make matters worse, no matter how many gifts she took with her to Kerala, Prasanna remained unhappy.

"Hmm! What have you done for me, Amma, all these years? You don't care about me at all."

With the passing of time, her husband's death and old age had softened Sethulakshmi Amma. These days, she was rather affectionate to Kaali.

"Now that your husband owns a shop, why do you still work as a maid? Just stop and rest at home, Kaali."

Not a day went by without Sethulakshmi Amma asking her this question.

Sethulakshmi Amma's second son, Rajan, had eloped with Chinnathaayi's daughter, Mottai. No one knew where they had gone. All they knew was that the couple now had three children. Rajan did not visit his mother. The next time Sethulakshmi Amma saw her son was when her husband died. He came home on the day of his father's funeral. Her older son, Gopi, did all the rites earnestly. To his credit, Rajan did not leave his brother's side that day. He stayed till the end and carried out all the rituals. He came once more to the house on the sixteenth day after his father's demise for the Hindu prayers but he did not linger or stay to find out if his mother needed anything. He left as soon as the prayers were over. His wife, Mottai, who had accompanied him did not make any attempts to comfort Sethulakshmi Amma. Mottai kept out of her mother-in-law's way. She did not have the courage to face her mother-in-law.

Someone in the crowd called out, "Mottai!" which annoyed Rajan's wife to no end. Her sharp retort came in seconds.

"My name is Raani. Don't you dare call me 'Mottai' again! I will not respond."

With those words, Mottai left Sethulakshmi's house. Kaali had to fight to hide her giggle that erupted from within her. She was, after all, at a prayer for a departed soul.

21

KAALI'S NEXT STOP was Chithamparam *Ayya's* house. As usual, Chithamparam *Ayya's* wife Meena Amma opened the door for her.

"Come in, Kaali. Come and eat something."

Meena Amma affectionately served her hot idlis with a generous scoop of tasty coconut chutney on a plate. Only after she had eaten and had a cup of coffee did Kaali pick up the broom in her hands to start on her chores.

Meena Amma went back to packing the things in the house. The sight of the things being put away made Kaali sad. It dawned on her that the following week at this time, Meena Amma would not be here. Chithamparam *Ayya* had changed too. The talk of the town in Sembawang was that Chithamparam *Ayya* would never get married. Lots of families vied for his attention and secretly hoped that he would marry their daughter. He was a good catch after all. He had a good job and was also the president of the Workers' Union as well as an Executive Committee Member at Holy Tree Sri Balasubramaniar Temple. He was oblivious to the years that had rolled by as he worked long hours. By the time the hair near his ears started greying, he was thirty-two years old. That's when he received a telegram from India that his mother was not well.

The Sembawang folks were convinced that, this time, when Chithamparam *Ayya* returned from India, he would return with a wife in tow. But their hopes were dashed once again when Chithamparam *Ayya* returned as a bachelor.

When he had gone home after receiving the telegram, his mum was truly ill. She looked frail and her heart was weak. She was too weak to even cry when she saw her son. She could barely move from her bed. He held his mother's hands and sat next to her for a long while before revealing his secret to her. He did add a caveat though.

"But I won't get married without your permission, Amma."

There was no fight in Chithamparam's voice. It was just a child's wish. His mother listened to him patiently without saying a word. Tears gathered in her eyes. She gave him her blessings in a whisper for she had no strength to speak loudly.

"Do as you wish but before my time is over on this earth, bring her to me. I want to see her."

Chithamparam touched his mother's feet with his hands and brought his hands to his eyes seeking her blessings. He left soon after that and boarded the ship to Singapore.

A month after he returned, he married Meena at the Holy Tree Sri Balasubramaniar Temple. Meena's grandfather sat on a chair not taking his eyes off the dais where his granddaughter and the bridegroom sat. Her grandfather was a very respectable man who looked like royalty.

The wedding was well attended by the members of the Union that Chithamparam *Ayya* belonged to. His colleagues from the magazine as well as his friends and neighbours from Sembawang had flocked together for the occasion. It was no surprise that almost everyone from Sembawang had gathered at the temple for the wedding as they were very fond of Chithamparam *Ayya*.

He had helped a lot of people. In Murugan's case, he helped him to get a job as a road sweeper. Murugan had been jobless for a long time despite his best efforts.

Vellaya too had come for the wedding with Mumtaj. Vellaya now ran Usman's shop. The next time that Usman turned up at the house to hit Mumtaj, she yelled out for help. Mumtaj revealed Usman's true colours to her neighbours and pleaded with them to help her get out of the unhappy marriage. She was adamant that she would not live with Usman any longer. Sensing that she was in danger of getting beaten again, Vellaya stood guard right next to her. Moved by her story, the neighbours advised Usman to leave the house. Their words must have enraged Usman as, at the next moment, he lunged forward suddenly to slap Mumtaj. Vellaya's quick reflexes saved the day as he dragged Usman out and threw him to the ground before beating him to a pulp.

"Why are you showing your manhood to a helpless woman? Show it to me! *Dei*, if you're a man, show it to me!"

"Oooh!!" yelped Usman as he stood up. He let out a string of expletives at Vellaya. Vellaya hit him again. Unable to bear the beating any more, Usman ran away with his tail between his legs.

After giving it a lot of thought, Mumtaj decided that her father's meat shop could not be kept closed on account of Usman. She asked Vellaya to take over the running of the shop. Vellaya was able to ease into the role with the help of the existing workers. His business acumen served him well as he saw business boom after he added more meat items such as chicken as well as masala or ground spices for sale. Those who recognised him made snide references about his past. One or two even referred to him as the 'ex-con'. But soon, word got around that fresh meat was available only at Vellaya's shop. People started coming to his shop slowly.

Little was he aware then that Mumtaj's heart was burdened.

Then another scandal broke out at 13th Mile.

This time it was Meenatchi Paati. No one thought she had it in her to react the way she did. Meenatchi Paati started working as the 'flower lady' who tied the flowers into garlands and sold them at the Holy Tree Sri Balasubramaniar Temple. Whenever time permitted, she swept and cleaned the temple too.

Maasilamani too worked at that temple. He did odd jobs around the temple including writing out receipts for those wanting to pay for prayers to be chanted by the priests. It was Maasilamani who told Meenatchi Paati about the temple looking for someone to help out with the flower shop. Little did he expect that Meenatchi Paati herself would turn up the next day for a job interview. She didn't ask for much in return. All she wanted was a little bit of *prasadam* or food offerings that was made daily for the deity. Maasilamani felt really sad when he watched her eat the *prasadam* at the corner of the temple.

Maasilamani knew that his friend, Sangkaralingam, treated Meenatchi Paati pretty badly. He had witnessed the fuss his friend kicked up when Meenatchi Paati spilled a little bit of water on him accidentally once when she was serving Sangkaralingam his meal. As Maasilamani could not bear to witness anyone using such derogatory language to address a woman, he had left the place right away. Meenatchi Paati really had no real financial need to earn a living. Maasilamani wondered what prompted her to take up the job.

Maasilamani thought that Meenatchi Paati looked particularly anguished that day. Maasilamani watched her from a distance. They barely exchanged pleasantries unless they came face to face with each other.

That morning, the noise emanating from Meenatchi Paati's room woke up everyone in Sethulakshmi Amma's house. Sethulakshmi Amma peeped into Meenatchi Paati's room. Her eyes widened at the sight that greeted her. Meenatchi Paati was known for her calm and collected nature. Nothing ever fazed her. But the sight in the room that morning spoke another story. Meenatchi Paati stood there with a parang in her hand, raised high over her head. Her normally tightly wound up hair was untied and flowing wildly like the goddess Kaali.

"Tell me! Tell me! Am I a prostitute? How dare you say that word to me? How dare you call me a prostitute? What right do you have to say that to me? Are you a man? What did you say? Tell me what did you say? How can you say that to me to my face? You die today!"

Meenatchi Paati had to be dragged out of her room away from her husband. She left for the temple shortly after that.

The straw that broke the camel's back was Sangkaralingam's suspicion. Sangkaralingam did not like Meenatchi Paati taking on a job. But Meenatchi Paati did not want to beg him for two dollars every day. Sangkaralingam was rather stingy and he would only give her money for household expenses after giving her an earful. Unable to bear the lashing from his vicious tongue, she escaped for a few hours to the temple. He treated her as though she was a worm under his feet. *Am I just a worm? Doesn't he realise that I am a human being made of flesh and blood with emotions?*

Sangkaralingam's tongue was worse than a vicious cobra's fangs. The venom in his words enraged Meenatchi Paati that day.

Someone had reported to Sangkaralingam that Maasilamani and Meenatchi Paati were seen walking out of the temple, laughing and sharing a joke. No one knew if that was true. Sangkaralingam did not pause to think or clarify if there was any truth to the matter.

"Adiye! I am not enough for your face? You want that Maasilamani too?"

Meenatchi Paati was startled at the words that spilt out of his mouth. She could not believe her ears at what he was accusing her of. She was silent for a split second before her body felt as though it was in flames.

"Who? Me? What did you say? What did you say to me? What!"

She dashed into the *kusini* and picked up the parang from the counter top and returned in less than a minute. She raised the parang and threw it at him with all her strength. She heard him give out a spine-chilling scream. Thankfully, he had the foresight to move away at the crucial moment before the parang could land on his neck. Meenatchi Paati picked up the parang again and charged towards him with a blood-curdling cry.

"*Dei*, you will die today!"

She was a frightening sight indeed. As both of them were elderly, it was hard for anyone to comprehend why Sangkaralingam would even entertain the thought that his wife was having an affair. Her unprecedented outburst set tongues wagging in Sembawang. Everyone in Sembawang remarked how calm Meenatchi Paati was and what a virtuous wife she was. Even Kaali felt angry at Sangkaralingam. *How could*

Sangkaralingam even think or say such a thing about her? What a low-lying creature he must be to even think these things?

Meenatchi Paati moved out of the house that day. She rented a small room near the Holy Tree Sri Balasubramaniar Temple. No one knew where Sangkaralingam went after he vacated the room.

Seeing the guests approach the wedding couple to give the ang pow, Vellaya too stood up to join them. But Mumtaj stood quite a distance away from him amongst the women. She did not even turn around once to look at him.

Chithamparam stood up and put both his palms together to say '*vanakkam*' to thank his guests for coming. It was then that Vellaya finally got a good look at Chithamparam *Ayya*'s wife. It struck him that she looked familiar. *Isn't that Siam* Thaatha's *granddaughter? Or am I mistaken?* He could not stop staring at her. The bride kept her eyes fixed on the bouquet and did not make eye contact with her guests at all.

Vellaya could not take his eyes off her.

22

CHITHAMPARAM'S FRIEND, MANICKAM, came by the Workers' Union office seeking his help as he was the President. Manickam introduced the elderly man in the wheelchair to Chithamparam.

"*Ayya*! This man was one of the workers who had a narrow escape from the Siam Railway. He is from a small village in Kedah's Bujang Valley."

Chithamparam invited both of them to sit down.

"I lost my leg when I tried to escape," explained Sangayya.

When the Japanese entered his village in Bujang Valley, they hunted down the frightened village folk and dragged the men away to work on the Siam Railway. Sangayya was caught and made to board the train at rifle-point. The prisoners were treated rather inhumanely and many men died of hunger or illness before they reached Siam. The Japanese soldiers threw the dead bodies out of the train and continued with the journey. Sangayya felt his blood go cold as he watched the soldiers.

The Japanese had gathered Tamils, Ceylonese, Malays, Chinese and Burmese to clear the jungles for a railway line. Despite the back-breaking work, the prisoners were not given enough food. What they were served looked rather cheap and often unhygienic. Not surprisingly, dysentery was rampant amongst the prisoners. Others passed away after being violently sick for days.

The days were long as they toiled hard. Sangayya was surprised to see the European who was the Senior Manager in his estate working alongside him as a coolie of the Japanese. His *Chinna Durai*, Albert, too worked as a coolie here. The sight of whites working as cooks surprised Sangayya. *If they can make these white men coolies, what will they do to me?* Sangayya half-died at the mere possibility of what awaited him. Men were dying like flies around him from exhaustion, starvation and illness. Those who were not able to work were shot with no mercy. The dead bodies were gathered and dumped into a shallow hole that was dug out by the remaining prisoners and covered with sand. The heartlessness of the Japanese soldiers frightened Sangayya.

The food was truly unbearable. Their meals usually consisted of a small portion of rice, a soup of some sort that he did not recognise and, on rare occasions, a small piece of salted fish. The salted fish had a strange odour to it and Sangayya could not bear to eat it. The first time he ate it, he threw up uncontrollably. There was no one to tend to him. Everyone was in the same boat. None of them was in a position to pity the other.

Sangayya threw up the next day too. The man who served him noticed this. He must have felt pity for the petite Sangayya for the next time dried fish was on the menu, he gave Sangayya an extra portion of boiled wild potatoes instead of fish. But Sangayya wasn't able to stomach that either. Without much food, he wasn't able to work well either. He was fatigued and in constant pain. One day, he fainted at work.

A Japanese soldier hit him repeatedly with the rifle trying to get him to stand up. Sangayya was in no state to protest.

A few of the other prisoners dragged him to a shelter close by once the soldier left the scene. There was a white man at the shelter who administered a concoction to him. Sangayya did not feel any different after taking it, but it helped him to fall asleep right away.

The next day, he wasn't able to eat the food either. It must have irritated the guards. But he was oblivious to the hard stare that the man serving him gave him. That day, while he was at work, his diarrhoea started. He was barely able to stand straight. Watching him suffer, the man working next to him, Marakkanam from Madurai, took over his assigned tasks as well. He signalled to Sangayya to pretend to work whenever the Japanese soldiers came by. But their farce didn't last too long. Unable to bear the repeated runs and overcome by fatigue, Sangayya fainted once again.

His body had taken a beating and he lay there on the ground looking lifeless. The Japanese soldiers thought that he had died. They tried poking his body with the rifles, flipped him around and one even stepped on him and walked over him. He had no energy to protest. Thankfully, one of the three prisoners working close by noticed Sangayya move slightly. He alerted the rest and three of them tried to lift him. Sangayya's body was burning up. They tried to make him take a few sips of water. Finally, when Sangayya woke up, one of the men had a suggestion.

"In four hours, a steam train carrying goods will go by this way. There will only be two or three compartments. It will be filled with imported items like food, alcohol, towels, sometimes oversized clothes, pots and clothes made out of rough materials. These are all the things that the Japanese order from overseas. They unload the items at the railway station and load the train with things that need repair, machines that don't work or damaged rifles fill the carriages. The compartments will be filled to the brim with these things when they leave the station."

A coolie, whose name he could not remember, put him on this train. There was just a narrow window to board the train. Once all the carriages were filled to the brim or they had loaded all the items they needed to, a soldier would start closing the compartment doors. Before he reached the third compartment, one had to board. One had to do it in the blink of an eye. Sangayya managed to jump onto the third compartment somehow.

He didn't know when the train stopped. He heard a loud sound in the jungle and woke up. He must have fainted. Sangayya was terrified. Someone was banging the compartment doors shut and he could hear the loud thuds coming closer. He hid at the back of some boxes. In the split second when the soldier shut the second compartment door, Sangayya quickly jumped out of the train. The Japanese soldier turned around at the noise from the jungle. His eyes did not spot anything but he did see the plants move and thought something was amiss. By instinct, he aimed his rifle in the direction of the sound and fired away.

When Sangayya awoke, there was blood spurting out of his legs where he had been hit. Maybe it was the sight of the blood or the pain, he could not tell. All that he knew was that he fainted again. Several days later, he woke again. He was lying motionless in bed. A Siamese lady lifted him up from the bed and got him to sit up. She fed him some food. Only when he moved a little was he able to see his legs. It was then that he realised that both his legs had been amputated. He did not even have the strength to cry or speak anymore. Exhaustion took over.

His pain moved the young lady who brought food to him. She knew that she had no words to console him. Nevertheless, she tried in her own way to comfort him in her language. She knew that he could not understand her but it was worth a shot. Even then, he did not move.

She placed her fingers on his forehead lightly and then cupped his face with her hands for a few minutes. She then traced the stubble on his cheeks with her knuckles. She lifted his face up gently and buried it on her chest, resting her cheek on his hair. The gesture broke Sangayya's resolve. His sorrow erupted like a volcano into tears. When his tears subsided slowly, she ran her fingers over his legs gently caressing and massaging his bandaged legs. She brought both the legs together and held them for a little while before burying her face on his legs. She placed a tiny kiss on each leg stump.

Sangayya could not put a finger on when it really started. The Siamese lady had captured a permanent place in his heart within a short span of time. She lived with her mother in the small hut that he too now inhabited. Her mother left the house in the wee hours of the morning to travel to the next village where she sold woven mats and winnowing baskets. She only returned in the evening after she had sold all her wares. He spent the day with her. As he could not pronounce her Siamese name, he gave her a Tamil nickname that he considered beautiful: 'Mala'.

When Mala gave birth to a baby girl, Sangayya named his daughter after his mother. His happiness was short-lived. When his daughter turned ten, Mala passed away from a bout of viral fever. By then, Sangayya had learnt the family business of weaving baskets. It was a job that he was able to do despite his disability because he did not need to move around. But his heart was no longer in it.

The Japanese troops had retreated. The barriers between the countries were not as heavily guarded as they used to be. With the help of a friend, he returned to Johor Bahru. He knew that he would not be able to cope in his hometown, Bujang, with his disability. Upon his friend's recommendation, he joined as a factory worker cutting paper in a factory. The boss only gave him just enough money for food, clothing and accommodation. Nothing else was provided for. Sangayya was a patient man and he worked diligently without a word of complaint for four years. His Chinese boss was touched by his dedication. Feeling sorry for Sangayya, he bought him a simple wheelchair and paid him a proper salary.

He was indeed in a better place when a friend from Singapore came to visit him. Seeing his well-endowed pretty daughter, his friend Raajam asked if Sangayya would consider giving his daughter's hand in marriage to his son. Sangayya burst out crying. She was just fourteen years old. But it was not that she was too young for marriage that made him cry. He had been far more fearful that, since his wife was from Siam, no Tamil man would want to marry his daughter. This marriage alliance was God-sent. When Sangayya explained that he wouldn't be able to help out with the marriage expenses, his friend brushed his concerns aside.

"I will take care of all expenses. You just come with me."

Ramasamy was a good boy most of the time. He just went mad when the sun set. He stumbled home with a bottle of *samsu* from the Chinese shop every evening. He would barely be able to walk in his drunken state but that didn't stop him from verbally abusing his wife every chance he got. Even a corpse would have raised itself up to escape the words that came out of his mouth. The helpless Sangayya shed tears every night, hearing his son-in-law's filthy language that filled the house. But he was just an old man who could not move from his bed without help.

Rajathi was barely a child herself when she became pregnant. She did not even have the strength to deliver the baby. Three days after childbirth, she died of a fever.

The committee of the Holy Tree Sri Balasubramaniar Temple came forward to help Sangayya. They handed over the newborn to a widow by the name of Pappamma. They found Sangayya a job in a factory nearby too. All he had to do was to operate the lift at the factory. Although he was wheelchair-bound, Sangayya did not shy away from working hard. When he wasn't well, his friend, Salim, who worked as a *jaga* helped him out. Sangayya and Salim shared a room. Sangayya visited his granddaughter, Meena, once a week.

Meena was a good student. But for some reason, she did not obtain a full certificate at the Senior Cambridge Examinations. In her second attempt at the Senior Cambridge Examinations, she had decent scores. Within one month of the results being released, she secured a job as a clerk at the Jurong Town Council. Siam Thaatha's prayers were fulfilled and he carried out prayers for all the deities at the temple. He had ordered sweet *kesari* and chickpeas as *prasadam* and served the devotees who came to the temple that day. His heart was content.

Sangayya had forgotten that he was once called 'Sangayya'. Everyone in Sembawang called him Siam Thaatha. Funnily enough, he too referred to himself as Siam Thaatha.

Six months after Meena started work, Siam Thaatha went to the President of the Workers' Union seeking help for a delicate problem that Meena and other female workers faced at her workplace. There was no toilet designated for women in her office. Both men and women had to use the unisex cubicles. The women at the workplace were uncomfortable with this arrangement. Despite having raised the issue with senior female officers, no action was taken to rectify the matter. That was the issue that Siam Thaatha had come to meet Chithamparam for.

"Thambi, can you help in any way?"

Chithamparam felt that it was a reasonable request.

"Do write it down as a formal request and go, *Saar*," he said.

About two months later, a young lady turned up at the Union Office as he was about to leave for the day. He did not recognise her. The first embers of love hit him that day. He walked around with her face embedded in his heart. He could not tell what it was that caught his attention. *Was it her calm demeanour or her wide eyes or even her lips or perhaps, her thick curly hair? I think it was when she lifted her head and our eyes locked for a second.* He lost himself in that moment.

It was only a few minutes later when she started speaking that he realised that she was Siam Thaatha's granddaughter. She told him that the problems at work had been resolved and she wanted to thank him for putting in the request. But long after she left, her face lingered in his eyes.

With time, their hearts grew fonder of each other. Their love grew by the day. His parents grew tired of sending him photographs of eligible women from his village. His mother's health soon started failing.

"Before my time is over on earth, bring her to me. I want to see her."

He kept his word to his frail mother. He took Meena to his village one week after their marriage.

His mother gave her stunningly beautiful daughter-in-law the family heirloom of a gold-coin chain and two gold bangles.

Despite being feeble, she took it upon herself to show Meena around the house and taught her the practices of the family. She demonstrated to Meena how to make a sweetmeat made out of *kavuni* rice that Chithamparam liked very much. Meena was an eager student wanting to please her husband and his mother. She had a hand in cooking all the traditional dishes of Chithamparam's household under the supervision of his mother. She accompanied her mother-in-law to the family deity's temple.

Chithamparam's mother's long-term desire to bring her son and daughter-in-law to pray at the sanctum of their family deity was finally fulfilled. She threw a grand wedding feast for the entire village before the newly-weds returned to Singapore. She dressed the bride and the groom in their finest gear, seated them on a stage and treated the guests to a sumptuous meal. Everyone blessed the couple. Chithamparam's mother's wishes were fulfilled. She sent her son and daughter-in-law back to Singapore, having fulfilled her wishes.

His mother passed away soon after that without even seeing her grandchild. Kaali helped out with both of Meena Amma's deliveries by cooking food that suited the lactating mother. Kaali was tasked to bathe both mother and children and do all the household chores in Chithamparam *Ayya*'s house. Kaali took great pride in the fact that she had been chosen to look after Chithamparam *Ayya*'s family.

About the time when Meena became a mother, a beautiful new nurse by the name of Sarojini was appointed to the Maternal and Child Health Clinic. After what the trio, Vellaya, Chinnadurai and Murugan, had done, the government had closed the twenty-four hour Maternal and Child Health Clinic in that area. Instead, they appointed nurses who visited new mothers to help them. Sarojini was one of these nurses. She advised Meena that, while traditional food was good, it was important that she have nutritious meals as well. Everyone at 13th Mile treated Sarojini like a doctor. The residents believed that Sarojini played an important role in raising awareness amongst the women in Sembawang about family planning. The men too treated the nurse with respect. It was rare to see an Indian female nurse as Indians rarely went into nursing.

What surprised Kaali was that Meena Amma never aged. She looked just as she did on the day of her wedding. There was no change in her demeanour either. People in 13th Mile, 14th Mile and 15th Mile flocked to Chithamparam *Ayya*'s door for advice. Both Chithamparam *Ayya* and Meena Amma never turned anyone away. As word spread, their relatives and acquaintances from all parts of Singapore came to them for help.

Hmm… it's all just for a few more hours. The flock of visitors to this house will end today. They are leaving this area and moving into their own house that they had bought in another area. If I want to see them, I will have to go to where they live from now on.

Tears rolled down Kaali's cheeks.

23

"Give me one *kati* of mutton with no bones"

In those days, mutton, fish and chicken were all sold according to *kati*, not in kilogrammes. Vellaya was busy chopping the mutton chunks into smaller pieces. He looked up for a second to see whom the voice belonged to before turning his attention back to the task at hand.

"Hang on a minute. I will serve this customer first."

Soon it was her turn. He chopped up the mutton with his gloved hands. He put in extra effort to select the best cut without any bones and weighed it. It was just one *kati*. He handed it over to her and noticed her hard stare. He turned his attention back to the task at hand. Soon it was time to close the shop for lunch. As he walked out of the shop, he spied a figure in front of him. Words escaped him as he stood rooted to the ground like a prisoner.

"Hmm! Even after you came back from jail, you didn't look for me? You just pretended to NOT see me in the morning. What sort of man are you?"

Vellaya felt his throat tighten. "That…" he could not continue. He had heard that Mallika had got married when he was in jail.

"Why can't you talk? Do you remember all the things you said to cheat me? What a huge cheater you are! That day I saw you at the 15th Mile beach. You were lying there on the bench. I wanted to tell you off that day! But my older child was with me. I had to leave without saying anything that day."

She vented the frustrations that she must have been holding on to for years. He did not make any attempt to defend himself. He had wronged her. He had cheated her of her dreams and hopes. He had made promises that he never kept. He had lied to her.

"Until my mum explained what you did, I didn't even realise what it was. How could you say you love me and go out and rape the nurse? What sort of scoundrel are you? You will never have a good death. Just see!"

Her curses rang in his ears the whole day. Vellaya did not go home for lunch that day. He went back to the store to rest in the back room. He lay on the ground for a while. For the first time since he got out of jail, he bawled. A distant memory took him to the hot springs again. He leaned against a tree trunk. It wasn't a particularly hot that day with the huge trees providing some shade. He must have barely closed his eyes for a minute when the sound of children woke him. The sun was setting.

There was a bigger crowd at the hot springs these days. Some people filled bottles with water from the hot springs to sell. Otherwise, nothing else had changed. There were women washing their clothes in a corner and others giving their children a bath. There were men in short towels taking a shower almost as though they were seated on their mother's laps. A Chinese Paati was boiling eggs with the water from the hot springs. Moosa *Ayya*, who frequented his meat shop, was there with his friend. Vellaya saw him taking a gulp of water with his hands. Moosa *Ayya* was deep in conversation with his friend and heading in his direction. Not wanting to engage in a conversation, Vellaya quickly closed his eyes again. He could hear the conversation when they came closer to him. Moosa *Ayya* was reminiscing about the good old days of the hot springs.

"In those days, we had to come through Gambas Avenue to get to the hot springs which was at the airbase. The surrounding village was known as Kampong Ayer Panas or Village of Hot Water.

"After the fall of Singapore, the Japanese military seized the place and converted it into recreational thermal baths or onsens. They say that many Japanese took their showers here. During World War II, bombs destroyed the facilities around the hot springs. It was only after several years that there was any activity around the hot springs again."

"What is special about this water?"

"You may not believe me if I tell you. That's why I brought you here to show you the crowd. See how many people are here? The water that comes out from the hot springs has more sulphur than normal tap water. This has been proven. This water helps people with osteoarthritis and skin problems.

"Despite the scorching sun, people gather to bathe in the hot springs. Children, too, come here with their parents. Children who suffer from chest phlegm, fever and wheezing take a gulp of the water and bathe in this water. If they do it for three days, you will see the children running around and playing with no care in the world on the fourth day. This is what our experience tells us."

The foreigner friend of Moosa *Ayya* filled two bottles with water from the hot springs to take with him. Seeing even foreigners collecting the water warmed Vellaya's heart. *It's been so long. Tomorrow, I shall come here and have a bath as well.* He did not know when he had dozed off.

Mumtaj was waiting at the doorway when he got home. She stood up abruptly when she sighted him. But her heart sank at the expression on his face.

"Why didn't you come home for lunch today? I felt so sad."

Her voice was really low. She looked upset too. Vellaya did not have an answer to the questioning look in her eyes. He sank into the chair in the living room. She walked towards him and knelt down by him and started crying. Vellaya too felt like crying. The sadness that had been weighing his heart down since the afternoon made him burst into tears.

"I am a sinner. Mumtaj, I am a sinner. Even God will not forgive me, Mumtaj."

Mumtaj's body shivered.

"Why? Why are you crying? Ya'Allah my dear, don't cry. Show me a man who hasn't made any mistakes. It's in my scriptures too. When a man repents his mistake, he is forgiven and he becomes a good man. Why are you crying? You have already paid for your sins!"

Mumtaj reached out to him and drew him to her chest.

Vellaya's sobbing grew louder now. He pulled away from her and brought his hands to cover his face. His body shook as he cried. He thought about his Thaatha whom he had lost because of his ways. He thought about the mistakes he had made. They all stood in front of him as ghosts with fingers pointing at him. He cried for release.

Mumtaj held his face up with both her hands as she wiped his tears away with her fingers. Vellaya pulled her close to sit next to him, held her waist and laid on her lap and sobbed his eyes out. Mumtaj didn't know how to comfort him. She stroked his hands and she too cried.

She melted into him that moment and became one with him. If she could, she would have absorbed all his sadness into her. She held him tight and melted into his embrace. They found comfort in one another and that helped to ease both their pain somewhat. After several hours, as both of them slowly eased out of the stupor of their honey-soaked union, the first thought that hit them was hunger. Neither of them had eaten the whole day. Vellaya ate more than he would that day.

A few months later, the neighbour, Chinna Akka, came to visit Mumtaj. Her name was not actually Chinna Akka. Muthaliyar's wife had two daughters. Everyone called the elder daughter Periya Akka which meant Big Older-Sister and the young daughter Chinna Akka which meant Younger Older-Sister. No one at 13th Mile knew nor remembered their real names any more. Chinna Akka was Mumtaj's best friend from childhood. Chinna Akka did not waste time beating around the bush and got to the point right away.

"What is this? What does this mean?"

Mumtaj had a faraway look in her eyes.

"What about the life I lived a long time ago? What did it mean?"

"There is one difference. When I asked you the same question a long time ago, you had an answer for me. You were in tears and you were lost. Today, your tone isn't right. You answer me rather arrogantly. That's what's different."

"Here, I just made it this afternoon, *ketti urundai*. Eat and see whether it is nice."

Mumtaj placed a few evenly-rolled hard *ketti urundai* on a plate.

"What is this? You made sweetmeat today? What's the occasion?"

"I had a craving... been having these cravings for a while. I don't have anyone else to make this for me, do I?. That's why I made it."

Her words saddened Chinna Akka.

"You are not alone. We are all here, aren't we? But there's a place and time for things, Mumtaj. Things should be done properly."

That evening, Chinna Akka's husband spoke to Vellaya.

Mumtaj was not willing to convert. Neither was Vellaya ready to accept Islam. Mumtaj was three months pregnant by the time they registered their marriage in the civil court. They both kept their faiths. When their baby was born, Vellaya named him 'Rajah'. Mumtaj had no objections. She too thought that her son looked like a king. The child was very good-looking with his mother's light skin and his father's sharp features. The sight of his baby in the cradle overwhelmed Vellaya. He fell in love with his wife all over again. He swore to himself that he would take very good care of his wife.

Of course, there were naysayers who resented their marriage. But no one dared to approach or confront Vellaya. He was an ex-con whom no one wanted to trifle with. How could they expect him to do the right thing? In any case, what did it matter what happened to him? If he needed any help and came to them, they would give him a hard time. For now, they let the couple live in peace.

Murugan was finally able to quit his job as a rubbish truck driver. He finally landed a better job at Chithamparam *Ayya's* friend's office upon the latter's recommendation. None of that would have been possible if Vellaya had not introduced him to Chithamparam *Ayya*. In gratitude, he helped out at Vellaya's shop in his spare time.

Vellaya added a masala and spices section to his shop. Mumtaj hired Elizi, her maid, to tend to the masala and spices counter as Vellaya was adamant that his wife not frequent the store nor help out at the masala and spice counter. Although Elizi was hardworking, she was not the brightest bulb on the porch. Kaali often found Elizi and Murugan lost in a conversation at the shop when she came by. The store hand would chop up the mutton into small pieces for her while Murugan would pack it into a plastic bag.

Vellaya was not at his shop as much these days. His Chinese friend, Gilbert, and he had started a union for ex-cons. Through the union, they found small jobs for many people. Gilbert had spent six years in prison. Thankfully, Gilbert's father owned a garment shop so when Gilbert was released from prison, he did not have to look for a job.

These days, 'Butcher Vellaya' was well-respected in 13th Mile. Apart from the meat shop, he also ran a sundry shop that he registered under Mumtaj's name in Bah Tan Road. He hired ex-cons. His wife too gave a helping hand to those in need at 13th Mile.

Vellaya had started a food stall too. Upon the recommendation of Gilbert, he hired Muhammad as the cook for the stall. It had been a chance meeting. Gilbert had introduced Muhammad to him as an experienced cook. For some reason, Vellaya had taken an immediate liking to Muhammad. Muhammad had arrived in Penang at the end of the Japanese Occupation in search of a job. He had first joined a spice store as a store hand. Later, through the help of a relative, he moved to Singapore and worked in hawker centres. Gradually, he learnt to cook many dishes and became the chief cook. When his regular customers saw him behind the wok, they would order an extra plate. It was hard to beat the magic of his cooking. Confident that he could pull it off on his own, he started his own food stall. But Muhammad was a bad businessman. He did not charge his friends and acquaintances who visited him. The shop folded in six months leaving many customers reminiscing about the tasty dishes that their tongues remembered.

Hawker stalls were far more popular than restaurants. It was hard to compete with the sheer number of stalls around the island. The hawkers, too, had a reputation of working at the speed of the light to get the meals on one's plate. One moment the lamb leg piece would be hanging from a skewer and, in the blink of an eye, it would be chopped up into tiny pieces as keema by the assistant cook. The chief cook would toss these pieces into the wok with noodles and other garnishing before scooping up the *mee goreng* onto a plate for the customer. The taste was out of this world and would linger on the tongue for days.

Vellaya's faith in Muhammad was not lost. The food stall had long queues and his food had great demand as Vellaya predicted. In 13th Mile, Vellaya was like a small-time businessman. Mumtaj and Vellaya had finally earned their place in society. Those who had sniggered about Mumtaj and Vellaya's lives now treated them with great respect.

Kaali returned with the chopped pieces of lamb from the store and started lunch preparations. She was an excellent cook. She gave the traditional recipes a twist by adding additional ingredients. In addition to the onions, ginger, garlic and masala, she also included raisins, dal, cashew and other ingredients that produced an irresistible fragrance. The ingredients had to be ground to the right amount and consistency. When she finished cooking the lamb curry, the other curries and side dishes beckoned. She paid careful attention to preparing each and every one of the dishes. Once she had finished cooking, she went to shower feeling rather pleased with how the lunch spread had turned out.

By the time she walked out of the shower, Raasu Boy and his Chinese wife had arrived and were seated at the dining table. Munusamy was incredibly fond of his son. When his son had announced that he was in love with a Chinese girl, it was Kaali who was taken aback by the news. Munusamy, in contrast, felt rather proud. His son had accomplished something that he could never have been able to.

None of the Chinese shop owners next to his shop had spoken to him or treated him as a fellow shopkeeper for several years since he had set up his own shop after Seeni Chettiar left. His customers in the early years had been Indians. No one else came by asking for a loan. It took him a long time to build up trust in the community. It took him even longer to receive a friendly word from his neighbours as their equal.

Munusamy invited all the shop owners of the neighbouring stores to Raasu's wedding. Only one of them came to the wedding. The rest of them dropped by the shop briefly to hand over an ang pow packet to convey their well-wishes to the wedding couple.

The couple had their meal under the eagle eyes of Munusamy. Munusamy was rather proud of his son. His daughter-in-law, Mei Ling, ate just what her mother-in-law served her. She did not go for seconds. Kaali had cooked the dishes keeping Mei

Ling's taste buds in mind and had reduced the tamarind and spice level of the curry.

Raasu got up from his seat with a satisfied smile after his meal. Both Mei Ling and her mother-in-law had never spoken to each other. Kaali did not have the language skills to speak to her daughter-in-law. Mei Ling was an overworked teacher who did not have the time to study Tamil. Love had blossomed between Raasu and Mei Ling when they met as colleagues. Mei Ling was clueless about Tamil dishes. Kaali was hoping to teach her all the dishes that her son loved, but sadly, Mei Ling showed not an iota of interest in learning them.

About an hour after they left, Munusamy got ready to step out of the house. He dressed in his best shirt and put on his perfume. Out of the blue, he was overwhelmed with fatigue and flopped down on his bed. He lay down for a bit on his bed, hoping for the feeling to pass. He could not sleep. He could not pinpoint where the pain was from. It seemed to be emitting from either his back, his shoulders or his chest.

Kaali was not aware of any of this. She had retired to sleep in her usual spot outside the entrance of Munusamy's room. When she got up in the middle of the night to use the washroom, she saw Munusamy lying on the floor. Her shrill screams woke up the neighbours. They helped her bring Munusamy to the Thomson Road Hospital. By then, dawn was breaking. There was no sign of Raasu yet.

24

THE DOCTOR SAID that it was a stroke. The muscles on his right hand and leg had weakened. People around her talked about his condition amongst themselves. They said that his hand "had fallen".

Kaali was beside herself. *Why did it matter that Munusamy barely said two words to me or slept with me?* None of that had mattered to Kaali. But it broke her heart to see Munusamy lying in bed, completely helpless.

It was way past midday before Raasu arrived. "*Ayya!*" called out Kaali running towards him to give him a hug. But she stopped in her tracks when she heard what her son had to say. Raasu looked as though he was fuming mad.

"What is this, Amma? Why are you crying and creating a scene in the hospital? Appa is still alive, isn't he? When you get old, you need to discipline yourself. You shouldn't be eating fish every day or chicken and mutton every other day! Okay… okay… stop crying."

Kaali could not bear to keep quiet anymore. She had to know.

"I sent someone to inform you last night. What happened? Why are you arriving now? Where were you?"

"Yeah, Suppiah Maama came by to tell me what happened.

But I had a lot of work to do in school today, Amma. I couldn't go to work late today. Everyone is here. Why do you need me?"

His nonchalant tone and scant regard for his father's health irked Kaali. She had not had a drop of water to drink from the time she had brought Munusamy to the hospital. Neither had she moved from the entrance of the ICU ward where Munusamy lay. Even strangers had stopped by with comforting words seeing her distraught face.

Exactly two weeks later, Munusamy was moved out of the ICU. His Chinese friends from the shops next to theirs came by to visit him. Their old neighbours from Sembawang too called on him. It was when he was moved to the general ward that she heard him say her name for the first time in years.

"Kaali…"

Her heart skipped a beat. It had been years since he had acknowledged her presence. Now he spoke to her affectionately.

"When will Raasu come? Once he does, you should go home and rest. You can come back later."

"I'll go. You sleep," she said, with tears threatening to storm her cloudy eyes once again.

When Munusamy returned home, he wasn't able to move about as quickly as he used to. It certainly helped that his home and shop were in the same place. He moved slowly and managed to get to the counter of the shop. It wasn't his health that Munusamy fretted about these days. *Do sons change after they get married? Do they stop caring for their fathers? I didn't raise Raasu like other children, did I?* Raasu had arrived at the hospital rather half-heartedly behaving as though he was visiting an acquaintance. What happened at the end of his stay at the hospital left Munusamy shaken to the core. While preparing the discharge papers, the senior nurse had come in to check with the family about the formalities including the payment of the hospital bill.

"My father will take care of all those expenses. Just ask him. Tomorrow you can ask him to sign the bill and the paperwork when you discharge him."

Munusamy could not believe his ears. He could afford to pay the hospital bill but he found it hard to swallow the fact that his son had said that in front of him. Chinnadurai dropped in for a visit. Murugan did too. Vellaya sent his friend, Murugan, on his behalf, with food cooked with herbs and a bag full of fruits. It was on the day that Murugan came to visit that Munusamy was discharged. Munusamy held Kaali's hand and leaned on Murugan as he walked slowly out of the hospital.

Kaali massaged Munusamy's right hand and leg that had lost its strength from the stroke every day. Paarukutty Amma had taught her how it needed to be done with traditional ointment from Kerala. After the massage, Kaali placed a towel in a bucket of hot water, squeezed the towel dry and while hot steam seeped out of the towel, placed it on Munusamy's hand and leg. It was like a hot compress massage. She also cooked his meals according to the advice of the doctors and nurses.

Munusamy needed her help to shower as well. She helped him at the shop counter after his shower and his meal. For some unknown reason, once he was seated at the shop counter, Munusamy felt stronger. His business picked up again as soon as he returned.

One day, Mathai *Ayya*'s wife, Margaret, came by asking for a loan with her jewellery as collateral. Kaali was taken aback to see her at her husband's counter.

It appeared that once Mathai had finished building his

dream home in Kerala, he began to visit Kerala more frequently. During one of his trips, when his eldest child was about eight years old and his younger child six years old, he had met with a car accident and died on the spot. Margaret could never forget the sight of his badly injured face when they brought the body to her wrapped in a white cloth. She had not stopped crying for days. Six days after the funeral rites were over, a few of her relatives dropped a bombshell on her.

"This is not an accident, Margaret. Mathai's younger brother hired men to kill him. Do you know what happened the day before he died? His brothers fought with Mathai, asking for a share of his wealth in this house he built. Mathai was so angry. He slapped his younger brother across the cheeks in front of so many people. Then the brothers got into an ugly fist fight, just like in the movies. The next morning, Mathai was on his way to see the family lawyer to set the record straight. He said he wanted to be sure that his property and money would only go to his children and wife when he died. Before he could reach the lawyers, he met with an accident. It is not a coincidence! They did it!"

For a moment, Margaret could not believe her ears. *Could it be true? Would anyone kill their flesh and blood for money? What sort of low-class human being would do that? Chee!* With the help of her family members, Margaret sold off everything that Mathai had bought with his savings over several years in Singapore. *I will never return to this land again. Come what may, my life and death will be on the Singapore land.* True to her word, she never did return to Kerala ever.

The years flew by. Margaret made a living as a tailor stitching clothes for her neighbours. With the income from her tailoring job and the money Mathai had left her, she put her children through school. Margaret's eldest son found a job at the shipyard. Her second son was studying medicine. Despite the dual income, she faced great difficulty in paying her son's medical school fees. The vicissitudes of fortune brought her to the pawnshop often. It was only now that she had come to a moneylender.

Once Kaali told Munusamy about Margaret's predicament, he loaned her the money without charging any interest. Instead, he worked out a repayment plan specially for her. All she had to do was pay a small sum of money a month. Kaali took her to the back of the shop and made her a cup of coffee and hot dosa.

Vellaya was in a petulant mood. A Peranakan Tamil man, Gunasekaran, had opened a shop next to his and, for some reason, was hell-bent on giving him a really hard time. For the life of him, Vellaya could not understand why a stranger would take an instant dislike to him. Gunasekaran spoke predominantly in Malay. His father was Tamil and his mother a Malaysian Malay. Vellaya was tempted to put Gunasekaran in his place with a good thrashing but things had changed a lot over the years. Everyone respected him in Sembawang these days. He had to think twice before he acted rashly. But Gunasekaran's antics did not cease. Gunasekaran stood outside his shop and yelled out at Vellaya's customers.

"How can you respect that jailbird and go to his shop? The stuff in my shop is good too. Come here, lah."

He heckled Vellaya's customers. Vellaya ignored Gunasekaran. But, one day, Gunasekaran misbehaved with

Elizi who worked at his shop. That was the straw that broke the camel's back. Vellaya confronted Gunasekaran.

"If you want to run this business properly, you better behave!"

That was it. The floodgates had been opened. Like a rooster awakened from its nap, Gunasekaran leapt out of his shop yelling at the top of his lungs in Malay.

"Ooi, you first better behave."

Vellaya had enough. He gave Gunasekaran a tight slap. In return, Gunasekaran punched Vellaya's chest. The neighbours came running out of their shops to pull the men apart.

That evening, both of them stood in front of Chithamparam *Ayya* and Gilbert and narrated their sides of the story. Both Chithamparam *Ayya* and Gilbert listened patiently. It was Chithamparam *Ayya* who addressed them first.

"We are all here to make a living. Why are you targeting him? He's already paid for his sins. Ask anyone in Sembawang. They will tell you that he is a role model for all ex-cons. He has made the lives of so many ex-cons better. Why are you angry at him? What did he do to you?

"Don't think we don't know what you have been up to? We know you left your wife — whom you had a love marriage with — all alone in Malacca and came here. Do you think we don't know that you're living with someone else's wife with three kids? But that's your personal matter, right? You are not perfect. So, what right do you have to talk about him?

"Why did you misbehave with a girl who works in his shop? And how can you expect him to keep quiet? We are angry with you too. You... you first say sorry to him."

Rather reluctantly, Gunasekaran apologised to Vellaya. Gilbert made both of them shake hands. After everyone had dispersed for the evening, Gilbert pulled Vellaya aside and spoke to him at length.

"Do you know during the Japanese Occupation, how the Japanese tortured the Chinese, Vellaya? You guys always say that Tamil men were taken to Siam Railway and were tortured by the Japanese. In fact, during the Japanese Occupation, more Chinese were tortured by the Japanese. Our ancestors will tell you many stories. That's history.

"You know, they told the Chinese folks to turn up at Jalan Besar for compulsory registration. There were so many men, from young men to the elderly, who could not even breathe as the Japanese kept pushing more and more people into the place. The Japanese soldiers inspected them, tied their hands behind their back, loaded them on lorries and took them to Tanah Merah Besar Beach. There, they were made to walk towards the beach. As the men were walking, the heartless soldiers shot them in their backs with machine guns. The men fell like worms to the ground.

"Their bodies were left there to rot. Some were pulled into the sea by the waves and some rotted by the seaside. Some bodies were claimed by screaming and crying relatives who managed to find them. There are many stories like that. The Japanese went on such killing rampages and admitted to them much later. But what can we do to them? Aren't we all living? Look at how much my community has progressed!

"Think about it. If we can forgive murderers, can't you forgive one another? After all, both of you run businesses right next to each other. How can you fight with each other? It doesn't matter who is at fault here. Can't you ignore him and do your own business?"

Gilbert spoke for a long time before parting ways. It was a matter of learning to live and let live.

The confrontation brought another matter to light.

Murugan and Elizi were in love. When the news reached Vellaya's ears, he was delighted for the couple and bore all the wedding expenses.

Chinnadurai attended the wedding too. Chinnadurai had initially worked at his Akka's husband's shop where he was subjected to derogatory words and humiliating sneers. Unable to bear them any longer, he went to see Chithamparam *Ayya* with his educational certificate that he had obtained in jail. He was first given a low-paying job at the Union Office. While he was there, he learnt how to drive and obtained his driving licence. When the Union Office hired him as a driver, his fortunes changed.

It also sparked a fire in him to study further. He was obsessed with wanting to improve his life and circumstances. Like a possessed man, he dived into his studies at the night classes. This time, he enrolled himself in night classes out of his own volition. He completed a polytechnic diploma successfully. Contrary to what he had envisioned, it wasn't as easy to find a job with his polytechnic diploma. Luckily, after some time, he was able to secure a job at the Naval Base with a decent salary.

Chinnadurai worked really hard. His European boss liked Chinnadurai's work and dedication. Despite that, he did not get the promotion he had been eyeing. His sister secured him a marriage alliance with a girl who was far prettier and more educated than his childhood sweetheart. The years had mellowed everyone. His family and the community had a favourable opinion of him. Life was, for once, peaceful. He was content. He arrived at Murugan's wedding with his new bride.

The three men, Vellaya, Murugan and Chinnadurai, were happy. After sending Murugan off to the bridal chamber, Chinnadurai and Vellaya grabbed themselves a bottle of beer before retiring for the night. In the stillness of the night, Chinnadurai voiced out what was on both their minds that night.

"Vellaya, if only we had listened to our parents, we wouldn't have gone through all these problems, would we? Maybe it was fate, huh? Why did we do this? We had to suffer. Where can we go and hide now?"

Vellaya sat staring at the sky long after Chinnadurai left. His thoughts were on his grandfather. His heart was heavy.

"You wanted me to do well in life. You wanted to see me do well, Thaatha, but you're not here."

Mumtaj found him sobbing away at the wedding hall. She did the one thing that she knew would help to calm him down. She sat by his feet and hugged both his legs with her arms. She placed her head on his lap as his tears caressed her face in the stillness of the night.

WHAT'S WRONG WITH her? She must be mad! Why else would an old woman have such desires at her age?

Munusamy did not want to go to India at all. *Who do we know there?* He was born and bred in Anjarai Kattai. He had completed six years of education at Anjarai Kattai. His mother had found him a girl to marry in Anjarai Kattai. The only reason he left Anjarai Kattai was to make a living at 13th Mile. He had to admit that he had not done too badly with the move. *But she knew full well that if we had lived our lives at the rubber estate, we might have died there and been buried there, having never left the place. We are getting by here, aren't we? Why do we need to go to India now? If she was going to make a vow, why couldn't she have taken the vow at a temple here? Why do we need to go to India, for heaven's sake?*

Chinna Akka had talked about the Sri Mutharamman Temple in her hometown in India to Kaali. It was the Kulasekhara Patnam village deity, Mutharamman Aatha. The villagers in that town believed that the deity had the power to defeat death by stopping Lord Yama, the King of Death, when he was on his rounds. With Chinna Akka recounting several instances of how fervent prayers to her deity had saved the lives of many villagers, Kaali had also prayed to her to save Munusamy from death.

The threat on Munusamy's life was averted with the grace of God. He had recovered rather quickly from the second stroke and only had to stay in the hospital for a few days. This time, Kaali was far more insistent about his exercise and food routines than she had been for his first stroke. She dragged him out for daily walks. She did not make any concessions regarding food no matter how hard he pleaded. She was very careful with what she added to the food when she cooked. She ensured that he took his medication on time. She followed the doctors' advice to the tee. She watched the exercises that the physiotherapist did with Munusamy and added those to his daily exercise routine at home. She was constantly on his back bugging him to do his daily exercises, which irritated Munusamy to no end.

"Once you pray and take a vow, you have to fulfil it. Otherwise, it is a grave mistake. Something might happen to you!"

Her threat was not really the reason why Munusamy relented after a few days, nor was it because he had already had two strokes in a short span of time. His heart had been heavy for the last few days. He hoped that the trip to India would perhaps help to ease the weight on his heart. Raasu had been persistent in his mission to get his father to sell his shop so that he could have a portion of the sale proceeds. Raasu wanted to invest the money in a business venture. He did not want to work as a teacher any longer.

"If you are not happy with your job, why don't you take over Appa's business?"

"Chee, chee! Who wants this? How can I do this business? I am an educated man, Appa. Mei Ling's Anna and I are planning to open a perfume store. You just give me the money. I will take care of the rest."

Munusamy was bitter that his son looked down on the business that had helped to put a roof over their heads and educate him. *Had it not been for this shop, we would still be living in a rented room in Sembawang. How will a perfume store do well in Sembawang? Who will buy perfume here? The boy does not know the nuts and bolts of business. How will he run the shop? Why was he listening to his Chinese brother-in-law?*

"What would happen to us after we sell the shop?"

"Why? Just come and stay with me. We can all live under the same roof."

For once, Kaali was not taken in by his act. *If this boy behaves like this now, how can we rely on him in the future?* She did not have to voice her concerns to Munusamy. He, too, could not imagine moving in with Raasu.

With Kaali rather insistent about going to India and Chinna Akka promising to take care of all their needs during their travel, he relented. He was relieved to see that Kaali was really happy after all these years.

Upon arriving at Chennai airport, they were greeted by a chorus of voices belonging to beggars from all directions. "*Saar... Saar!*" It was rather disorienting as, in a matter of minutes, they were surrounded by a team of them. It was a strange sight for Munusamy whose heart went out to their plight. But before he could react, one of Chinna Akka's relatives who was waiting to receive them at the airport, swatted the beggars away rather brusquely.

"We've given you enough. Go away!"

While their luggage was being loaded into the waiting car, a faint voice caught Munusamy's attention. It was a familiar voice — one from sometime or somewhere in his life. He stared closely at the beggar in front of him.

"*Ayya*! *Ayya*! It has been two days since we have eaten. Just give us something to eat."

"*Ayya*! *Ayya*! Aren't you… aren't you Thakkan? Aren't you Thakkan? *Dei*! Thakkan… *dei*?"

"Munusamy…"

The beggar ran into Munusamy's outstretched arms.

Kaali also knew Thakkan well. He was Munusamy's childhood friend. Both of them had been inseparable throughout their lives. Thakkan was responsible for introducing Munusamy to toddy at Anjarai Kattai. They were thick friends who colour-coordinated their outfits and their wives' saris for Deepavali and Pongal.

Thakkan's life changed with one rash act that he committed. He had returned home drunk and he must have uttered something terribly nasty to his wife. Later on, no matter how hard he tried, he could never recall what he had said to her nor why she had made such a rash decision. Maybe she did it in a fit of anger or she had just given up on ever getting him to mend his ways. That night, his wife consumed the weed killer that he had in the house. It was what he used on the *lallang* weeds at their estate in his job. Had he not been drunk, he could have saved her. But he was too intoxicated to keep his eyes open. When he woke up at dawn and searched for her as it was time for them to head off to the *peratu*, he found her in the *aluru* near the *kusini*. There was froth dripping out of her mouth. He yelled out for help from his neighbours and to the unseen Gods above. Mustering all his strength, he placed her icy-cold lifeless body over his shoulder and ran as quickly as he could to the estate dresser. It was too late. Everyone in the estate blamed him for what had happened. Thankfully, they had no children. Thakkan never remarried.

"Why do I need to marry again? I killed her, didn't I?"

Soon it was a common sight for the residents to see him bawling his eyes out and beating his chest repeatedly like a possessed man after a few drinks at the toddy shop at Anjarai Kattai. Munusamy and his friends would then bring him home, holding him carefully between them, with his arms around their shoulders.

"Why has this Anna come to Chennai? He was working as a rubber tapper in our estate, wasn't he?"

Munusamy did not have the answer to Kaali's question. He too was puzzled at the turn of the events.

When the British government left, they sold off the land to rich Chinese and Tamil locals. Unfortunately, not all rubber tappers managed to secure a job with the new landowners. Most of them were let go with a paltry sum of money as compensation for their life-long service. Most workers were stuck between a rock and a hard place. They had nowhere to go. Many were not granted citizenship in Malaya and they had, at most, weak links to India. Then there were those who had not applied for citizenship who were not able to obtain jobs in the cities nor could they enrol their children in schools. Many Indian men joined gangs while others took on demeaning jobs. So many lives were destroyed on so many levels.

Thakkan was one of the rubber tappers who was turned out of his estate. The only relative he had was a Maama in India. With very few options at hand, he moved to India. When he first arrived, with money in his pocket, nothing was amiss. His Maami was loving and sweet-natured. On the surface of things, she was fond of him. But her true colours reared its ugly head when the money in his pocket ran out. He had not fritted the money away. He had, in fact, spent most of it on the household expenses. Her demeanour changed afterwards. Derogatory words and insults were thrown at him on a daily basis chasing him out into the streets.

"I was insulted and insulted…"

His feeble voice cracked up with uncontrollable sobs. Thakkan could not go on any further. Tears gushed out from Munusamy's eyes as Thakkan spoke. He pulled out some rupee notes from his pocket and pressed it into Thakkan's hands.

Kaali's face too was wet with tears. *How fragile life is! How can someone's life take such a bad turn in a span of a few years?* She knew that she could not blame him for not staying in Malaysia. Thakkan did not have a choice.

It was Kaali's first trip to India. She was touched by the affection and sincerity of the villagers in Chinna Akka's village. In order to fulfil her vows, both Kaali and Munusamy showered three times a day and offered *pongal*, a sweet rice dish, to the deity.

Munusamy went through the motions with a burdened heart at the fate of his childhood friend, Thakkan, and of his ancestors. *The British brought our ancestors to clear the forests and work in the sugar farms and estates. But none of our ancestors knew what they were getting into. They could not even read the documents they signed. They were treated worse than slaves and stripped of their dignity… made to live in homes smaller than cow sheds. Several generations did not have any amenities in their homes. Many died in these estates, not once returning to their homes or ever seeing their loved ones again. Why? Not even the kranis, who were Indians themselves, had any respect for the coolies. They treated us as worms beneath their feet that they stamped on.*

Munusamy came to a decision. He returned to Chennai a day earlier than he was due to depart to meet Thakkan. He went back to the same spot in front of Chennai airport. But there was no sign of Thakkan or his friends anywhere in sight. No one knew where they were. No one had noticed them. Chinna Akka's husband managed to speak to someone who gave them an insight on what had happened.

"These beggars… one day, they will be here, but as soon as they hear that there is money in another area, they will move there. It is very difficult to see the same group of people in the same place two days in a row, *Ayya*!"

The words dashed Munusamy's hopes of reaching out to Thakkan. He berated himself for not telling Thakkan to wait for him.

Munnusamy and Kaali returned home to a rapidly changing landscape. Their neighbourhood was changing with everyone they knew moving into flats. Even men who had left their wives in India and lived in shared accommodation moved into flats. The biggest draw these flats had was the modern toilets in the privacy of their own home. They felt free.

The government built rental flats as well as three-room, four-room and five-room flats for sale. Those who could not afford to buy their own flats continued to rent. There were amenities right by the flats such as wet markets, supermarkets, paediatricians and parks. There were benches at the void decks under every block for people to gather in the evenings. The amenities were a big hit with the residents. Despite the conveniences, they could not shake off the feeling that they had left something far more precious behind: their kampong and neighbours.

The faces that greeted them outside their doors belonged to Chinese or Malay families. Many of them were housewives who stayed home the whole day. But there was no room for conversation as most did not speak English or Malay.

Kaali and Munusamy had their fair share of battles to deal with. All that they were familiar with was changing. Their community at Sembawang was disintegrating as they moved into flats in different parts of Singapore. Then there was Raasu, who showed no signs of letting up on his insistence that he wanted his share of the family's property. His incessant pestering was unbearable.

Unable to let go of everything that they had built up from scratch, Munusamy and Kaali held onto their shophouse for as long as they could.

I⊤ was ⊤ime for the British forces in Singapore to return to England. Before the British pulled out their forces, they granted British citizenship to all those who worked at the Naval Base for at least five years. Those who worked for the British were nostalgic about the life at the base.

"The British were very good bosses. They had very good hearts. No matter what others say, they won't come close to that."

Not surprisingly, many chose to emigrate and left for England and, from the letters that they sent home, they seemed to have adapted well in their adopted land. Chinnadurai re-read the letters from his friends who had emigrated. He was eligible for British citizenship. Given that he was a diploma holder with relevant job experience, there were several good jobs for those with his qualifications. But his heart was set on going to London like his friends had done. His wife too was eager to migrate and was constantly on his back to make the move soon. With very little else holding him back, both Chinnadurai and his wife picked an auspicious day to set off for England.

The rent in those days at 14th Mile was merely eight or ten dollars. There were two-room and three-room flats with *kusinis* that required you to walk down the stairs to get to. The flats with low rents had common bathrooms. When the British forces pulled out of Singapore, many of those who lived in these flats moved into Jurong Town Council or JTC flats. Some bought their own flats. The flats at 14th Mile were earmarked to be demolished. Today, this area lies between the Admiralty Estate and Sembawang Road.

Security was always tight at the Naval Base. Before one could enter the Naval Base, one had to register at the Sembawang Gate which was one of the entrances to the Base. Visitors handed over their identity cards to the guards before being allowed in.

The area outside of the Sembawang gate was 13th Mile. Although the houses at 13th Mile were large landed properties with five or eight rooms, they were called kampong houses. But there are no remnants of this area anymore in Singapore. The entire Sembawang area had changed.

Murugan too lived in one of these flats in 14th Mile after his marriage, with his wife and parents. He was one of those who moved to the JTC flats. Now, Murugan joined Vellaya's meat business and worked there full-time. Through Chinnadurai's letters, they knew that he was very happy with his life in London.

Vellaya and Mumtaj bought their own house and moved out of Sembawang. They continued to help everyone who came to their home seeking help. Chithamparam *Ayya* was now elected as the Member of Parliament of the Sembawang area. This came as no surprise to the residents who had known him for a long time as he was a well-loved member of the Sembawang community. Most importantly, he introduced many beneficial schemes in Sembawang that addressed the concerns of all races.

Meena Amma's home continued to be besieged with visitors as usual. She never failed to serve everyone who came to her home with a broad smile, a cup of coffee and titbits. Once in a while, when friends like Kaali dropped in, Meena Amma would make a sweetmeat made out of *kavuni* rice, a delicacy of the Chettiar community that Chithamparam's mother had taught her. Chithamparam *Ayya* continued to be the person that Kaali would go to when she needed help.

Muhammad, who had worked in Vellaya's shop for several years, decided to retire and spend the remaining days of his life with his wife and children in India. Vellaya did not have the heart to stop him. When the time came to bid Muhammad goodbye, Muhammad teared. Vellaya hugged him tightly for a few minutes. He had been good to Vellaya. Under Muhammad's care, the food stall had been a success. He had paid Muhammad well and that helped Muhammad to build his own house in India for his family. Before he left, Vellaya rewarded Muhammad with a substantial sum of money in gratitude for his many years of loyal service.

Vellaya's growth from an ex-con to a successful businessman of a food stall, a meat store and a sundry store warmed the cockles of Chithamparam *Ayya*'s heart. For some unexplainable reason, Chithamparam *Ayya* had a special place in his heart for Vellaya.

Raasu, on the other hand, was incredibly unhappy and grouchy. He constantly lamented that he had made the wrong career choice and missed the boat to migrate.

"I should have joined the Naval Base as well. If I had a job at the Naval Base… never mind what… any job… I could have gone to London."

Raasu's incessant complaints were getting on Munusamy's nerves. All their friends who lived in kampong houses had moved into flats. Many of those who lived in Sembawang moved into flats in the Marsiling or Yishun area. Some managed to snag newly built flats in the Sembawang area too. Many Sembawang residents were unfortunately only able to buy flats in other parts of Singapore which were far away from Sembawang. A handful of them moved to the other ends of the island or wherever their jobs took them.

The flour and spice mill owner, Unnithan *Ayya*, passed away. His sons took over the running of the store. They now sold a variety of spices and food items under the label 'House Brand Curry Powder'. The mill had grown many folds with several employees.

Sethulakshmi Amma passed away ten years ago. In her final days, Paarukutty Amma had been bedridden and was barely conscious. Upon the advice of the doctors, her family admitted her to Sree Narayana Mission, an old folks' home. Kaali took to visiting Paarukutty Amma whenever she could. During one of her visits, she was surprised to see Sangkaralingam, whom no one had seen in several years, seated there. Meenatchi Paati was seated next to him, patiently feeding Paarukutty Amma rice porridge.

"Paati!" Kaali hurried towards Meenatchi Paati. She signalled with her eyes to Kaali to sit down in the chair across her. Meenatchi Paati only turned to Kaali after she had finished feeding Paarukutty Amma.

"My husband had a heart attack, Kaali. When I heard the news, I went to him. Only when you have strength in your body, will you be arrogant and treat others badly. Once your nerves die, men won't bother you. But, for the life of me, I never thought this man will change like this.

"Now he is always weeping. Whenever he looks at me, he tries to put his palms together to apologise. He doesn't have any of those habits anymore... you know those filthy habits. His right leg and hand are rather weak now. He can't speak anymore. Life is peaceful. I can look after him till I die."

Hearing Meenatchi Paati speak of her own death and the sight of her frail form after all these years proved to be too much for Kaali. She could not stop the tears that flowed down her cheeks.

"What a forgiving soul! This is what a virtuous woman looks like. And no one can be a better wife than Meenatchi Paati in Sembawang."

Kaali repeated that statement to everyone she met for a long time after that meeting.

Many of the elderly from Sembawang who moved to Marsiling found a spot at the void decks to gather in the evenings. Their favourite topic of discussion was to reminisce on what life was like in Sembawang. They described the plants at the back and front of their houses and wondered what had become of the rambutan trees, banana trees and guava trees that they had left behind. Some of them recalled the mature fruit-bearing durian trees too.

Then there was the matter of space and the size of the house. The rooms in their Sembawang houses had been huge, unlike their current flats. They had to fight for space to grow a small rose plant or even the essential auspicious basil plant of the Hindus, the tulsi. There was simply not enough room in the common corridor to place the plant in front of their flats. Like birds with clipped wings, they had to learn to live in the confined space of the high-rise flats.

The elderly found it hard to bear that they were so disconnected. In Sembawang, neighbours dropped in without any notice. It was a village where their lives were interconnected.

The warmth of neighbourly relations was missing in the 'bird cage' that they had moved into. Their conversations often left an ache in their hearts for the paradise that they had lost. In fact, many Malayalees had avoided this fate by returning to Kerala when they saw the changing landscape of Singapore and realised that they had to move into flats.

What was more painful was not living close to their beloved Hot Springs anymore. Many of their daily activities had revolved around the Hot Springs. Now when children fell sick, mothers took them to the polyclinics but wished that they could make a trip to the Hot Springs instead. The water from the Hot Springs was available for purchase in the shops though. Kaali resorted to buying a bottle for herself from a Chinese shop when she wasn't well.

In the 1960s, there had been talk that the Hot Springs might be converted to a spa or a tourist attraction with a hawker centre to boot. But nothing came out of it. In 1985, the government made plans to expand its air force and this meant that the hot springs would be in an enclosed area for a while. But many of the Sembawang residents wanted it to be made accessible to the public. So finally, in 2002, the Hot Springs was open to the public again. But it wasn't exactly how it was in the past.

Everything had changed. Sembawang's 13th Mile was no more. In its place were many other buildings. The spot where the Holy Tree Sri Balasubramaniar Temple stood gave way to the Sembawang MRT Station. The Sri Maha Mariamman Temple at Mandai Road moved to Yishun. The entire Sembawang area, as Kaali remembered it, had been carved out to become different constituencies.

Even those who lived in rented rooms were able to purchase a flat of their own. The buttermilk-seller Anjalai's granddaughter was interviewed on television where she talked about how the act of owning their own place had given many Indians a sense of belonging.

But Kaali felt beaten by the circumstances of their life. Even after Munusamy had sold his shop and had given Raasu the proceeds, Raasu was not satisfied. He sank the money into a perfume business that failed. He now made ends meet as a private tutor who travelled to his students' homes. Kaali was tasked to look after her grandchildren while Raasu and Mei Ling were at work. Kaali and Munusamy could never reconcile themselves with the fact that Raasu had given up his government job to chase after a futile dream.

It was the time when Singapore welcomed foreign graduates and skilled workers with open arms and offered them jobs with a handsome salary. Knowing how troubled Kaali was about her son's sharp vicissitudes of fortune, Chithamparam *Ayya* introduced Raasu to Professor Chandralekha from London. The professor encouraged Raasu to enrol in a part-time degree programme at the university. Raasu did so and his action even served to encourage many of Raasu's friends who were teachers to pursue a degree as well. Professor Chandralekha had to be truly credited for encouraging Indian students in Singapore to further their education.

Though he didn't know it at that time, Raasu's decision to pursue his studies helped to save his marriage as well. Mei Ling respected Raasu for taking the plunge and for wanting to improve their circumstances. Their children were older now and didn't need constant supervision. Mei Ling kept their children in their home, rather than leaving them under Kaali's care while she was at work. During that time, their household ran on Mei Ling's salary. But it was just a matter of time before things would turn around for them. Raasu proved to be a committed husband and father. Kaali was relieved that Mei Ling ran the household well. Her son was in a good place now.

Munusamy had lost a lot of weight worrying about his son but his health recovered by leaps and bounds at seeing Raasu turn his life around. Thankfully, Munusamy had had the foresight to buy a four-room flat in Marsiling so their lives carried on without the need for support from his son.

Out of the blue, a white-haired elderly lady came by their home wanting to see Munusamy. Neither Kaali nor Munusamy recognised her. The old lady sat at Munusamy's legs and sobbed away quietly.

"Don't you recognise me, my prince? I am Shanti. Shanti... from Kedondong Road. Shanti... My son is going to America. I am going with him. I may never see you again. I wanted to see your face one last time before I left. I wanted to let you know that I was leaving for good."

Munusamy didn't say a word. But Kaali understood what was not being said in that room. Kaali could not stifle her giggle. The more she thought about it, the more heartily she laughed. *Ha ha, so this is his woman? I am so much prettier than her crooked face.* The mystery was solved. Kaali was relieved on many levels.

Munusamy was now eighty-five years old. He had severe memory loss. He was completely dependent on Kaali to carry out his daily chores. Kaali gave him an earful if he annoyed her. She was still sprightly for a seventy-eight-year-old Paati. She did all her chores and cooked all the meals in the home. Once a week, a Bangladeshi domestic maid came by to help out.

She had Munusamy on a strict diet these days. She added far less salt, tamarind and chilli to their meals. But Munusamy still wanted tastier food and would yell at her about the cooking. Kaali was not too perturbed by his demands. She wondered how long they had left. Once Munusamy showed his displeasure by throwing the plate of food she had placed in front of him at the wall. Kaali did not say anything. Instead, she ignored him for the next two days.

On the third day after their fight, they heard on the news the government announcement about a special scheme for the pioneer generation to pay less for medical expenses, transportation and entry fees to many places. This brought a wide smile to both their faces.

Kaali was really happy that day. As first-generation migrants, their lives had turned out well. She was in reasonably good health which she attributed to working long hours as a maid when she was younger. She was also grateful that they had moved to Singapore at the right time. There was a tinge of sadness about the life they had left behind at 13th Mile. Those days would always have a special place in her heart.

When the news ended, she went into the *kusini* to prepare a bowl of oats for Munusamy.

The old woman's heart was content.

PEOPLE & PLACES

T. Kanapathipillai supervising a rubber tapper at 12th Mile, Sembawang
(circa 1960s). He arrived in Malaya in the late 1930s from Kankesanthurai,
Sri Lanka.
Courtesy of Santha Kumari.

Balakrishnan Pillai and his wife, Chellamma Amma, who lived at 13th Mile,
Sembawang, with their family at Tong Lam Studio (1952).
Balakrishnan Pillai arrived in Singapore in 1920 from Kerala, India.
Courtesy of B. Aravindakshan Pillai.

Chellamma Amma in her kitchen at 13th Mile, Sembawang (circa 1950s).
Courtesy of B. Aravindakshan Pillai.

13½ Mile, Sembawang (circa 1970s).
Courtesy of George Hardington.

A post-wedding gathering at Achutan Pillai's 13th Mile home, Sembawang (1968).
Achutan Pillai arrived in Malaya from Parur, Kerala, in the early 1940s, and at
Sembawang in the 1950s.
Courtesy of Balan s/o Pillai.

Canberra Primary School (circa 1950s).
Courtesy of B. Aravindakshan Pillai.

Sree Narayana Gurukulam Malayalam teachers and students awaiting the arrival of
Swami Mangalananda's arrival (circa 1950s).
Courtesy of B. Aravindakshan Pillai.

Chandran and Ravindaran Pillai were born and raised in Lorong Maha (circa 1940s). *Courtesy of B. Aravindakshan Pillai.*

Selvarani Suppiah (bottom middle) at Naval Base Quarters (1972). *Courtesy of Sivasankar Suppiah.*

Naval Base dock workers on their way home after work (1966). *Courtesy of David Ayres.*

Sembawang market, Chong Pang Village (1966).
Courtesy of David Ayres.

Ramu's Clinic at 10th Mile, Sembawang.
Courtesy of Old Sembawang Naval Base Nostalgic Lane Facebook Group.

Maternal and Child Health Clinic, Sembawang.
Courtesy of Sofea Abdul Rahman.

Pasar malam at 13th Mile, Sembawang (1968).
Courtesy of Jack Hockey and Paul Hockey.

Outdoor seating for food stalls in Sembawang (1967).
Courtesy of David Ayres.

A stall holder with an airmail envelope tucked in his lungi at
Sembawang Village Hawker Centre (1967).
Courtesy of David Ayres.

A bar at 14th Mile, Sembawang (1966).
Courtesy of David Ayres.

A *thongal* shop at Sembawang (1966).
Courtesy of David Ayres.

A provision shop run by Richard Ng's family (1973).
The shop was located at 58 Jalan Ketuka, Sembawang.
Richard's grandparents arrived in Singapore in the 1930s from Canton Province,
China. The shop ceased operation in June 1986 when they relocated to Yishun town.
Courtesy of Richard and Veronica Ng.

A drinks stall at 14th/15th Mile, Sembawang.
Courtesy of Tony Dyer and Sofea Abdul Rahman.

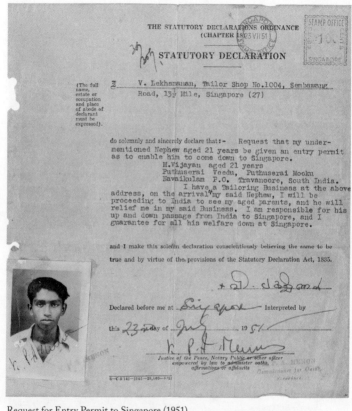

THE STATUTORY DECLARATIONS ORDINANCE
(CHAPTER 18)

STATUTORY DECLARATION

(The full name, estate or occupation and place of abode of declarant must be expressed).

I V. Lekhsmanan, Tailor Shop No.1004, Sembawang Road, 15½ Mile, Singapore (27)

do solemnly and sincerely declare that:— Request that my under-mentioned Nephew aged 21 years be given an entry permit as to enable him to come down to Singapore.
    M.Vijayan aged 21 years
    Puthuserai Veedu, Puthuserai Mooku
    Navaikulam P.O. Travancore, South India.
    I have a Tailoring Business at the above address, on the arrival my said Nephew, I will be proceeding to India to see my aged parents, and he will relief me in my said Business. I am responsible for his up and down passage from India to Singapore, and I guarantee for all his welfare down at Singapore.

and I make this solemn declaration conscientiously believing the same to be true and by virtue of the provisions of the Statutory Declaration Act, 1835.

Declared before me at Singapore   Interpreted by

this 23rd day of July 19 51

Justice of the Peace, Notary Public or other officer empowered by law to administer oaths, affirmations or affidavits

Request for Entry Permit to Singapore (1951).
Courtesy of Shanavas Vijayan.

Sembawang Beach at 15th Mile (1960s).
Courtesy of Tony Dyer and Sofea Abdul Rahman.

President of the Naval Base Labour Union, Narayana Kurup Dharmaseelan (far left)
signing an agreement at the Naval Base (circa 1950s).
Courtesy of Jaya Pillai.

Chief Minister of Kerala, Shri R Sankar, when he visited the Naval Base (1961).
Courtesy of Santha Sreedharan.

Kesavan Narayanan Unnithan with the first machine at KNP Trading in Sembawang.
Courtesy of Jayadev Unnithan.

KNP Trading lorries at Sembawang.
Courtesy of Jayadev Unnithan.

Executive Committee of the Holy Tree Sri Balasubramaniar Temple, 29 May 1965.
Courtesy of Santha Kumari.

The wedding of the author, Kamaladevi Aravindan,
at the Holy Tree Sri Balasubramaniar Temple (circa 1970s).
Courtesy of B. Aravindakshan Pillai.

The author, Kamaladevi Aravindan, and her husband, B. Aravindakshan Pillai (circa
1970s). The photo was taken at Tong Lam Studio, which was in Sembawang.
Courtesy of Kamaladevi Aravindan.

Thaipusam day at Sri Maha Siva Muniswarar Temple at Tampoi, Malaysia (1975).
Courtesy of B. Aravindakshan Pillai.

The author, Kamaladevi Aravindan (second from left), and her sisters-in-law (circa
1970s). Photo taken at Tong Lam Studio at 13th Mile, Sembawang.
Courtesy of B. Aravindakshan Pillai.

Sangaram Sita and Sitharam Sankaradas (June 1957). The couple lived at the Asian Settlement quarters in the Naval Base, Singapore. Their roots are from Andhra Pradesh and Tamil Nadu, India.
Courtesy of Gajandran Das.

Krishnasamy Suppiah and Solochana Davi Suppiah, 15 July 1961. Both of them had moved from Malaya to Singapore in the mid-1940s. Krishnasamy Suppiah worked as a storekeeper at the Naval Base. His roots are from Tamil Nadu, India.
Courtesy of Durai Singam Suppiah.

Sub-lieutenant Selvarajoo and Amuthaveli @ Kanchana (1960s).
The family lived at Sembawang Springs Estate.
Courtesy of S. Devendran.

Mr & Mrs Ramasamy Selvarajoo Thevar (extreme right) at HM Naval Base (circa 1960s).
Courtesy of S. Devendran.

Gajandran's father and Suryndaran in front of Block 1 of
the Royal Naval Armaments Depot or RNAD (1968).
Courtesy of Gajandran Das.

Abdul Rahman @ Nar Singh s/o Kudar Singh. He worked as a driver at the Naval
Base. He arrived in Singapore before World War II from Punjab, India.
Courtesy of Sofea Abdul Rahman.

It was customary for colleagues and friends to take a studio photograph with anyone who was travelling or migrating to India. The travelling party wore a garland and held a bouquet in hand.
Abdul Rahman @ Nar Singh (standing 2nd row, extreme left) with his Naval Base colleagues (circa 1960s).
Courtesy of Sofea Abdul Rahman.

KG Sreedharan with his peers from their Hindi class (1956).
Courtesy of Santha Sreedharan.

Dance Class at Sree Narayana Mission (1950s).
Courtesy of B. Aravindakshan Pillai.

Malayalam Class at Sree Narayana Mission (1950s).
Courtesy of B. Aravindakshan Pillai.

Ismail bin Ahmad's home at 15th Mile, Sembawang (1960s).
Courtesy of Tony Dyer and Sofea Abdul Rahman.

Jane Varghese at the veranda of her house at Lorong Maha (circa 1960s).
Courtesy of Grace Sebastian.

Sembawang Springs Estate at 13th Mile (1960s).
Courtesy of Tony Dyer and Sofea Abdul Rahman.

The *SS Rajula*, 20 January1968. It ceased operations in 1973.
Courtesy of Sreedevi Rajagopal.

VS Chellappan and family (1970). Photo taken at Tong Lam Studio in Sembawang.
VS Chellappan migrated from Kerala, India in 1938 and worked at the Naval Base.
Courtesy of Santha Sreedharan.

Lelitha Krishnapillai and Narayana Pillai (1971).
Photo taken at Tong Lam Studio, 13th Mile, Sembawang.
Courtesy of Sujatha Pillai.

Photo taken in front of Vasu Dash's home at 13th Mile, Sembawang,
just before his sister and her family migrated to the United Kingdom (1970).
Courtesy of Vasu Dash.

Sulekha Das and Sunu Sivadasan-Ghani in front of their home
at Sembong Road, 13½ Mile, Sembawang (1980).
Courtesy of Sunu Sivadasan-Ghani.

Block 4, Sembawang (circa 1978).
Courtesy of Dr Mercy Karuniah Jesuvadian.

Blocks 2 and 3 from old Sembawang Jurong Town Council (JTC)
at 14th Mile (2004).
Courtesy of Chan Kai Foo.

HISTORICAL NOTES & REFERENCES

THIS SECTION PROVIDES some background information and facts related to the events and places mentioned in this novel. A full list of the references is available on request.

Map of Sembawang

The map was drawn up based on the 'Singapore Guide and Street Directory' (1950–75), Singapore Survey Department and verified by Wan Chan Peew, B. Aravindakshan Pillai and Sofea (Nora) Abdul Rahman. It was drawn up by Thng Shalyn and Mohamed Fairoz Bin Nordin.

Prologue

- For Sir Thomas Hyslop's quote, see *Malaya's Indian Tamil Labor Diaspora: Colonial Subversion of Their Quest for Agency and Modernity* by PA Spencer (2013).

- Migration of coolies to Malaya
  In *Indians in Malaya: Some Aspects of their Immigration and Settlement (1786–1957)*, KS Sandhu draws on official documents by HJ Strokes, an Acting Sub-Collector (1870) and an article in the Police Weekly Circular (Madras) dated 4 February 1865 to describe the conditions in which coolies

were recruited and sent to Malaya. He states that between 1844 to 1941, 2,725,917 Indian labourers moved to Malaya to work. The first record of Indian labour immigration into Malaya in 1844 is 1,800. This number grew rapidly over the years and by 1957, the total number of Indians in Malaya was 4,245,990.

- Kanganis in Malaya
The Kangani system was established in Ceylon and later extended to Malaya. KS Sandhu (see above) describes the Kangani labour immigration system into Malaya as one that was 'an entirely south Indian phenomenon'. In his article, 'Indian Emigrants: Numbers, Characteristics, and Economic Impact', MC Madhavan states: 'It vastly improved the labour supply to those countries, but its method of recruitment came under severe attack for gross violations of law. Although labourers were supposed to be free, in practice they were not mobile, mainly because of cash advances that tied them into a cycle of debt bondage. The system was finally abolished in 1938, when the Indian government placed a ban on assisted labour migration.' He goes on: 'In the waning days of the Kangani system of recruitment, independent labour migration, both assisted and non-assisted, emerged as an important source of migrant streams and became significant after the depression.'

- Tamil indentured labour
In his article, 'Indians Overseas? Governing Tamil Migration to Malaya 1870–1941', SS Amrith states: 'There were around 30,000 Indians in Malaya in 1870, concentrated in and around Penang; by 1891, 75,000; 120,000 by 1901 and 275,000 by

1911. By 1911, the majority of Tamils in Malaya worked on the plantations of Perak and Selangor. ... Until the 1890s, the majority (between 70 and 80 per cent) of Tamil migrants to Malaya were under formal contracts of indenture; thereafter ... other forms of recruitment, based on debt, became more common.'

CZ Guilmoto, in his article 'The Tamil Migration Cycle, 1830–1950', tells us that: 'A typical feature of Tamil emigration was the "Kangani" system in which labour recruitment from India and supervision on the plantations were in the hands of Tamil headmen.' He follows that with: 'The migrants were organised by an overseer, the Kangani, who was responsible for them at every stage of their journey to the plantations. Originally, he was also the recruiting officer in Tamil Nadu, who visited the villages of his native region to persuade agricultural labourers and indebted peasants to accompany him to work on the plantations for varying lengths of time. The Kanganis travelled with the groups of Tamils all the way from the place of recruitment to Sri Lanka, advancing them the money required on their journey to the plantations. Once there, they continued to act as supervisors and were responsible to the plantation owners or managers for the workers they had brought, who were usually also indebted to them for the advances given. The role of the Kanganis was very important because of the social and financial powers they exercised within the limited geography of the plantations.'

- Indian immigration to Malaya
  According to KS Sandhu (see 'Migration of coolies to Malaya' above), the English-educated Indians and Jaffna Tamils were hired to work as clerks, dressers, plantation and office

assistants, teachers and technicians. North Indians such as the Sikhs were hired as soldiers, policemen, watchmen and caretakers.

• References
The following research papers and books informed the historical details described in the prologue: G. Ramasamy's *Opantha koolikalum Kanganikalum Unpublished Diary* (1989); Singapamuthu's *Unpublished Diary from Visakapatinam* (1949), *Anthology of Malaysian Tamil Poetry* by Nedumaran (1997), *Journeys: Tamils in Singapore* by N. Murugaian (2018), and *Tragic Orphans: Indians in Malaya* by CV Belle (2015).

Chapter 1
Interviews with Mr Sothinathan (Malaysia) and Dr Chandrasegaran informed the historical details as described in this chapter.

Chapter 2
• Sembawang
In his unpublished diary, *Reminiscence of the Old: H.M. Navel and Sembawang, 1919–1971* (1975), Mokia Manikam states that there were four areas near the Naval Base in the 1960s. They were 12th Mile (Chye Kay Village), 13th Mile (Chong Pang Village), 14th Mile and 15th Mile.

• Naval Base in Sembawang
According to Singapore's National Heritage Board and the Housing and Development Board: 'The former Singapore Naval Base built by the British in the 1920s used to stretch all the way from Sembawang Road to the Causeway at

Woodlands. Sembawang was the site where the most intensive military build-up took place under British rule. The Singapore Naval Base came equipped with facilities such as barracks, workshops and hospitals. When the graving dock of the base was officially opened in 1938, it was the biggest naval dock in the world then.'

KK Liew tells us in his article, 'Labour Formation, Identity, and Resistance in HM Dockyard, Singapore (1921–1971)', that the Naval Base was where the 'largest concentration of labour was located, with an estimated of 10,000 employees, many of whom were ethnic Malayalees from southern India.'

In 'British Withdrawal from Singapore', the National Library Board states that most of the British forces pulled out of Singapore in 1971 and the remaining few members left five years later.

- Holy Tree Sri Balasubramaniar Temple
  In his book, *Hinduism in Singapore: A Guide to the Hindu Temples of Singapore*, JP Mialaret says that the Holy Tree Sri Balasubramaniar Temple was originally from Sembawang Naval Base. In 1963, it started off as a small shrine against a tree. The structure was built in 1966 for the Hindu workers at the Naval Base. It moved to its current location at Yishun in 1996.

- Sembawang Hot Springs
  V Chelvan (in 'Sembawang Hot Spring to be developed into 1-hectare Park by 2019') and National Library Board (in 'Sembawang Hot Spring') report that the Sembawang Hot Spring was discovered in 1908 on the grounds owned by a

Chinese merchant, Seah Eng Keong. It was a thermal bathhouse for the Japanese during World War II. The flow of water at the hot springs was interrupted briefly during World War II when a bomb fell near the well during an air raid. Chelvan also reported that the signboard in front of the Sembawang Hot Springs credits a British soldier, William Arthur Bates Goodall, with the discovery of the hot springs in 1908.

* References
The following research papers and books informed the historical details described in this chapter: Mokia Manikam's unpublished diary *Reminiscence of the Old: H.M. Navel and Sembawang, 1919–1971* (1975) and *The Man Behind the Bridge: Colonel Toosey and the River Kwai* by P Davies (2013).

* Interviews
Information from the following interviewees provided the historical details described in this chapter: Dr Murasu Neduraman and Dr Chandrasegar (Malaysia) and ex-Sembawang residents: Radhakrishnan Menon, Vela Yudan, Kannan Devakaran, Raasu Karuppan, Shantha Letchimi and Aravindakshan Pillai.

Chapter 3

* Siam-Burma Railway
The Siam-Burma Railway came to be known as the Death Railway because of the thousands who died during its construction. A former Prisoner of War, Sir Harold Atcherley, recounted the five-day trip with no toilet facilities or ventilation. None of the men could sleep during the journey. Reaching the location, they were made to work eighteen

hours a day with very little food. See the newspapers articles from Tom Rowley ('Burma Railway: British POW Breaks Silence over Horrors') and Suzanna Pillay ('Remembering the "Romusha" who Built Death Railway'.)

• References
Some historical details described in this chapter were obtained from Maasilamani's unpublished diary, *Kaaname Ponne en Purushan*.

• Interviews
Ex-Sembawang resident, Ammakannu, provided some of the historical details described in this chapter.

Chapter 4
• Pulau Senang
On 12 July 1963, Daniel Dutton, Arumugam Veerasingam and Tan Kok Hian were murdered by the prisoners at Pulau Senang. Seventy-one prisoners who were involved in this crime were charged on 20 August 1963. (See the articles from *The Straits Times* on 20 August 1963, 19 November 1963 and 26 November 1963.) To read more, refer to *Pulau Senang – The Experiment that Failed* by Alex Josey (Marshall Cavendish Editions, 2020).

• Interviews
Some historical details described in this chapter were gleaned from the interview with ex-Sembawang resident Mohamed Malik.

Chapter 5

The interview with ex-Sembawang resident, Karuppan Raaman, informed the historical details described in this chapter.

Chapter 6

The historical details described in this chapter came from interviews with Sivaraman Nair and P. Sreedharan Nair (Appu Nair), both from Singapore.

Chapter 11

• Interviews

The following interviews provided the historical details described in this chapter: A. Palaniappan (Singapore), Dr G. Raman (Singapore), Sarojini Chandran (Australia) and ex-Sembawang residents, Karuppan Raaman and Vasu Dash.

• Rape of the Two Midwives

Four men, Gopal Krishnan (23 years old), R. Subramaniam (18 years old), A. Verraya (19 years old) and T. Tarmar (20 years) were charged with raping two midwives and stealing a transistor radio and $24 at the 24-hour Maternal and Child Health Clinic on 16 October 1968.

On 12 September 1969, all four were found guilty. Three of them (Krishnan, R. Subramaniam and Verraya) were given three counts of ten years imprisonment that they could serve out concurrently as well as several strokes of the cane. Tarmar was given a seven-year jail term and fewer strokes of the cane.

During the trial, it was reported that R. Subramaniam threw his shoes at a police witness. (See *The Straits Times* reports on 12 August 1969, 28 August 1969 and 12 September 1969.)

Please note that none of the characters in this novel are the four men described above. To read more, refer to *Beyond a Reasonable Doubt* by N. Sivanandan (Marshall Cavendish Editions, 2019).

Chapter 13

- Registered Passport to go to Malaysia (from 1967)
'Due to the high number of people commuting from Singapore to West Malaysia, a 64-page Singapore Restricted Passport (SRP) was introduced in 1967 to ease the travelling process. The SRP was eventually made invalid on 1 June 1999 when the number of commuters dwindled over the years.' (From the National Heritage Board's article, 'Singapore Restricted Passport'.)

- 'Chopped'
According to Dr Lisa Lim, a well-known linguist, the word 'chop' refers to a 'passport stamp' and is a term used in Hong Kong and Singapore. It originates from the Hindi word 'chaap' which means stamp, imprint or seal. The word 'chop' entered the English language in the 19th century though this word is no longer found in contemporary English. The word continues to be used by many Singaporeans and residents of Hong Kong. (See Lim's article 'Where Does the Word "Chop" Come From?'.)

Chapter 14

- Pongala Festival at Attukal Bhagavathi Temple

  The prayers for Attukal Pongala are described by Lekshmy Rajeev as such: 'most Malayalees wait for the Attukal Pongala like they wait for Onam or Vishu, the two major festivals of their land. Plans for the celebrations [are] made well in advance.' (See *Attukal Amma: The Goddess of Millions* by L. Rajeev.)

Chapter 16

- Teluk Intan

  The global depression in the 1980s reduced the demand for tin and rubber exports. The fall in demand for these two commodities diminished the importance of Teluk Intan. With fewer job opportunities, the population decreased from 62,393 in 1991 to 41,200 in 2010 as many left the place and sought better job opportunities in other towns. (See YT Wong's article, 'Telok Anson: The Faded Gem of Lower Perak' and N. Aandiappan's book, *Thiraikadalodi: Oor Ezhuthalarain Vazhai Suvadukal.*)

- Karaikudi Chettiars

  The Chettiars were early settlers of Teluk Anson. They are described as 'the most important Indian group of the town'. They played a significant role in financing small-scale Chinese rubber planters. They also erected a temple in Teluk Intan in 1899 that's known as the Nagarathar Sri Thendayuthapani. (From the article 'Telok Anson: The Faded Gem of Lower Perak' by YT Wong.)

- Racial Riots

  The *South China Morning Post* reported that the official death toll of the racial riots on 13 May 1969 was 260 people (mostly Chinese), with many suffering gunshot wounds. About 6,000 were injured and hundreds of buildings were burnt down. At the urging of Dr Mahathir Mohamad, Tunku Abdul Rahman stepped down as Prime Minister after the riots, and Abdul Razak took over. (*South China Morning Post*, 14 May 2007 and *The Straits Times*, 13 July 2015).

- Affirmative Action in Malaysia

  Dr Lee Hock Guan argues that the preferential treatment for Malays in Malaya was put in place by the British for the elite administrative service. 'What changed after 1971 was that a Malay-dominated state formulated and systematically implemented a comprehensive ethnic preferential policy to benefit the Malay community. The ethnic preferential policy has invariably generated intense controversy in Malaysian society, with the majority of Malays, Chinese and Indians taking diametrically opposing views. This inflammatory public issue and the emotionally charged debate it has generated, however, has not deteriorated into outright ethnic violence as had happened earlier in 1969.' (See Lee's article, 'Affirmative Action in Malaysia'.)

- Interviews

  N. Aandiappan provided the historical details described in this chapter.

Chapter 17

- Unnithan Mill

  KNP Trading Pte Lte (Ltd), which was popularly known as Unnithan Mill, was established in 1958. In the 1950s, spices were blended and ground manually for cooking by the end users, mainly chefs and housewives. It was a tedious process. Mr Unnithan wanted to ease the burden of the end users so he started blending and grinding spices using machines. While this was a business opportunity, the inspiration for this venture was not in creating a product but providing a service. So, House Brand was not merely in the business of producing ingredients for food but providing a service to enhance the food experience. Today, the company offers more than 200 products and has ventured into Ready Meals and Ready Gravy. (From the personal email communication with Mr Jayadev Unnithan in December 2018.)

- Mess in Sembawang

  Several messes were run in the Naval Base and Sembawang, with many owned by Malayalees. These were largely frequented by bachelors who paid $7.00 in the 1950s for three meals and tea. For an additional dollar, these meals were delivered to the office in tiffin carriers. Guests of these bachelors did not have to pay for the meals at the messes.

- Interviews

  The historical details described in this chapter came from the following interviewees: Jayadev Unnithan, Jayakumar Unnithan and KN Janamma.

Chapter 22

- References
The following documents informed the historical details
described in this chapter: J. Raman (2006), *Yuthathaal vantha
Yutham* by KP Suppiah (1946), *Malaysia Indiyaarkalin Samuka
Arasiyal Vaazkai Pooratankal* by P. Janthirakaantham (1995)
and *Nizhalum Nijamum* by SP Anbarasu (2009).

- Interviews
The following interviewees provided the historical details
described in this chapter: Tamil Selvan (India), Sarojini
Chandran (Australia), Meera Aandiappan, K. Pakiam
(Malaysia) and Sundrambal (Malaysia).

Chapter 23

Mohamed Kassim Shanavas and ex-Sembawang resident
Mohamed Malik provided the historical details described in
this chapter.

Chapter 24

- Operation Sook Ching
In February 1942, a Sook Ching Operation was conducted
where Japanese soldiers gathered Chinese men to search for
'members of volunteer forces, communists, looters, those
possessing weapons, and those whose names appeared in lists
of anti-Japanese suspects maintained and distributed by the
Japanese'. One of the centres where these men were gathered
was the Jalan Besar Centre. (From 'Operation Sook Ching is
Carried Out on 18 Feb 1942' by HistorySG.)

- Interviews

Ex-Sembawang residents, Muniamma and Janaki Amma, provided the historical details described in this chapter.

Chapter 25

The historical details described in this chapter were gleaned from the following interviewees: Kullinan (India), Sila Das (Malaysia), Prof Ramalingam (India), Mulagai Amma (India) and Muthupattar (India).

Chapter 26

- Pioneer Generation

The Singapore government introduced the Pioneer Generation Package in 2014. The package provides medical and other subsidies to those who were more than 65 years old in 2014 and those who obtained citizenship before 1986. (From the Pioneer Generation Package website, Government of Singapore.)

- References

Mokia Manikam's unpublished 1975 diary, *Reminiscence of the Old: H.M. Navel and Sembawang, 1919–1971*, provided the historical details described in this chapter.

- Interviews

Millat Ahmad Maraikkayar and Aravindakshan Pillai provided the historical details described in this chapter.

CRITICAL REVIEW OF *SEMBAWANG* (IN TAMIL)

SEMBAWANG BY KAMALADEVI ARAVINDAN is a fascinating narrative that is valuable not only as lively fiction but as a realistic documentation of a forgotten segment of Singapore history. It is also invaluable in that it both excavates and recreates subaltern history that has the feel of authenticity, is women-centric and is fictional history narrated from the underside. The Italian Marxist theorist, Antonio Gramsci, applied the term 'subaltern' to describe 'the unorganised masses that must be politicised for the workers' revolution to succeed'. The term 'subaltern' was first used out of its military context of inferior ranking soldiers by Gramsci as he adopted it to refer to the subordinate classes that made up the Italian peasantry in his 'Notes on Italian History'. The subalterns are always the 'represented' without means of representing themselves and hence understood as those whose voices never typically enter the discursive zone. Subalterns are also usually the marginal 'objects' of historical discourse, the pawns who appear in the sidelines of mainstream narratives.

In the 1980s, the Subaltern Studies Group, a collective of radical historians in India, appropriated the term, 'subaltern', focusing their attention on the disenfranchised peoples of India. The coolies of Malaya form a critical segment of this group. The Subaltern Studies Group had a long-standing commitment to highlight subaltern themes in South Asian history. The editor, Ranajit Guha, declares that 'this has meant not only publishing articles on the historical practices of subaltern groups', but also pursuing their inquiries into subalternity 'beyond conventional boundaries'. Guha states: 'We have always conceived the presence and pressure of subalternity to extend beyond subaltern groups; nothing — not elite practices, state policies, academic disciplines, literary texts, archival sources, language — was exempt from effects of subalternity' (2003 p. v). As Shanthini Pillai, when discussing Malayan coolies, points out, there are 'two important and relevant issues present' in Guha's observations above. 'The first is that the effects of subalternity and the representation of its effects transgress disciplinary boundaries and are not merely evident in historical documentation of the subaltern. The second is that language and literary texts are subject to effects of subalternity as much as the subaltern groups themselves." (Pillai, 2007, pp. 22–3)

Seen from this perspective, *Sembawang* not only becomes an artefact that foregrounds these marginalised histories through a literary, fictional text, but it approaches them from a distinctly unique angle. As S. Pillai observes, most information on the subaltern Indian immigrant stems from what has been written by colonial or state representatives. The politics of such representation serves mainly to augment the subaltern status of the coolies at every turn (Pillai, 2007, p. 20). Distinctively, though, *Sembawang*, though it narrates the lives of the South Indian coolies, does so in ways that celebrates their lives and retrieves their subject status. Brought as indentured labourers to Malaya during the colonial era to work in rubber plantations, build roads, construct bridges, and so forth, and who formed the first wave of colonial migrants from India, their lives were hard. As the narrative clarifies, these indentured labourers were as brutally treated, as exploited, as African slaves. To extricate them from their objectified locations and to excavate their subjecthood becomes a remarkable exercise, one that *Sembawang* enacts with not just commitment but exuberance.

The narrative thread is loosely tied to the figure of the twice-colonised subaltern woman, Kaaliyamma (Kaali), the wife of a drunken rubber tapper. It tracks her illicit love affair with Chandran, an unskilled labourer and details their subsequent elopement to Singapore, where she comes to live in squatter quarters in a communal house in Sembawang. The plot is composed of fiction interspersed with true events, such as the shockingly brutal 1963 riots in the former penal colony of Pulau Senang, when Superintendent Daniel Dutton, an Irishman, who believed he could reform criminals through hard labour without the use of weapons to control them, was brutally murdered and mutilated by the detainees, who proceeded to burn the island-colony to the ground. Another factual event that is recounted is of the gang rape that occurred in Sembawang village in the late 1960s, when four drunken men, probably high on drugs that were readily available in the dimly-lit bars of 'Sembawang 14 milestone', went on a rampage in a 24-hour Maternal and Child Health Clinic and gang-raped and brutalised two nurses working there. What adds value to these historical accounts is the way in which these histories are shown as imbricated in the lives of the subalterns. These are lived accounts recited by members of the subdominant citizenry.

In her famous essay 'Can the Subaltern Speak?', Gayatri Spivak raises the now legendary question in literary and postcolonial theory: 'On the other side of the international division of labour from socialised capital, inside and outside the circuit of the epistemic violence of imperialist law and education, supplementing an earlier economic text, can the subaltern speak?' Spivak persuasively argues that the histories of the subalterns are subsumed by hegemonic voices that speak for them and their histories remain unrecoverable leaving only traces in the annals of official history. Thus, subaltern histories are drowned out not only by the official top-down elitist histories but by the very erasure that is the effect of the clamour for survival that crowds the daily lives of the subalterns, where distinctive events are not bronzed by romanticised moments of heroism but emerge as shadows subsumed within elitist modes of historicising.

In *Sembawang*, it is precisely the nuanced excavation of this din of ordinary, 'inconsequential' incidents that pervade and make up the everyday life of those forgotten in the national archives that reanimates the ephemeral, unrecorded histories of the subaltern voices of Singapore's past.

Another remarkable feat of *Sembawang* is the foregrounding of women's histories. These women are 'obscure' homemakers, abused wives and recalcitrant mothers, whose lives never conform to the modes of conduct dictated by patriarchy. They are not the long-suffering, idealised wives constructed by patriarchy. These are 'real' women, whose far from ideal circumstances drive them to breach regulated modes of conduct for reasons of sheer survival. For instance, intelligent, efficient Kaali, the wife of Munusamy and the mother of Raasu, is the opposite of the long-suffering submissive wife so dear to patriarchal narratives. She is a feisty, courageous woman who sees the hopelessness of her plight and grasps her opportunity to flee with Chandran. The narrative makes no bones about the fact that their elopement, at least on Kaali's side, is not the result of great physical chemistry,

love or even a passing attraction. It is undertaken by Kaali for
the mundane, pedestrian need for survival. What is interesting
is also that Kaali breaks the mould of the ideal maternal. She
abandons Raasu to seek a better life albeit with qualms of regret
for leaving her son behind with a drunken, useless father. When
Kaali finally arrives to stay in a communal squatter home in
13th Mile, Sembawang, it is the other women who live there
who bring comfort and a measure of happiness to her life. These
wives who are kicked, beaten and routinely abused by their
husbands take the measure of their self-worth from their female
companions and not from their oppressive husbands. Their
bond of sisterhood transcends differences of religion, caste and
language. In this 'little Kerala', Tamil women like Kaali are
made welcome by the Malayalee women, like Manju's mother,
and Hindus like Kaali and Christians, such as Margaret, the
Malayalee Christian, alike go to drink the health waters close
by. Neither are the women rendered pitiable, as victims of fate.
On the contrary, they are shown as decisive and agentic. That
largely tabooed subject under patriarchy, women's sexuality,
is robustly visible in this tale made up of life's little incidents,
where daily life is filled with the challenge of endurance. Kaali's
neighbour, Muthuletchimi (Muthu), for instance, married to
the sexually passive Supramulu seeks sexual excitement illicitly
with Appunni. However, true to Rajeswari Sundarrajen's
observations that the only way a subaltern can ultimately 'speak'
is through her self-immolation, Muthuletchimi's subalternity
is reinforced when, becoming pregnant with Appunni's
child, and predictably with Appunni abandoning her, Muthu
commits suicide. But what makes this subaltern gain a measure
of subjecthood is her friendship with the women. Her story is
no longer erased. Instead, she shares her sorry plight with her

friend, Kaali, and in narrativising her extreme predicament, she enters the discursive zone without fading into invisibility and silence.

Another important aspect of the narrative that garners agency for women is the acerbic humour that pervades their conversations. This is not the humour of the defeated but the banter of the resilient. When Muthuletchimi's husband solicitously enquires whether she will be alright alone in the house while he travels to Johor Bahru for work, the reader becomes privy to her caustic inner thoughts that snap wordlessly at him 'and what good are you if you are here'. However, these ironic sentiments are not reflected in her serene countenance. At times this mordant humour is the only resistance these women can offer to their colonised condition — colonised by both patriarchy and poverty. Another instance of this humour is when news of Kaali's elopement spreads like wild fire in the community. On hearing the news Mandor Maarimuthu feels deep chagrin, not because she has deserted her husband, nor even because she has contravened the conventional code of behaviour expected of a coolie's wife, but that she had managed to resist his sexual advances while succumbing to Chandran's. The layers of oppression that bind these women are brought to light through an ironic authorial interface that appears to actively participate in their inner and outer turmoil.

The readers are also permitted to share the inner worlds of these women and are able to realise their constant straining to break free of the social fetters that bind them. They are always pushing boundaries. Even the elderly Meenatchi Paati, ostensibly docile, begins her daily visits to the temple in the sure knowledge that her husband cannot constrain her movements when it involves religion. Her agency emerges from beneath the weight of patriarchal surveillance as she carves out a space of action that is all her own.

As Sembawang gradually changes, moving into modernity and urbanisation, these transformations are registered through the resistant and mistrustful perspective of the subdominant and not in a positive light. The rise of high-rise apartments, though it comes with built-in toilets and modern kitchens, finds no favour with these people, who acutely feel the loss of their community bonds. The bewildering fragmentation of their identities, when they find themselves in modern homes surrounded by Chinese and Malays as their neighbours, is sensitively sketched in the narrative. The isolation of the women, who, not having a common language to communicate with each other and who therefore become prisoners in their modern apartments, invokes a deeply felt narratorial moment. Despite being persuaded into modernity, these women feel bereft since the bonds that sustained them in their penury and hardships have been shattered. Thus, this insight into and excavation of the subaltern perspective undermines the triumphalist national narrative that underscores the seamless progress from third world to first. But it is not the perspective alone that bestows a unique status to *Sembawang*. Perhaps its crowning glory is the language.

As Anita Chakravarty observes, modern historians, especially from erstwhile British colonies have rarely considered the fact that the material in their official archives, with few exceptions, are all in the English language. The first attempts by Subaltern Studies historians, trying to work their way out of this historiographical tradition, were marked, most notably in Ranajit Guha's pioneering work, by innovative techniques to read the presence of an insurgent consciousness from what were the most forgotten (and overlooked) English-language colonial accounts. But the question of finding traces of subaltern voices in an Indian-language archive remained unanswered. Yet it was surely obvious to everyone that the vast masses of the Indian people did not think, speak, dominate or revolt in the English language (Chakravarty, 1995, p. 3320). It is in these significant ways that literary narratives leverage the gaps in historical archiving. *Sembawang* interjects its narrative into the ebb and flow of subaltern existence, recording the details of their 'pedestrian' existences filling it with excitement and vigour, reflecting the challenges of everyday incidents that make up their lives. Another reason that makes *Sembawang* such a compelling read is the authentic rendering of the various regional dialects of the characters who make up this chronicle. As Chakravarty rightly observes, we see reality reflected in their individual speech acts. In this fictionalised account of a slice of Singapore history, the exchanges between characters reflect their regional origins from Tamil Nadu or Kerala, and also in their Malayan dialectal variations. Raasu's "*Yeppa, kalar muttaayi*" (meaning 'father, colour sweet') and "*padangaadi vanthaachu, padangaadi vanthachhu*" (meaning 'the movie van is here! The movie van is here!') are examples of these dialectical variations. Use of words such as *peratu* (meaning roll-call) and *krani* (meaning supervisor) periodises an era and specifies a location.

Kamaladevi's *Sembawang* gains its place in both literature and history by its subtle questioning of the privileging of elitist history and by its thoughtful depiction of a slice of Singaporean life. The author subverts these versions through her revisionist construction of the historiography of the South Indian subaltern through what Guha terms as the 'politics of the people' who are left out of elitist historiography. By doing so, the author relocates the position of subordinate individuals from a condition of transfixed subalternity to one that is dialectical, thereby empowering them.

I would like to conclude by conveying my hearty congratulations to the author, Mrs Kamaladevi Aravindan, for her thoughtful and thought-provoking work.

Associate Professor Chitra Sankaran
National University of Singapore

Works Cited

Chakravarty, Anita. "Writing History" *Economic and Political Weekly: Discussion*, December 23, 1995.

Guha, Ranajit. *History at the Limit of World-History.* Columbia: Columbia University Press, 2003.

Pillai, Shanthini. *Colonial Visions, Postcolonial Revisions: Images of the Indian Diaspora in Malaya*, Newcastle, UK: Cambridge Scholars Publishing, 2007.

Spivak, Gayatri, C. "Can the Subaltern Speak?" [Revised edition], in *Critique of Postcolonial Reason*, Columbia: Columbia University Press, 2010.

Sunder Rajan, Rajeswari. *Real and Imagined Women: Gender, Culture and Postcolonialism*, London and New York: Routledge, 1993.

WRITING *SEMBAWANG*: THE AUTHOR'S JOURNEY

I ARRIVED AS a 'newly-wed Singapore bride' to my in-law's home in Sembawang which was also called Kochu Keralam/ Kutti Keralam (small Keralam). It was a home like no other until my in-laws migrated back to Kerala. It was a joint family where we did not have any of the anxieties that come with modern living. I still long for my life in Sembawang.

It was surprising that some of the Tamils and Malays who lived in Sembawang in those days were conversant in Malayalam. On Onam day, Tamils, Telugus, Chinese and Malays as well as other races enjoyed traditional vegetarian feasts at Malayalee homes. One's ethnicity did not come into play in the friendships that were forged then.

The children attended English-medium schools where they studied English along with Malay and Tamil languages. The Malayalee children attended Malayalam classes after school in the evenings at the Sembawang Gurukulam and Sree Narayana Mission. It was a period when the Malayalee children learnt their mother tongue along with Kathakali and dance rather fervently. Alas, this is just a memory now.

When the British left Singapore, those who worked at the Naval Base were offered British citizenship. Some took the opportunity and settled in London for good. Most returned to

Kerala. There were a few who did not want to leave Singapore and continued to live in Sembawang. Their patriotism deserves another novel itself.

Even after moving into flats, the elderly gathered in small droves at the round tables in the void decks under their flats to share their nostalgic memories about Sembawang. They were never able to forget their memories of their fruit trees like the durian, rambutan, banana, mango and custard apple, nor of their flowering planters like their rose, coriander, basil and hibiscus. They had to leave those plants behind when they moved into their new flats where there was not enough sunlight to grow one or two plants at the corridor. It was a struggle to accept that this was their new life.

On Fridays, the women at Sembawang seemed to blossom and appeared lively. As a newly-wed who had just arrived at Sembawang, I could not understand this phenomenon. It was only when their husbands returned in the evening with *kway teow goreng* and confectionery for the children, that I understood that Friday was payday at the Naval Base.

Once the coast was clear — or rather once my mother-in-law had retired for her afternoon siesta — my friend and neighbour would come by for a chat by my window.

Once, after ascertaining that my in-laws and everyone at the home had slept, my husband and I sneaked out for a date. We took a taxi to the beach at 15th Mile. It was a lovely night, and my feet and sari were caressed by the water as I walked hand-in-hand with my husband. Such memories of my life at Sembawang leave me yearning for those days.

How can I forget the fond memories of the hot springs, Jalan Kadai and the satisfaction of watching a movie at Sultan Theatre?

Many migrants from the then Malaya, Tamil Nadu, Kerala, North India and Sri Lanka moved into 13th Mile, Sembawang. As the vast majority were the Malayalees from Kerala, Sembawang was nicknamed 'Kochu Keralam'.

Sembawang tells the story of a laywoman, Kaaliyamma, who ran away from the rubber plantation in Anjarai Kattai in Malaya to 13th Mile in Sembawang with Chandran, set against the background of historical events, some heartbreaking incidents that took place in Sembawang and in Singapore. These events cannot be forgotten in this lifetime.

The citizenship problems faced by residents in Singapore and Malaya then, and the workers' struggle to travel from Johor Bahru to Singapore after Singapore's separation from Malaya were real life experiences for so many people.

For several years, I have been aching to document the historical events such as the lives of those affected by the Japanese occupation in Singapore.

Despite the support and encouragement from the National Arts Council, Singapore, it still was not easy to write this novel from my heart. In fact, it took more than two years to finally complete this novel. In the midst of the writing, I even had to undergo two surgeries that greatly weakened my body. But the characters in the novel, *Sembawang*, did not give me any reprieve.

I returned to the road in the name of my novel. I travelled to Kedah, Ipoh, Penang, Kuala Lumpur, Kluang, Seremban and Chennai for my research. Some parts of this journey were filled with painful experiences too. After travelling by air and by bus, I was once told, "I am not in the mood to talk today. Can you come tomorrow in the morning?" Although their response broke my heart, I returned the next day. Even then, I was made to wait. On another instance, I fell ill on the day that I arrived. Despite being ill, I made my way, under a scorching sun, to the interviewee's home in my friend's car. In spite of the difficulties I faced for the interview, the interviewee did not provide any useful information. I was frustrated at the futile venture but I did not display my disappointment then. I returned to my hotel room with a raging fever. I boarded the flight that night in that condition and returned to Singapore in my weakened state. I was not able to get up for the following two days. But that was not the worst part.

When I went to another place in Malaysia to procure some specific books for research, the lady did not have the book that I wanted. When I reminded her about our phone conversation where I had explained what I wanted, she smiled and replied, "So what? At least, this way we got to meet, isn't it?" That was clearly a rather pointless trip that took up a lot of my time.

But there are two organisations and so many people I am indebted to from the bottom of my heart.

I have wanted to write this novel for the last twenty years with no success. It was the encouragement and unwavering support from the National Arts Council, Singapore, especially Ms Kavitha Karuum, that prompted me to start writing this novel.

The publication of this book would not have been possible without the grant from the National Heritage Board, Singapore. I am deeply grateful to the organisation and Mr Gowtham Gopal for facilitating this.

I would like to express my gratitude to the editor of Crimson Publishing for walking hand-in-hand with me in the final leg of this journey. This novel has benefitted from their careful proofreading.

My heartfelt gratitude and thanks to Dr Chitra Sankaran, Associate Professor (English Literature) at National University of Singapore, for reading my novel from cover to cover and for writing the critical review for this book despite her busy schedule.

I am deeply grateful to Mr Arun Mazhinan for explaining in detail about the life in that era.

I cannot thank Mr Sothinathan *Ayya* enough for kindly lending me books from his bookshop without any hesitation whenever I approached him. "It is important for this novel to be published, Kamalam," he encouraged me tirelessly. Mr Sothinathan *Ayya*, a former lecturer and current publisher/editor of Uma Publications, arranged for me to conduct interviews at his office in Kuala Lumpur.

Mr Na Aandiyappan too gave a lengthy interview detailing many historical facts which helped greatly in the research.

I was beside myself when I faced another challenge of not being able to locate a rare book. It was then that an important literary figure in Malaysian literature and my friend, Dr Shanmugam Siva, came forward and procured the book for me.

I am extremely thankful to Dr Hameem Saleem, a Tamil academic and my friend, for translating Dr Chitra Sankaran's critical review to Tamil.

I am filled with immense pleasure to thank my beloved daughter, Dr Anitha Devi Pillai, an academic and author, for carefully reviewing this novel chapter by chapter, consolidating the research and translating the novel to English.

The people who helped me with this novel from Singapore, Malaysia and Tamil Nadu for providing me with books, information, and granting me interviews: writer K. Pakiam from Kedah province who identified several workers for an interview to obtain information, Mr B. Aravindakshan Pillai,

Dr Chandrasegaran, researcher Janakiraman Manikkam, Dr Murasu Nedumaran, Dr Pichaimuthu, Professor Ramalingam, Bhama Sutharman, A. Palaniyappan, Durai Manikkam, the late Woodlands P. Sreedharan Nair (Appu Nair), Sivaraman Nair, lawyer Dr G. Raman, Jayakumar Unnithan, Jayadev Unnithan, KN Janamma, Jayashree Karuppan Raman, Vela Yudan, Kannan Divakaran, Kullinan, Shantha Letchimi, Mulagai Paati, Mohamed Kassim Shanavas, Prema Mahalingam, Muhamed Malik, Muniamma, Chinnamma, Muthupattar, Radhakrishnan Menon, Millat Ahmad Maraikkayar, Raasu Karuppan, Sarojini Chandran, lawyer Sila Das, Tamilselvan, Ammakannu, Vasu Dash, Meera Aandiyappan, Janaki Amma, Dr Thulasi, Manokaran Krishnan and Suntharambal.

I would also like to thank the following people: Sokkan, Sumi Thomas for their help with administrative and research support, Revathi Gunasekaran for translating photo captions and *Historical Background and References* from English to Tamil, professors from Singapore and Malaysia for their help with research, Simi Baby Thomas for designing the book cover, Binod Therat for taking the cover photographs of this novel, my beloved husband for helping me with collecting information and ensuring accuracy in the description, and my younger daughter, Sunitha Devi Pillai for the technical help.

This novel which is being published in both Tamil and English at the same time has finally been completed.

Sembawang is my humble attempt to capture the essence of time, the vast amounts of research gone into this and the life experiences of many from my soil.

Kamaladevi Aravindan
Translated by Sumi Baby Thomas

TRANSLATING *SEMBAWANG*: TWO YEARS IN MY MOTHER'S SHOES

Do you know what it's like to be raised by a mother who is a writer? I do.

Like many writers, my mother too moves between the worlds that she creates in her writing and reality. Often, my mother's characters in her novel become our dinner time companions. The conversations about plot and make-believe scenarios continue into the night with my mother's number one fan, my father.

A couple of years ago, I watched as my mother became engrossed in yet another novel. Only this time, the project was all too close to her heart as it was a story based on Sembawang, a place which both my parents often reminisce about. My mother spent hours in research by interviewing former residents and making several trips to libraries in Malaysia. It took several years before she finally relented to letting me read her final draft in March 2018.

I was hooked from the moment I read the manuscript then. There were several stories within the novel of love, loss, laughter and disappointment. There were vivid descriptions of a village from a different time and one that I recognised from black-and-white photographs in the albums of my parents and their friends.

Balancing Fact and Fiction —
Foregrounding People and Places

The novel, *Sembawang*, occupies a fluid space between reality and fiction, and to understand the relationship between the two worlds, I had to know the historical events that occurred in that time period, envision the landscape of Sembawang and understand the lives of the residents in that era.

While my mother had kept detailed notes on her sources, they were not cited nor represented in the conventional manner that I was accustomed to as an academic. Given that this was a work of fiction — albeit set in a historical context and based on people's memories of life in Sembawang, including the author's — I felt that it was essential that we made it clear where the line between fiction and history lay. Historical fiction novels often tread a fine balance between reality and fiction. Detailed notes and references allow readers to distinguish the fictional elements from facts. I asked for permission to include historical notes, photographs of people who lived in Sembawang as well as references to all the sources. These were written in English and translated to Tamil afterwards.

The photographs of places, homes and people who lived in Sembawang as well as the sketch of Sembawang provide an additional useful dimension to understand the novel. The sketch comprises the key locations mentioned in the book and were drawn up based on a street directory of the 1960s and verified by members who had lived in that area.

As it is a book with many characters — with long Tamil names — I included a list of characters for the benefit of the readers.

I must concede that, on most days, it was clear that my mother thought my approach to deconstructing the novel and foregrounding people and places was unconventional, but she was open to my suggestions. We both agreed that, with a book of this nature, the foregrounding of people and places would provide another dimension. But, then again, there were some days that I counted my lucky stars to be alive after our lengthy discussions on the plot, theme and additions we were including.

Translating and Editing

Next came the task of translating the novel to English. While I have published poetry, short stories and academic papers of my own, this is indeed the first novel that I am translating.

I drew on my background and training as an applied linguist for most parts of the translation process. At first, I translated the text line by line. But this proved to be an arduous task. I soon gave up after about twenty pages or so. I returned to the drawing board after a few weeks, and this time read the novel aloud to myself and made copious notes on the characters and the chain of events. Things started falling into place.

I sought the help of one of my students, Ravathi Gunasegaran, to read the novel aloud and had it recorded. Listening to an audio recording of a novel takes one's attention away from the visual text. It forces you to focus on the story at a different level. I must have listened to the recording of the entire novel at least four times before I felt ready to take on the task at hand head-on. By now, the characters in *Sembawang* had started to be with me in my silent moments and lived with me as they had done with my mother.

I was finally ready to translate the novel once again.

I played the audio recording aloud, pausing at every line to verbally translate it, to English, while my research assistant,

Sumi Baby Thomas, typed it out. I found it beneficial to start the translation at clause level. It was a slow process but not having to deal with typing or moving between the screen and the text, helped me to focus on choosing the right phrase and the most suitable word for the given context. Sumi and I met almost every day for several hours and for an entire month.

I then edited the text by checking if I had gotten the meaning right at the paragraph level and then at chapter level by comparing both the Tamil and English texts side by side. Once I was satisfied that the content was accurately translated, I moved on to examine the lexis more closely.

I did not want to overuse the same words such as 'in those days' which appeared several times in the original and combed through the text slowly to see if I could use a more appropriate word to capture the nuances accurately.

Words that could mean multiple things had to be re-read in the context that they appeared and corrected if need be; for instance, the word for 'honey' and 'nectar' was the same in Tamil.

Then there were words, like Chua, whose name was written as 'Swah' in Tamil because there was no equivalent character to represent 'ch' in Tamil and my translation had to be corrected. Having access to the writer — at all times of the day — to consult as I translated was a boon. Often these discussions led to longer ones on elements of Tamil that often get lost in translation.

I also made an editorial decision to italicise inner thoughts to distinguish them from dialogue in my translation.

The Revision Process
Once the novel was edited and proofread, I had another important decision to make before I could start on revising the

text. How authentic should the translated text be? My mum's answer to my query was short and crisp, "Do what you think is best for the 'English audience'."

My main purpose in translating this book was to ensure that it reached out to a wider audience and at the same time, for non-Tamil speakers to get a glimpse of the nuances of the Tamil language and culture. But therein lay the dilemma, I was not just translating the language but also the culture for a varied audience. How does one balance the two? The answer came from a chance conversation over Bru coffee and *Chettinad kuzhi paniyaram* (made with *Kavuni* rice) with Associate Professor V. Nagarajan and Associate Professor P. Madhan in Karaikudi, Tamil Nadu, as I was returning from delivering a keynote address at a conference at Alagappa University. The more we talked about the translation process of Tamil texts, the clearer it became that transcreation played an equal role in projects like these. As experts in translation and literary criticism, they pointed out that word for word translations may be accurate to some extent but they are rarely as impactful as transcreated texts, which are created with an understanding of the Tamil culture and language. Unintentionally, the trip also gave me a chance to understand many of the cultural elements in this novel better as Karaikudi is the birthplace of a few characters. That ninety-minute conversation then helped to propel the revision process.

This next part — the revision stage — was the hardest and kept me up at night. I was constantly waking up and replacing words and phrases with ones that suited the context best. As Ernest Hemingway once said, "The only kind of writing is rewriting."

I shortened some sentences and dialogues so that the text was tighter.

Metaphors and expressions that loosely translated to 'like
a starving moon', 'shaved the horns of the bull', 'she/he felt
like pulling out her tongue and dying', 'beat him like a dog',
'stamped on him/her', 'earning capacity' and 'talking casually',
all needed more context for a non-Tamil reader to understand
the implications. And yet, as a translator, I felt that my hands
were often tied because I could not possibly add too much in the
English version and still be true to the original.

Nevertheless, I had to substitute some idioms with the
meaning such as in the case of an idiom that loosely translates
to 'an old blind woman opened the door again'. It means
'old habits die hard' or a habit that is repeated. Since it was
impossible to discern the meaning from a direct translation, I
chose to replace the idiom with the meaning.

Then there were expressions such as *ull pavadai* (petticoat)
implying that a man was henpecked. In such instances, where
it was possible to provide a very brief explanation without
interfering with the text, I added sentences such as 'It was a
roundabout way of calling him henpecked'.

This novel is written in accessible language and even
incorporates phrases and words that were used in that time
period. Words such as *aluru* ('drain' in Tamil), *kati* (unit of
weight) and 'chopped' (stamped) — rarely used in current
times — were kept intact in the original language. In fact,
Associate Professor Chitra Sankaran points to the language
used in the original Tamil version of the novel, *Sembawang*,
as 'its crowning glory'. Given such an observation by the
reviewer, I have decided to retain the original words in the
English translation.

Likewise, the characters in the novel were often referred
to through their nicknames which when translated to English

sounded odd and often outdated but they reflect a time when people were given such nicknames without censure from others. These nicknames referred to where they lived (Maadi-veedu Amma — the lady who lives above or the lady who lives in a two-storey house), their jobs (Clerk Thambi — younger brother/young man who works as a clerk) or their ethnicity (Chinese neighbour).

Unfortunately, the one element of the language in the novel where it was not possible to capture the nuances is the dialectal differences amongst residents of Sembawang once the novel was translated to English.

The Two-year Journey Ends

It took me two years to translate the novel which included many long weeks of abstinence from the novel either because of work demands or that I needed space to think through the translation process.

And, for the first time in my life, I spent hours with my mother discussing the novel, debating the research and writing process of historical novels and talking through the challenges in translating a text from Tamil to English.

This journey has also given me two years of schooling into a writer's creative process of crafting a historical novel and a greater insight into my parents' past.

Dr Anitha Devi Pillai

ACKNOWLEDGEMENTS

THEY SAY IT takes a village to raise a child. A book in so many ways is a child — born out of an author's mind, in this case, this child, Kamaladevi Aravindan's *Sembawang*, comes to life in English through the many hands of kind souls who believed in the book.

To members of the *Sembawang* village:

(Listed in the chronological and overlapping order of appearance in the book's life cycle.)

The reviewer, **Associate Professor Chitra Sankaran**'s references to the subaltern studies in relation to this novel made me remember postcolonial literature classes at UNSW a lifetime ago and how much we learnt about the world and people especially through the reading of translated books. Your critical review was instrumental in my decision to translate *Sembawang*.

Managing editor and friend, **Anita Teo,** who believed in the book from its infancy. It's a blessing to have a dedicated editor who listens and offers answers or solutions. Thank you for not just cheering me from the sidelines, but for running along with me in the 'book marathon'.

Marketing manager and my former student, **Mindy Pang**, whose cheerful personality and creative ideas light up any room she's in, **Patricia Ng** and **Bernard Go** for getting this novel ready as well as the rest of the Marshall Cavendish International (Asia) team, for their faith in me from my first book. Your support kept me going throughout the last two years of this book.

My research assistant and former student, **Sumi Baby Thomas**, for helping to carefully dot the i's and cross the t's across all levels of the project from the start to the end, and for translating the author's bio into English. By taking on the additional role of being the brave bridge between my mother and me, you kept both of us sane during this process.

A Ministry of Education (Singapore) Tamil language scholar and my former student, **Ravathi Gunasegaran**, for kickstarting the process by reading the novel aloud and for translating my historical notes and photo captions into Tamil. I can still hear your voice sometimes as I look at the Tamil text.

My first reader, my father, **Mr Aravindakshan Pillai**, who was born and raised in Sembawang and hence proved to be a valuable fountain of knowledge and a luggage full of photographs of the Sembawang village. I am grateful that he read the book carefully, examining the descriptions of the historical events and places in Sembawang to ensure accuracy. By reading the manuscript multiple times without complaints or being squeamish about the intimate scenes, you have proven once again that you are my biggest fan.

My friend and mentor, **Shalini Damodaran**, for reviewing the translated text to ensure that it can be presented to the world. As always, your feedback was spot-on and constructive.

Tamil teacher and my former student, **Khaanchennah Gangadaran**, for coming onboard to read the final manuscript, check the Glossary and for researching on the epistemology of some of the tricky Tamil words and idioms. Your love for Tamil is contagious.

Geography teacher and my former student, **Fairoz Bin Nordin**, and art teacher, **Thng Shalyn**, who meticulously drew the map of Sembawang based on the memories of past residents, events in the book and the official map. Your map in this book has brought the landscape of the novel alive and that's no easy feat.

The members of the Sembawang community: those in the online **The Old Sembawang Naval Base Nostalgic Lane** Facebook group, especially **Sofea (Nora) Abdul Rahman** and **Wan Chan Peew**, for the hours of discussion and input, photographs and verification of details, as well as other past resident members who graciously donated photographs that appear in the 'People & Places' section of this book. Your help has given multiple layers of meaning to *Sembawang*.

Family, former students and friends, who took on the following roles: photographer, **Binod Therat**, and models for the book covers and publicity photographs, **Geetha Muthuramalingam, John Praveen Raj, Visithra John, Sangeetha Tamilarasan, Vasudevan Thottekkatt, Swapna Koranchath, Arpitha Vasudevan, Akash Vasudevan, Theijes Therrat Menon, B. Aravindakshan Pillai, Mohamed Nazirudeen bin Malik** and **Letchmie Thambusamy**, for gamely experimenting with a 1960s/1970s look for the photographs. You have helped to recreate a different time period in the unforgettable visuals.

The team that gave a cinematic twist to the novel *Sembawang*: **Sandeep Krishna, Sumi Baby Thomas, Pavethren Kanagarethinam, Lijesh Karunakaran, Sajin Ravi, Khaanchennah Gangadaran**, as well as the duo **Aileen Chai Siew Cheng** and **Levine Ong**, who took a documentary lens to examine the author's and translator's journeys — all of you have taken *Sembawang* beyond our wildest imagination.

My teenage son, **Theijes Therrat Menon**, who gave me looks of disbelief and plenty of raised eyebrows as he read the manuscript, unable to fathom that his grandmother and mother could conspire to write about matters of the heart! My dear friend, **Dr Mary Ellis**, who patiently listened to all the trials and tribulations of translating this novel over our morning coffee sessions. I am very grateful for the hours of conversations this book has generated between all of us.

My kind endorsers who read the novel and wrote a few lines for me, I am deeply appreciative of your gesture. All of you and your work has inspired me at different stages of my life.

Emeritus Professor Bill Ashcroft, the founding exponent of postcolonial theory and my former professor for introducing postcolonial literature and a wide range of books to me during my undergraduate days. Twenty over years ago, I never thought that I would one day come to you with a postcolonial narrative myself. If not for your classes, this book may never have happened.

Professor Sunil Amrith, a renowned historian and the 2017 MacArthur Fellow, whose research has reshaped the way we understand the migration of South and Southeast Asian studies, for taking the time to read this manuscript in the midst of a major move. I am over the moon that you enjoyed reading the novel and wrote an endorsement.

Associate Professor Rajesh Rai, the leading expert on the history of Singapore Indians and friend for always making time to help. Your passionate description of the migration of Indians to Malaya and the long reading list that you gave me in 2015 spurred me on to study the connection between history and heritage with language. Your graciousness towards fellow scholars and students is inspiring and heart-warming.

Felix Cheong and **David Davidar**, prolific and talented authors whose books on Singapore and India have brought me a lot of joy in the past. I am delighted that you are the first few readers of *Sembawang*. It's a fan's dream come true.

Gita Krishnankutty, a prolific translator, whose work gave me an insight into many critically acclaimed Malayalam literary books that would otherwise have been lost to me given that I do not read Malayalam. I now understand that thrill of bringing a book to life for a different set of readers and have truly enjoyed our conversations.

Dr Angus Whitehead and **Dr Ann Ang**, fellow academics and experts in world literature, I am over the moon that you enjoyed reading *Sembawang* and for your unwavering support. One could not ask for better colleagues.

I am very thankful to all of you!

Sembawang will be published in English and Tamil almost synchronously as the translation and the editing of the original text took place simultaneously. While I translated, my mother, Kamaladevi Aravindan, fine-tuned her original text. She added portions and strengthened other areas as a result of our discussions and research undertaken together. For that reason, I do feel connected to the 'making' of the original text as well, but that also meant that both books evolved many times during the translation process.

It's been a long journey but one that my mother and I have been privileged to share with many people. The story of *Sembawang* is yours now.

Dr Anitha Devi Pillai

ABOUT THE AUTHOR

KAMALADEVI ARAVINDAN IS an award-winning bilingual (Tamil and Malayalam) writer and playwright. She has studied postmodern literature from Koothupattarai Muthusamy from Tamil Nadu and from Ramanujan, professor from Thanjai University. She also specialised in Parikshartha drama literature in Tamil Nadu.

In addition to Singapore and Malaysia, her short stories have been published in periodicals from Tamil Nadu, USA and Switzerland such as *Kanaiyazhi, Yukamayini, Uyirmmai Thendral* and *Oodaru*.

At fifteen years of age, she was awarded 'The Best Writer' in the Johor state and was praised to be the pride of Tamils by K. Sarangapani. She has received many awards in the field of drama for her short stories, scripts for drama serials over radio and television, as well as scripts for dramas on stage. Besides short stories, she has written plays for radio, television and stage, and won several awards in the theatre as well.

Kamaladevi's short story collection, *Nuval*, which has been published in Tamil and English, has been specially selected as a curriculum book for undergraduates at the University of Malaya. Likewise, her other short story collection, *Karavu*, is studied by students pursing their Masters at the same university. Many of her short stories are studied at universities and selected as texts for examinations. Her research articles are also recommended at university level as important study materials for female literary works in Malaysia.

Her short story collection, 'Soorya Grahana Theru' (A Dark Street), was published in the book *Fiction of Singapore* in 2014.

In 2014, her creative non-fiction book documenting her life in the literary and theatre field, *Nigazhkalayil Naan*, received the Jeyanthan Foundation Lifetime Playwright Award. Her short story, 'Mugadugal', from the collection *Nuval*, was chosen as 2014's Best Tamil Short Story during the Singapore Writers Festival and released as a short film, which won three awards. Her short stories are also published in Malayalam, English and French. Kamaladevi won the Karigarsozhan Award from Thanjai University in 2011. The Tamil Language and Cultural Society's Bharathiyar-Bharathidasan Award, Association of Singapore Tamil Writers' Tamizhavel Award during Muthamizh Vizha in 2016, and Artists Association's Best Playwright Award are some of the other awards she has received.

She has also won the Indian Muslim Association's Societal Literature Contributor Award during the annual literary recognition in 2000 and the Research Award for Malaysian Tamil Female Writer in 2013.

Similarly, Kamaladevi has also received many awards in Singapore for her literary works in Malayalam. Her Malayalam plays have been staged at various venues in Singapore and have acclaimed awards. She won Singapore's Best Playwright Award, Best Director Award and Best Author Award at the drama competition organised by Kairalee Kala Nilayam, Singapore, in 1992. Her play, *Silanthivala* (Spider Web), has brought her fame in the Malayalam literary scene for being a female scriptwriter and director.

The author, Kamaladevi Aravindan (right), with her daughter and translator,
Anitha Devi Pillai.

ABOUT THE TRANSLATOR

ANITHA DEVI PILLAI (PH.D.) is an applied linguist and teacher educator at the National Institute of Education (NIE), Nanyang Technological University (NTU), Singapore, where she teaches courses on writing pedagogy and writing skills.

She is the recipient of three Teaching Awards. She received the *Excellence in Teaching Commendation 2018* from the NIE, NTU (Singapore), and the *SUSS Teaching Merit Award* in 2013 and 2014 from the Singapore University of Social Sciences (SUSS). In 2017, she received the *Research Excellence Award* from Pravasi Express for her research on the Singapore Malayalee community.

Anitha has authored five books, including *From Kerala to Singapore: Voices from the Singapore Malayalee Community* (2017), *From Estate to Embassy: Memories of an Ambassador* (2019) and *The Story of Onam* (2020). She has also published academic papers, poems, stories and newspaper articles.

Some of her creative writing publications in 2019/2020 are 'Monsoon in Kolkata' (poem) in *Wanderlust: The Best of 2019 Anthology*, 'That Kiss on Your Forehead' (poem) in *Poetry Moves: An Anthology of Poetry*, 'Home is a Three Syllable Word' (poem) in the *Southeast Asian Review of English Journal*, 'Mother Tongue' (poem) in *Asiatic: IIUM Journal of English Language and Literature*, 'How Do You Want Your Dumplings?' (short story) in *Food Republic: A Singapore Literary Banquet* and 'Voices' (short story) in *The Best Asian Stories 2019*.

Anitha is bilingual in English and Tamil and speaks Malayalam. *Sembawang* (2020) is her first translation of a Tamil novel into English. She is currently writing a collection of short stories about the Malayalee community in Singapore, editing a short story compilation for young adults titled *An Asian Tapestry of Colours: A Collection of Contemporary Short Stories* and co-editing a collection of short stories with Felix Cheong, titled *A View of Stars: Stories of Love*.